Forever, One Day

Forever, One Day

Samantha LaPointe

Copyright © 2024 Samantha LaPointe.

All rights reserved. No part of this book may be used or reproduced by any means, graphic, electronic, or mechanical, including photocopying, recording, taping or by any information storage retrieval system without the written permission of the author except in the case of brief quotations embodied in critical articles and reviews.

This is a work of fiction. All of the characters, names, incidents, organizations, and dialogue in this novel are either the products of the author's imagination or are used fictitiously.

Archway Publishing books may be ordered through booksellers or by contacting:

Archway Publishing
1663 Liberty Drive
Bloomington, IN 47403
www.archwaypublishing.com
844-669-3957

Because of the dynamic nature of the Internet, any web addresses or links contained in this book may have changed since publication and may no longer be valid. The views expressed in this work are solely those of the author and do not necessarily reflect the views of the publisher, and the publisher hereby disclaims any responsibility for them.

Any people depicted in stock imagery provided by Getty Images are models, and such images are being used for illustrative purposes only. Certain stock imagery © Getty Images.

ISBN: 978-1-6657-5841-3 (sc)
ISBN: 978-1-6657-5842-0 (hc)
ISBN: 978-1-6657-5843-7 (e)

Library of Congress Control Number: 2024906192

Print information available on the last page.

Archway Publishing rev. date: 6/28/2024

Prologue

Sicily, 1900

The Sicilian countryside glistened in the dissipating moonlight. The fields were subtly coated with a faint frost, sure to be forgotten once the sun began to peek over the mountains. Filomena, only a few weeks from delivering what would be her only child, pulled herself out of bed. As she eased herself off of the cot, she felt the floorboards creak beneath her. The wooden slabs felt rough and cold underneath her swollen feet. It was early morning, but her husband Vittorio was already out and working. She did her best to maintain the level of help she was to him, but she grew weaker and more fragile the bigger the baby got. Her back ached and she hadn't slept well for weeks. It was hard to lie still with the weight of a baby pressing up against her bladder. Her muscles twinged from exhaustion. She would give anything to stay off of her feet and part ways with the laborious duties ahead of her, but she couldn't leave Vittorio to fend for himself. Not while the *Mafioso* was on the prowl to shakedown any landowners for debts owed, or assumed.

In its inception, the initial *Mafioso* derived from a group of people who had banded together to fight against the various wrongdoings to the land of Sicily. For thousands of years, Sicily was ruled by a wide variety of cultures - the Romans, Greeks, Spanish, Arabic - who had invaded and exuded influence. The *Mafioso* began with good intentions, or so that's how the story goes, but soon the *Mafioso* was reigning over those they could easily take advantage of. Filomena and Vittorio didn't stand a chance. Poor farmers whose crops grew only when luck prevailed, yet still, they were indebted. The collectors came every other week to gather a percentage of what little profit the couple would see.

Filomena yearned for a different life, away from Sicily. She loved her home, but the region had turned into nothing but poverty and she knew there was no other foreseeable future in her lifetime. She and Vittorio would only know being poor and having to pay money to those they rightfully did not owe. She wanted to run to America, the land of promises, with her husband and soon-to-be child, but she knew that was impossible.

While Filomena got herself together, slowly, before heading out to help her husband, she rubbed her belly.

"My boy," she whispered in Sicilian, "You will get far, far away from here and you will have a beautiful life. You will do things that I can only dream of." Filomena stood for a few seconds, hoping to feel movement. The gender was unknown, but she believed she would have a son. In the seconds of silence, she felt the subtlest of kicks, causing her to laugh.

"Yes, my child, that's right. You will go to America and live a wonderful life full of love and happiness, and you will create your own destiny."

Filomena pulled her hair back, put on her shoes, and opened the door to yet another dawn.

Part One

Chapter 1

1949

It was one of the warmest Sundays in October that Luella could recall. The distinct change of seasons in New Jersey was what she loved most about the garden state - fall being her favorite. From right after the children returned to school in September, straight through early November, she embraced the beautiful change, welcoming the full, bushy trees vibrant with color, eventually enjoying the crunch of the dead leaves on the ground as she walked through town. There was nothing she didn't enjoy about the fall. But this Sunday was even more special. Her brother was getting married, and there was this effervescent excitement among her and the rest of the bridesmaids of Elena.

Luella's soon-to-be sister-in-law was a Godsend. She was lighthearted and easygoing, but she could flip on a dime when it came to something she got passionate or heated about; a true Calabrese. Elena and Vinny had met at a church dance two years earlier and had been inseparable since. Vinny fell instantly for Elena's big green eyes and her body shaped truly like an hourglass. They were set up through a mutual friend, Skip, who thought it'd be a good idea to introduce them. He knew based on Vinny's sly demeanor that someone with Elena's quick wit would be the perfect match.

As Luella and the rest of the bridal party waited on the steps outside of beautiful Saint Anthony's Church, the sun was at its peak, beaming warmth onto the bridesmaids' shoulders. A shadow of the cathedral crawled on the sidewalk. Elena looked breathtaking with her long, dark hair held back by her veil, in tightly wound finger waves. She looked exactly as she described she had wanted to on her wedding day - like a dream. Luella had admired her sister-in-law who was only seven months older, and she felt she had truly gained a big sister. Elena was strong, and independent and certainly gave Vinny a run for his money.

"Lu, my lipstick?" Elena pointed to her mouth, awaiting Luella's response.

"It hasn't moved at all, just as the counter girl said it wouldn't! You look beautiful."

"You think your brother's ready for this for the rest of his life?" Elena giggled as she offered up the somewhat rhetorical question.

Luella threw her arms up jokingly: "If he's not, I'll marry you!" And the women laughed.

The bells began to ring and the women lined up in formation. Elena, in the back, and Luella right in front of her; the chosen maid of honor. As the women entered the church with their bouquets, everyone anxiously turned to see what choice was made when it came to the color and fabric of the bridesmaids' dresses. Luckily, Elena had spared no expense at her bridal parties' glamour. Elena's mother was a seamstress and worked in a high-end factory, so she was able to get the most beautiful satin fabric at a discount, but still a higher-than-average price point for 1949. Elena's mother designed the dresses from scratch. A pale blue satin with slight touches of ivory lace draped over the shoulders so that no one had to worry about a bare arm in church.

Church weddings were quite amusing in the 40s. Locals would come if they were familiar with the family, or knew someone who knew someone; afterall, no one was going to turn you away from the ceremony. As neighbors "*oohed*" and "*aahed*" at the bridal party walking down, Vinny and the groomsmen waited patiently at the altar. When Luella was ready to walk down the aisle to greet her brother, just seconds before his bride walked in, she felt his energy. The entire room felt his energy. At twenty-two years old, not having known her own mother, nor having seen an example of true love, she now saw it in her brother's eyes. Vinny was euphoric, emotional, stricken with anxious energy, but in a thrilling way. The kind of nerves that make you think about taking the jump without knowing whether or not there's a harness strapped to you; but being more excited to see what's on the other side. As Luella approached her brother, she realized he had been sweating. She offered him her kerchief and gave him a gentle kiss on the cheek while they embraced for a quick second in a doting hug.

"I love you, Vinny, and I'm very proud of you. You're going to make a great husband." Luella released her brother and as she did, his hand grabbed hers as if he were going to say something.

"Your wife looks stunning, just wait," she said, then took her place at the altar.

The organ began to roar, with the tune that everyone was waiting for. As the wedding march bounced off the walls and through the pews, the audience rose to their feet and turned to face the oversized, wooden doors. As they opened, the room filled with the push of incense and a fall breeze. It smelled familiar and new, all at once.

Elena, arm-in-arm with her father, Gaetano, waited as the doors opened. The dramatic pause allowed for the gasp of awe when they saw the bride. Elena and her father began to walk slowly down the aisle, the onlookers admiring every step that she took; she was radiant. As Elena glided down the aisle towards her husband, Luella was filled with nothing but happiness. Happiness for her brother and his new bride, happiness for herself having gained a sister, for her father who gained a daughter, and for their future as a family. Elena was a perfect addition to the small but mighty Greco clan, and Luella knew that she'd be the glue to keep them all together. Luella turned to soak in her brother's expression as his bride approached. To her amazement, she saw her strong, tough, older, macho brother, with tears welling up in his eyes. Luella had never seen her brother cry, and in that moment, she knew that she would strive to have the same love that she was witnessing. Luella knew that she was meant for a great love story; it was undeniable at that moment, the feeling that she would not let her life go by without knowing this same kind of love.

Chapter 2

1950

It was about nine months after the wedding, and one of the hottest summers in New Jersey. While many were escaping to the shore or Atlantic City on the weekends, to soak up the rays, or gamble their week's pay on slot machines or boardwalk games, there was still always a unique bustle around Greco's Market in July.

Vincenzo Greco, Luella and Vinny's father, had opened Greco's in 1932. Vincenzo Greco had made his American Dream into a reality when he signed the lease and turned the "open" sign on for the first time. Luella and Vinny grew up in the market, passing off Italian bread or freshly butchered meat at the young ages of four and six. It had just been Vincenzo and his two children since their mother died shortly after giving birth to Luella. Luella quickly grew to be as tough as her father and brother, but also maternal, because she realized that they needed the love and nurturing that only a woman could provide.

It was nice to have Elena officially now working at the store as Elena Greco. Elena did an excellent job in taking on the bookkeeping with Luella and assisting the customers when they were busy. But Elena enjoyed the back of house work; she liked the organizational aspect of the business, and a lot of the behind-the-scenes work was where she felt she could offer the most. The Grecos, by nature, were in-your-face kind of people. They enjoyed being the face of the market and gathered with their loyal customers daily. They had unique relationships with the vendors and everyone felt like family. They knew everyone by name, and the Grecos were a constant in everyone's lives. For holidays, birthdays and any joyous occasion, their loyal customer base came to Greco's looking for menu suggestions, ingredients, or any extras. Similarly, for the ominous and heavier occasions - funerals, repasses and succumbing to illness also brought their customers in. Greco's was perpetual. Greco's was a home away from home. Greco's saw community members through joys and tragedies.

"Lu!" Vinny shouted from the cellar, "Can you get back here? Elena ran to the bank and I'm helping *Papa* with the inventory. A delivery is here and I'm tied up."

"Vin, you know I don't like leaving the front unattended," Luella shouted back, raising her hands in frustration if only for her own shadow to see.

"Lu! Come on! Cut the shit, alright? The guy's here. Let's go!"

Reluctantly, Luella grabbed a pen from the drawer, and headed towards the back door. She looked down the cellar stairs to see if her father and brother were in sight. While they were not, she could hear the clambering around and her father's mutters, spewing Sicilian curse words. Luella turned the knob and pushed the door open, hit fiercely with the sweltering heat, only to find there was no delivery man there. As she stepped out onto the pavement of the back parking lot, she noticed the delivery truck, one she hadn't seen in quite some time; Andriotta's. Andriotta's delivered their linens. Aprons, towels and cloths for wrapping the breads in. As Luella took a few steps towards the truck she heard the deep voice of what sounded like it was coming from a bear sized man.

"*Ciao, ciao.*" The delivery man was leaning back against the brick building behind the door, under the awning that stretched only to the left. "I was too hot to stand in the sun so I made my way to the only shady spot I could find."

"Oh, sorry to have kept you waiting that long, but why didn't you just go back in your truck? And where's Anthony?"

"My truck? Well, because I'm new and don't want to use up too much gas just to keep the air conditioner on. The old man would kill me if I needed to gas up already after only three days in the field." The man pushed himself off of the wall.

"So where's Anthony? And who are you?" Luella sharply responded. She didn't like feeling as if she were being snuck up on, and she certainly did not like it when her vendors sent unexpected delivery men. She enjoyed knowing who was going to be showing up to the backdoor of the store.

"Me? I'm Giuseppe. Joseph. Joe is good." Joe was a brolick man. He was stocky with jet black hair and matching eyes; wide and deep. He had a little belly on him and stood at nearly six feet, a stature that matched his deep baritone voice. "Anthony is officially retiring from the field. I'll be here weekly now."

Luella, intrigued, yet still facetious in her own right responded, "*You're* Joe. And Anthony is retiring and done with the field? Why weren't we notified? We've been customers for years."

"You were. We notified everyone. My pop is tired. He doesn't want to do the deliveries anymore." Joe smirked and hauled the bag of linens over his shoulder like Saint Nicholas. "So, lucky for you, you've got me."

Joe made the swinging of the heavy linens in the heat seem effortless. The load was large, but so was he. Luella was undeniably attracted by his braun, and instantly her annoyance subdued to interest. She quickly followed only to scurry in front of him, leading her new delivery man to the regular drop location.

"Here's where we left everything for your father. I didn't realize he had a son in the business."

"My father told me I'd appreciate *Il Mercato de Greco*. Family run, like us. I've been trying to establish my own thing for the better half of my youth, and, well, here I am." Joe loaded the dirty linens and unloaded the neatly folded ones, tucking them away tightly so they wouldn't fall to the floor from the leaning shelf rack. "I learned that I do want to continue my father's legacy, so I decided to get more involved. And by getting more involved, my pop decided to take a step back."

"Hey! There he is!" Vinny and Vincenzo came up from the cellar to greet Joe, seemingly knowing one another. "We were wondering when you'd be here and start stepping in for your old man." Vinny embracingly hugged and kissed Joe on the cheek. Luella was taken aback. She had never heard any news of Anthony retiring, or stepping away, nor was she aware Andriotta's was a family business, let alone there being a son to be sent as a replacement.

Luella inspected the friendly exchange before quickly chiming in. "When was anyone going to tell me to expect a new delivery man?" She snarkily asked.

"Lu, you don't ever even accept deliveries. What are you bitching about?" Vinny responded while gathering the boxes he and his father had just brought up.

"I'm just saying, it would've been nice."

Luella was finding things to keep her hands moving and her head in the opposite direction while her brother and the secret, unannounced Giuseppe Andriotta conversed. She enjoyed the sound of his voice; deep and resounding. It was as if his voice took over the entire room, vibrating the wall that she leaned against. He wasn't loud, not by any means shouting, but his voice had strength. It was less than a minute before Vincenzo returned to the back of the market.

"*Ciao, Giuseppe! Come stai e tuo padre?*"

How the hell does my father know Anthony Andriotta's son too? Luella thought.

As the pair exchanged pleasantries for another few minutes, Elena arrived back from the bank.

"Oh my, seems my office has been overrun by laundry and meat!" She said.

"I know, unexpected delivery today. Seems the new guy is learning the linen route. We usually get the drops on Monday's." Luella responded.

"Oh, Joe? He finally took over, huh? Go easy on him, he's probably just trying to make his rounds and do right by his father's loyal customers." Elena removed her black leather satchel and placed it on her desk, followed by the removal of the faux leather money pouch before she carefully placed the cash in the safe. "Come on, Lu. You of all people understand what that means."

"How the hell did everyone know that Anthony Andriotta had a son and that he was going to be doing deliveries except me?" Luella raised her hands up, shaking them in the sky before assertively landing them on her hips.

"Lu, how the hell did you *not* know Anthony Andriotta had a son? He talked about him all of the time. He's mentioned him every time he came to do drops since I've been with your brother. I'm pretty sure he's even shown Vinny and I pictures. Plus, for the last few months, Joe had been tagging along with Anthony to learn the routes and customer preferences. Maybe it's because you're always in the front." Elena rolled her desk chair out and fluffed her cherry red furry pillow before sitting back down on it.

"Oh," Luella quietly responded as she tried to get a peek at Joe one more time. "I don't know. I guess I've missed that memo. Yeah, it was probably because I was in the front." Vinny poked his head in. "Lu, are you checking him out and signing or me?"

"I will!" Luella shouted. Quickly trying to cover for her unexpected heist. "I mean, I'm going to. I got it, Vin." Luella rolled her eyes and grabbed a pen off of Elena's desk. Vinny, almost simultaneously with Luella, rolled his eyes and pulled his head out of the door. "Alright Joe, I'll see you later."

Elena caught Luella's gaze and smirked at her sister-in-law. "I know, Lu. He's a hunk. You should flirt. Let your hair down a little."

"My hair is down, and I do flirt. I don't need to right now, but I can and I do." Luella felt herself stammering and her pace picking up. Was it obvious she was getting flustered? Elena always had a way of calming Luella's nerves. Elena smiled and gave Luella a slow blink, looked down, and chuckled as she began to pick her work back up.

"*Ugh*," Luella let out before turning to the door to meet the new delivery man.

Luella extended her hand for the clipboard.

"Oh, it's in the truck, sorry. I couldn't carry it with the linens. I'll be right back." Joe said as he headed towards the door.

"It's okay, I'll come out with you so you don't have to make an unnecessary trip." Luella quickly rushed behind him to make sure they would have a few words exchanged while they were walking.

"So, you're new, huh? What was that about?" Luella mocked.

"Well, I'm new to you, aren't I?" Joe turned to face her as he closed his rhetorical question. As their eyes met, Luella felt something. It wasn't the strike of love that she had hoped for, but it was something. She couldn't deny that. Unsure if it was love at first sight, or lust taking over, or maybe it was the heat and the thick air that was settling in that afternoon. Whatever it was, it was undeniable.

As Joe reached in the truck to grab the clipboard, Luella quickly patted her head and tossed her hair. She leaned on the clipboard being held by Joe and began signing her name. Luella realized his strength even in that moment, his large arms were holding the clipboard so steady that she didn't even need to offer her other hand to support. The way Joe was holding it was as if she were leaning against a brick building. Solid. Unshakeable.

"Luella Greco," Joe read. "Nice to officially meet you Luella Greco, and I'm sorry about the confusion."

"It's ok, and sorry, also. That was me just being me. I didn't mean to come off snarky. I just…" Before she could finish the rest of her ramble, she stopped herself, looked down and laughed. "Nice to meet you Joe. I'll be expecting you next time."

"Well I hear you don't often take deliveries, so hopefully I'm this lucky next time." Joe turned and smiled as he opened the driver's side door, and jumped in. He turned the truck on, and gave Luella a warm smile and a wave as he turned out of their parking lot.

What just happened? What was that about? She'd met so many men throughout her time at the market. Delivery men, customers, and from all walks of life, but she hadn't ever been so caught off guard or thrown off as she just was. What Luella did know was that she yearned for the next time Andriotta's truck would pull into their back drive.

Chapter 3

1951

The following week, Luella began her routine in the market the same as every other day; turning the page on the calendar in the office.

Saturday.

Although their normal delivery days were on Mondays, she was hopeful that Joe Andriotta would pull up today. In fact, she was confident. She pulled half of her hair back and let her naturally highlighted bangs fall in front of her face. Typically, when Luella worked, she had all of her hair pulled back tight to avoid it from getting into her eyes as she served her customers during long days at the market. She'd get easily irritated if she felt something was lightly tickling her face, or was caught in between her vision and her guests' expectations. Hair in her face of any sort was bothersome to her and would almost instantaneously force her to snap. Wearing her hair tousling lightly in front of her was by design. Elena, her brother, and her father always complimented her when she had hair near her slender face. It would dull the rigidity of her hard jawline and lighten the big, deep-set eyes she had inherited from her father.

As she made her way to the front of the store, she switched the lights on from the back. The lights were in perfect, sequential order starting from the back hallway, and moving down the glass casings featuring miscellaneous baked desserts. They flicked on through the deli meat and butcher case, and lastly, over the shelves of baskets which housed the fresh made bread. She walked in tandem with the lightshow towards the front of the market. She pulled the gate up, turned towards the large coffee machine and fired up a fresh brew. The rich smell of the Italian blended coffee beans filled the air while the quiet murmuring of the pot began to work. The subtle buzz of the lights, the delectable scent of fresh bread, and her father singing faintly in the background were some of what comprised Luella's favorite part of the early morning ritual.

"*Ciao, tesoro mio*", Vincenzo greeted his daughter while hurling a tray of fresh semolina loaves onto the counter.

"*Ciao, Papa.*" Luella placed a kiss on her father's cheek as they embraced for a moment.

"Luella, please, can you unlock the door? I don't want no one to think we're not open". Vincenzo spoke in broken English.

"*Papa*, no one is going to think we're closed. We still have fifteen minutes before we open."

"*Per favore*, Luella. We don't have fifteen minutes. We only have seven!" Pointing to the clock angrily, Vincenzo had made his point when the hands read 5:53.

"Fine, *Papa*. Fine. We'll open already." Luella sighed and reluctantly set for the door. Flicking the "open" sign on and turning the lock to the right. She pulled the street sign from behind the counter and hoisted it on her hip as she made her way with the large advertisement out through the door. She opened the sign and propped both sets of legs evenly on the sidewalk, carefully avoiding the placement of the wooden pegs in the cracks on the concrete. The sign was bold and attractive; just as her father had imagined it when he thought up the creation. Large, red, half-moon-shaped words read "*Il Mercato de Greco*" against the bold, black, chalkboard-looking background, with bright green words translating: "Greco's Italian Market". Luella brushed her hands from the board, satisfied with its placement. She paused for a second and placed her hands on her hips, soaking in the early morning air. Luella returned inside, made her way behind the counter, tossed on her white apron and smiled at the thought of Joe Andriotta delivering their linens.

"Good morning, *mia famiglia*!" Vinny shouted as he and Elena came through the backdoor.

"Oh, is your son in a mood today." She pointed at her father-in-law making her way to her office and kissing him on the cheek as a formal hello. "And you," Elena nodded at Luella, "He said he had a dream that all of the Grecos bred little Grecos. So he's in a great mood and wants us to start trying to have a baby, and for some reason thinks that you should be quickly behind us. Don't ask. Happy Saturday." Elena laughed and shook her head. "He always says his dreams are like premonitions. It's as if he *'watches a movie from the future and he believes it'.*" Elena used her fingers to make air quotations. But, by the way Elena's smile stayed on her face, it was as if she, too, believed the dream, or at least was hopeful that a child was in their near future.

Elena had always wanted to be a mother. She'd dream about the day when she'd bring a little girl into the world. She'd embrace her with gifts, toys and all the beauty secrets one could share with their daughter. She was eager to have a confidant and best friend in her offspring; she believed that she and Vinny would have all girls. Vinny, on the other hand, prayed for boys. He wanted to have more Grecos to continue their legacy, and have a new generation's blood in the market.

Luella laughed at the dream, but hoped it was true for her brother and Elena. She wanted them to start a family quickly. Selfishly, it was because Luella was uncertain herself whether or not she was fit to be a mother. She didn't have a mother growing up, and she wasn't sure what she'd do with a child of her own. Would she love it unconditionally? Would she harbor resentment towards a baby taking everyone's attention? Would her maternal instincts kick in if something were wrong? All of the unanswered questions that a mother of her own could not reassure her of. She didn't have that luxury. The thought of the mother-child relationship scared her. Not because it was unknown, but because it didn't seem natural to her.

"*Ah, nipoti*! I wish you would have little *bambini* to run and jump on everything. Including me!" Vincenzo shouted and laughed.

"*Si, Papa*! *Nipoti*! See? See Elena? Everybody believes my dream will soon come true!" Vinny grabbed his father and hugged him.

"Alright, alright. As of now it's just a dream, hon. Please, let's not get crazy here. We haven't even started." Elena embraced both her husband

and father-in-law, laughing and cheering as she turned around and winked at Luella.

It was not uncommon for a Saturday morning to start out as such. The foursome was so frequently together, yet there was something unique about Saturdays. It's as if they rewarded themselves with laughter and love for making it through the overtaxing week. Each one of them loved being a part of the market. They loved the loyal customers, the relationships they all had and made, and they loved what they were able to provide the community - comfort, love, and good food. But they were often tired. It was not an easy business. The hours were long and the days were grueling. Sometimes, a day was neverending. And other times, if they didn't make enough money that day, they felt that the day had not been long enough. At the beginning and end of every day, though, they had each other. They did not let a day go by where they stayed mad at one another before leaving the store. They began each day with a cheerful tone and wanted to conclude each day the same. It was not easy being in business with family, and they knew that. They consciously chose to make an effort day in and day out, and it did not go unnoticed by any of them.

5:59 and in walked George Stirnacolous, a local who worked for the Board of Education as a weekend janitor. George was a lanky, Greek man who always offered a joke and a compliment when he came in on Saturdays.

"George, this is early for you. What are you going to do for lunch if you're already here for breakfast?" Luella said from behind the counter.

"They're performing some construction in the gymnasium, so I'll be working around their schedule today. I'll be overseeing what they're up to to make sure it's up to snuff, if you know what I mean. So, I can't leave for lunch today, I figured I'd have to come and see my favorite Italians for breakfast," George replied.

"Alright," Luella chuckled, "That'll do. What can I get you, sir?"

As George rattled off his order, the usual slew of regulars began to pile in:

Maryann Higgins, who always ordered fresh bread and meat

to prepare over the weekend for her twin boys and husband, James. Maryann, when her schedule permitted, would admit the dreams she once had for a career of her own, a beauty parlor offering the latest styles. Maryann had an eye for the upcoming trends. She would extend compliments when they were deserved, and alternatives when a style did not meet her standard. She'd also admit to abuse that she'd fall victim to from James occasionally. One time, instead of vibrantly walking in with her luscious, thick hair waving and free, eyes wide and lipstick freshly applied, she came in with a headscarf and large, oversized sunglasses to hide the black eye and scratches over her eyebrow. Once, Vinny overheard Maryann confide in Elena and rushed from the kitchen to the front of the store enraged. Neither Vinny, nor Vincenzo, could stand violence against a woman. Vinny offered to get involved however he could, but Maryann begged for them to forget she had even said anything. Typically, the Grecos would put two and two together if they didn't see Maryann for a few weeks, but she was consistent as of lately, so they delighted in pleasantries.

Bobby and Sue Patrowski lived up the street from Greco's and would walk there every Saturday morning for their coffee and fresh breakfast sandwiches. They were in their fifties, quiet and humble for damn near local celebrities. The Patrowskis inherited a large sum of money from Sue's parent's estate when the Polish immigrants passed away. However, you would never know that they sat on over a million dollars and held the title of savvy investors. The Patrowskis were lovely and would never make a fuss about anything.

Then came the Italians. There was Vito Sarro, who worked at the local car dealership and always came in for three coffees and a box of fresh biscotti before hosting his 7 o'clock Saturday morning meeting with the rest of his team. Rosa Invante always came in for deli meats sliced very fine, fresh bread and a box of pastries, which would make up her four children's lunches for the week.

Sarafina and Marco Del'Orio lived upstairs from the market. Either one, or both of them, came down almost everyday. They'd often come down multiple times a day if they forgot something they needed for supper that night, or to marinate over the evening. Marco and Sarafina were honorary Grecos, both Sicilian and first generation in New Jersey. Both sets of their parents also resided in Hawthorne and would frequent the market. They were in their mid-twenties and newly married, but had been together before they decided for themselves. Since both of their families came from the same village in Sicily, there wasn't much that was up for debate. It was a sealed deal when they had children around the same age, and when it was an appropriate time, the parents sat them aside one another and laid the law down that this was their future. So they very quickly got acclimated to each other. Luckily, Sarafina and Marco were very much alike and worked out wonderfully. They were expecting their first child, so it wasn't uncommon for Sarafina to get cravings throughout the days where she'd sneak down to snag a couple slices of salami and *sfogliatelle*.

Sarafina waddled through the door, still in her robe and slippers, with her hair held up in her rollers from the night before. Holding her belly yawning, she proceeded to the back of the market, and grabbed herself a lemonade.

"I can't sleep anymore. I just can't get comfortable." Sarafina was seven and a half months pregnant and had a rough pregnancy with odd cravings and consistent morning sickness. "I just can't wait to meet the little guy, and fall asleep together. That's all I want. ten fingers, ten toes, and sleep."

Luella knew that Sarafina was also going to be an excellent mother. She was excited to meet the baby and learn about what it'd be like to have a newborn around. "What else do you want aside from the lemonade? I hope not that same weird craving you had last week." Luella and Sarafina exchanged smirks and started laughing.

"No, not yet. Maybe in a few hours. Marco already left for work and I just really wanted a lemonade." Yawning and scratching her neck, Sarafina reached for her pocket and remembered she was in her robe. "Oh my God, I left my wallet upstairs. How am I in public like this right now?" Seemingly horrified, Sarafina tightened her robe and looked down. "*Ugh*, I don't even care anymore. Marco or I will be back at some point today with the money, Lu. Don't send the police after me. I'm pregnant and forgetful." Making her way towards the door, Sarafina looked at Luella pretending to be scared.

"Would you stop? Don't be silly. We'll see you later or Monday."

Sarafina exited in silence and waved her hand up as she walked through the door.

Francesco Petrelli and his wife Irma owned multiple buildings around the northern New Jersey area and were inadvertently deemed restaurant connoisseurs. Francesco was in his mid-seventies and had come to America from Naples when he was only seventeen years old with his brother Umberto. Neither Francesco nor Umberto were ever intimated by the unknown of what was to come. They didn't care that they didn't speak the language, or that the discrimination against Italians was at an all-time high in the early 1900s. They were determined. They had a dream and a vision - to introduce the taste of Naples to Northeast America. Umberto was the talented chef and Francesco, the savvy intelligence. They worked their way through learning English by working around restaurants and importing foods, knowing that they'd need a foundational understanding of the language. By 1920, they had two restaurants, one on the Hudson, overlooking the New York City skyline, and the other in Paterson. Umberto was in the busier of the two restaurants in West New York five days a week and hired a sous chef to cover for the other two days. The Paterson location's head chef was a mentee who had worked underneath Umberto for seven years before finally earning the title of head chef. The brothers worked effortlessly together. They had an external manager overseeing the operations of West New York while Umberto cooked, and Francesco managed Paterson while the head chef handled the kitchen. Both brothers tried to staff their restaurants with immigrants. They wanted to help and mentor young immigrants who were trying to make it in America, just as Francesco and Umberto had. They often asked for their first language when going through the interview process, to make sure that they could at the very least, communicate with each other.

At least one of the Petrellis would typically arrive at Greco's before

7:30 on Saturdays, but as the morning slipped away and the minutes turned into hours, before Luella knew it, no Petrellis. Similarly, there was another individual she expected to see that Saturday. The delivery truck with the son who took over his father's business had not yet arrived. Luella held out hope, anticipating an encounter with Joe in the second half of her day.

Chapter 4

1925

Vincenzo Greco had just started out his produce delivery company, and was trying his best to solicit business and land regular accounts. Greco Limited was only printed on the shirt that he wore on his back, and he had walked his cart around with the imports he had negotiated with his cousin, Dante, who was the one to travel back and forth from Italy. Vincenzo had only met with Francesco once briefly when he dropped by one of the Petrelli's restaurants. He caught Francesco managing his staff between lunch and dinner and he told Vincenzo to come back in a few weeks. The weeks have passed and Vincenzo was never one to miss a meeting, even if it wasn't set in stone. Vincenzo hauled his produce cart up the sidewalk and made his way around the back of the restaurant in hopes that the cellar door was open. It was 10:23 in the morning and Vincenzo knew there was a better chance in meeting formally with Francesco before his day started rather than in between crowds. To his surprise, what he turned the corner to see was much, much better. He saw a beautiful copper-skinned woman with long, waist length black hair sweeping the steps of the cellar. She only stood about five foot three inches and had a figure that looked inviting yet tastefully covered in her black shirt and black slacks.

"*Ciao, scusi.*" Vincenzo softly said, not to alarm the beautiful young woman.

"*Hola,*" She smiled and nodded her head. She was even more

beautiful when he was able to lock eyes with her. She had a bright smile and big brown eyes, the color of espresso beans.

"*Parli Italiano?*" Vincenzo asked curiously.

"*Yo no.*" The woman replied. As she did, Francesco came beaming out of the cellar doors. "*Ah, ciao Vincenzo!* I was hoping you didn't forget to come see me!" Francesco's English was that of someone who had been in America and studying for fifty-plus years, it was beautiful and impressive. His accent came through, but not in a way that was distracting. Vincenzo admired the man who seemingly lived a life he thought he wanted.

"*Maria, disculpe. Te improta?*" Francesco said to the mystery woman.

Maria thought Vincenzo, and before he knew it, *Maria* was softly coming off of his lips.

"How do you know how to speak Spanish so well?" Vincenzo asked genuinely.

"When I came to this country with my brother, I was determined to learn everything I could. I never wanted to feel that I didn't belong, or that someone else didn't feel welcomed. I work with and hire a lot of immigrants to give them a chance. And in return, I challenge myself to understand them all the best I can." Francesco's genuine reply made Vincenzo that much more eager to earn his business and begin working with him. "What do you have for me?" Francesco asked excitedly and guided Vincenzo inside the restaurant.

As the two swapped business negotiations and exchanged promises and obligations, Maria served them hot coffee. Vincenzo's attraction to Maria was obvious. His eyes danced in hers when they caught one another and he wasn't shy about it.

"Ah, I see you have interest in Miss Maria, *si*? She is a good girl. She comes here by herself from Mexico and I know she wants to learn the new world. She's eager, but struggles to learn the language. If you'd like, I can teach you some Spanish." Francesco's offer was more of an invitation and Vincenzo was ecstatic to accept.

It took Vincenzo nearly a month to learn enough Spanish to communicate, and for Maria to realize that his studies were all to make her acquaintance. It inspired her to learn Italian, and in turn, and surprisingly enough to the both of them, she actually learned English faster.

They'd communicate in their own way; in their broken words and misused phrases, but it worked for them. It wasn't long before the two became a couple and were going steady. This, however, was frowned upon in the Italian community. Italians should be sticking with their own kind, not inviting another immigrant race into the mix such as a Mexican. The Italians felt they had discrimination enough; why give the Americans another reason to put them down? Unbeknownst to them, the community's disapproval of Maria and Vincenzo was the same kind of discrimination they were experiencing from the American people. Vincenzo didn't care what anyone else said, and not only did he continue to see Maria, but after only eight months, he decided they should wed.

Since Vincenzo and Maria were in this country both struggling to make their dreams into reality, they decided to commit to one another in holy matrimony in front of the lord and skip the costly reception. They wed in a little church in Paterson and only invited a few people who mattered to them. Dante and Angelina Greco were Vinny's only relatives in the United States. Dante was Vinny's first cousin on his father's side, and his wife Angelina, who both came over just a short time before Vincenzo did. In attendance that day were Dante and Angelina and the Petrellis. Fransesco, Irma and Umberto.

Once married, Maria and Vincenzo were still very much alone. Not because they didn't want to get to know each other, but because they had cultural differences and the language barrier sometimes became a reason for their surface level conversations. They were two people, alone in search of the American Dream, but together in their shared isolation. They discussed what would be next for them, and how they'd ever feel fully at home. Vincenzo had dreams of opening a supply market where all of his customers from Greco Limited, would come to him for their produce, rather than him delivering on his cart. Maria, wanted to return to Mexico. She was never fully settled in America, and hoped that one day she'd return to her family, give them money, and tell them about how great her life had been in the land of dreams. But she never felt pure happiness in her life with her Italian immigrant husband. Plus, her broken English and Italian, began to blend and make her Spanish sound less native and more eclectic, which saddened her deeply.

When Maria was joyous, it was often over memories of love. Love that she had for her family, her culture or her country, alongside with her love of food. Food, and the commonality of not belonging, was ultimately what bonded the couple. Vincenzo tried to make Maria happy and continuously tried to impress her with bringing home the finest of imported goods and freshest delicacies from Italy, but they never quite added up. Maria tried to be hopeful, positive and forward thinking, but something was always holding her back.

When the pair would talk their best talks, it was over food and homemade wine. Maria wasn't much of a drinker, but she enjoyed a couple of glasses, enough to take the edge off and give her the courage of something to look forward to.

"Vincenzo, why do you think we were put on this earth?" Maria pondered as she looked out the second-story window of their two-bedroom apartment overlooking Paterson.

"What do you think our real purpose is? Is it to be a lover for someone else, or a friend to those in need?" She asked her questions one after another in her broken English. "Is it to work, to make money, and wake up every day to do it all again?"

"What's making you think of this, *mi amor*? Is it because you're unhappy?" Vincenzo never wanted to believe that he could be the cause of her occasional, undeniable despair.

"No, I'm just thinking." Maria paused. "I try to be happy. I think I'm happy, but I'm not sure most of the time. Most of the time I think I'm just going through the motions, and unsure of what exactly I'm doing here. Am I to have a family of my own someday? I know I'm not being the best partner to you. You want a nice Italian wife, a family and babies. As for me, I don't know what I want."

This was the first time Maria and Vincenzo had spoken of such things. Although the tone of the talk was dismal, the depth of their conversation elated Vincenzo, and he wanted more.

"Did you say a family… and babies? I don't want that with anyone but you. If that's what you want, that's what I want. Of course I want to have children and leave a legacy here, but you and I never spoke of such things. We never talked about babies…" Before Vincenzo could get a word out, Maria interrupted.

"Babies," Maria whispered the word and looked away from Vincenzo. "I will be honest with you, Vincenzo. I never thought I wanted to be married. At least, not married in America. Not married in America, to an Italian. I didn't want to be *owned* by someone. I didn't want to be legally bound to someone, like a slave. I didn't want to know I would be someone else's responsibility aside from my own." Maria took a breath and rubbed her head. "But, here we are. We're married, in America. And now, I think maybe talking about babies is something worthwhile."

"I didn't know that was how you felt, Maria." Vincenzo paused for a second before proceeding. "I didn't know *these* were all feelings you had. Maria, are you happy? You know, that is, deep down inside?" Vincenzo tried to get a read on Maria's face before reaching for her hand. "I know you're unsure of America, and what life could be like, but are you happy?"

Maria smiled, slowly, her gaze fixed on Vincenzo, but before he could let her respond, he continued with his thought.

"I don't know why we're here. All I know is that we are. We're here and it's up to us to make the most of our time here. Who knows how long or how short we've got, Maria. But I want to start living a life. A life with you, and a life of happiness and excitement. So whatever that may mean for you, think about it."

There was stillness and silence in the air and the two did not say much more over the remainder of their meal. They quietly conversed as they disassembled the meal and cleaned up. Once again, they were each alone with their thoughts. Together, yet alone, just as they had started.

After what should have been uncomfortable silence and awkward interactions, the pair went about their nightly routines. Maria and

Vincenzo had been so used to not speaking at times, that they didn't know how to communicate when things got turbulent, because they'd never really had to. Nothing that the couple discussed was that heavy or disheartening that it would cause them to be displeased with one another. The company that they were for one another was a warm body and a gentle touch, nothing that got to the depths of one another's souls. But Vincenzo tried. He yearned to be a good husband and plant roots in the country he now called home. He knew what it was that he wanted.

Because of the unsuspected heaviness of their dinner conversation, once everything was cleaned up, Vincenzo had opted for another glass of wine and dozed off on the sofa.

He had been out for nearly an hour on the couch, when he awoke to Maria straddling him. This was unlike any interaction they've had throughout their relationship. When they were intimate, it was not in a romantic, sensual way. Their sex was more of a passionless chore. This, however, was different. Maria gently kissed Vincenzo's cheek and whispered in his ear, "I want to have a baby." Vincenzo expected anything from the earlier conversation but this. He'd anticipated them quietly going about their business until some other form of commonality led them to their next conversation.

Vincenzo felt something he had never felt for Maria before. This was a feeling he would not be able to describe until he was much, much older and able to have gone through mature, emotional encounters. All he knew was that it was deep, moving and invigorating as he responded to Maria's statement with his body. By the way Maria had moved on top of him, it was as if she moved through him. He felt at that very moment that Maria did have love inside of her, and she most certainly had experienced it before. Perhaps a distant lifetime ago, and she was reliving it in that moment with Vincenzo.

Chapter 5

1951

It was minutes before closing at Greco's on Saturday. The place where a mere twelve hours earlier Luella impatiently anticipated their linen delivery service. Now, she annoyingly waited for closing time. As she began to clean off the countertop and collect the miscellaneous items not allowed to be left out overnight, the door swung open and in walked Irma Petrelli.

"Hey! I was wondering where my favorite landlords were this morning. Everything ok?" Luella greeted Irma. It was typical for either one, or both of the Petrellis to be in first thing in the morning. They typically bought in bulk on the weekends for the restaurant in Paterson. They gave Vincenzo his start, continued to guide him in business, and, in turn, became very loyal customers.

"Oh, Luella! What a day. Umberto is not doing well so I was tending to the restaurant all day and Francesco went to make sure he was okay. All is good now. I'm sorry we're so late. I'll still collect the order for the weekend and use it throughout the week."

"I'm so sorry to hear. I'll pray for a speedy recovery and please let us know what we can do." Luella went to the back, let her father know that Irma was there, and together they pushed the large cart with heavy crates full of produce, meats and flour out to the front.

Anytime either of the Petrellis were in, it was a nonnegotiable for Vincenzo to be notified. He enlisted his children with all of the duties of the market, but the relationship and debts that he felt he owed to the

Petrellis were not up for debate. Petrelli's was the largest and last account he landed while he had Greco Limited. Between providing fresh produce for both restaurants, the Petrelli account had given him so much work, he no longer needed to look for new business. Francesco, Umberto and Franseco's wife, Irma, all supported Vincenzo, mentored him where they could, and encouraged him to follow his bigger dream of opening a market. Francesco, unknowingly at the time, introduced Vincenzo to Maria who would be the unmatched love of his lifetime, and it was in the Petrelli's building that Greco's Market resided.

Luella quickly caught her father up on the news that Irma had just shared of her brother-in-law's health as they made their way to the front of the store with the order.

"Irma! What happened? Is everything alright with Umberto? What can I do?" Vincenzo offered.

"Oh, Vincenzo," Irma replied as she grabbed his face. "You are, and always have been, too sweet. Everything is alright now. We had a scare. Umberto fainted in the restaurant and they ran some tests. They said that he may have something going on with his heart, but he's in good overall condition. They want him to cut back on the meat... and the *vino*." Irma smirked. "Can you imagine? My brother-in-law, not having his steak and *vino*! He wouldn't be who he was!"

"Well I'm sorry to hear that, but I hope he listens to what the doctors say. It's important, you know, your health. It's all we've got and hopefully we've got it for a long time."

As Vincenzo responded, the room went dull, the unavoidable sorrow hit them all at once. The memory that Vincenzo and Irma had of Maria flooded their minds, and what Luella imagined of her mother, filled hers.

"You're absolutely right, Vincenzo. Wise beyond your years. We're all lucky to be here, and we miss Maria all of the time." Irma acknowledged that while dealing with her brother-in-law, she faced a husband and a daughter who knew the sadness of loss, in different respects.

"Let me run. Thank you both, as always. I'll see you next week, and

I'll have Francesco give you a call about Umberto's status if you don't hear from me." Irma kissed them both goodbye.

It was a little after six when the exchange with Irma concluded. Vincenzo followed behind her to bring the sign in, close and lock the door, and turn the "open" sign off. Vincenzo did not want his daughter to have to deal with the weight of his grief as well as her own at the thought of her mother being brought up. So he quickly continued with closing the store and in Vincenzo fashion, tried to lighten the mood.

"Luella, you look beautiful. I meant to tell you that all day today and I didn't want you leaving without knowing that. What made you pull it in your face? You never have it down in the market." Vincenzo gestured to his daughter's hair.

The imaginary portrayal of her mother that was taking up space in Luella's head was quickly replaced with irritation. She remembered her hair. She remembered Andriotta's. She remembered the linens, and she remembered Joe. She remembered he hadn't come today. She remembered how much her hair had brushed against her face throughout the day, and that she reluctantly pushed through it at the chance that Joe Andriotta would be back and admire her effortless look. Though it wasn't her father's fault, nor was he aware of the intent behind her look, she couldn't help but feel slightly deflated. She smiled at her father and found herself wrapped in one of his hugs.

"*Grazie, Papa. Te voglio bene.*" Luella loved her father, and he was the greatest single parent he could have been. He did everything, daily, to make sure his children knew how much he loved them. Even since they were young, he'd instill in them that both their parents loved them very much, and that since their mother was an angel now, he had to give her love through him, strengthening its sentiment.

The pair walked to the back of the store together, turning off the front-of-house lights, which all turned dark in unison. Elena came out from the back office and looked behind her, figuring she had forgotten something as she normally felt she had. Vinny came out of the bathroom adjacent to the office, drying off his hands with the towel as he pushed the door open. The foursome was headed home for the evening. Sundays were their day of rest. Elena and Vinny lived only two blocks from Luella and Vincenzo in Hawthorne, which had a tight knit Italian community in 1950. Vinny opened the back door, allowing everyone to go first, taking one last look back, as if he too, forgot something. As he went to close the door and lock it behind him, he couldn't help but notice the shelf that housed the linens.

"*Oh-wee*, those linens sure are piling up. I hope Andriotta is coming soon."

Chapter 6

1951

Elena and Vinny arrived around 11:15 a.m. every Sunday at Vincenzo's house, after attending the 10 a.m. mass. Vincenzo opted for the 7 a.m. worship. Luella would go almost every Sunday and meet with either her father or her brother and sister-in-law. There were some days she enjoyed the simplicity of the mornings and having no responsibility; though everyone would shame her for not attending the house of the Lord on the holiest day of the week.

Additionally, Sundays were filled with food and family, no different than any other day of the week in the grand scheme, but Sundays were, somehow, still unlike the rest. They moved differently, and felt lighter. Luella and her family were able to embrace one another with wine and not have to be bothered with any of the ancillary duties that go with running a business. Elena's parents often attended, where her father brought homemade sausage and her mother helped cure it in the kitchen. Vincenzo did not have any family in the United States aside from his children, and his cousin, Dante. Dante, his wife Angelina and their children Emilia and Sofia were over every Sunday. Sofia was twenty-two, the same age as Luella, and the unexpected Emilia was fifteen. All of the second cousins got along beautifully, and never referred to each other as such. Dante and Vincenzo made a tremendous effort to have their children grow up together and began having Sunday dinners when Luella was born. Not a Sunday passed that they didn't enjoy the company of their small, but powerful bond. Dante and Vincenzo's fathers were brothers, making the two of them first cousins and both carriers of the Greco name. Dante, two years Vincenzo's senior, had come to America three years earlier with his new bride, Angelina. Dante settled in Paterson, and helped Vincenzo when he first got to the states. Vincenzo, however, did not want to impose on the newlywed couple exploring their own path, so he set out on his own.

Once the two of them had their children, and after the loss of Maria, Dante and Angelina began showing up regularly to Vincenzo's with food to make sure the family was eating in their time of grief. Sometimes, if the market got busy, Emilia and Sofia would help out, and Sofia often hung out waiting for Luella to finish work before the two set out for a night of amusement. Before Elena, Sofia was the sister Luella never had. She had her *Zia* Angelina, who doted over her, but was very much a stern force in everyone's lives, typically laying down the law and reprimanding the young girls for being out late. Sofia was a ball of energy, and a fiery soul. She and Luella would constantly laugh together and enjoy going for ice cream, or to a drive-in film in the summer. When the two were together, they would only think about one another, and bountiful laughter followed wherever they went.

"*Ciao Zio*," greeted Elena. She was near the door shaking the flour off of her towel. Elena extended the door open from the inside, noticing Dante carrying a large cardboard box.

"*Ciao bella*. Help me with this, would you? Fresh tomatoes." Dante passed off the box as he reached behind him to grab another load. "From the garden."

Following closely behind, was Emilia with a smaller cardboard box with a generous amount of eggplant poking out from the top.

"Why on earth? You don't think we have enough produce? We have it coming out of our ears and eyes at this point." Luella remarked from the kitchen.

"Sh, Lu." Elena shot her sister-in-law a look, trying to keep her uncle from being offended. "Beautiful, *Zio*! Beautiful! *Papa* is going to love it!"

"I know, there's nothing like imports from Italy, but I'm very proud of my little but mighty garden here in New Jersey. The soil is not like

Sicily, neither is the sun, but the turnout is amazing! Use it as you wish." Dante replied, shrugging his shoulders as if he were letting his air of insult roll off with the shrug. "If you don't want to sell it, I understand."

As the family embraced one another, Vinny began to share his dream from a few nights prior with the group.

"So get this, I had this dream where Elena and I, and Luella all had babies! All boys. We were able to continue on with the Greco name and it was beautiful. Bigger Sundays, more food, and more Grecos. Sorry, Sof. You didn't have a baby yet in my dream. But maybe one day… if you ever find someone to tolerate your stubborn ass." Vinny said as he playfully punched his cousin's arm.

The crew had a sibling-like relationship, and the banter was welcomed. No one in the Greco bunch took things to heart, or got insulted when there were friendly wisecracks being made. No one got insulted, that is, unless it was about the food that someone didn't want to accept from another.

"Elena, how did he land you? You are too good looking for this chump!" Sofia cracked back. Vinny grabbed Sofia, pretending to mess her hair up and put her in a headlock. This was the usual tone of Sundays. Wisecracks, food, wine, laughs, and more wisecracks.

The day was nearing dusk and no one stayed much later, knowing that Greco's Market needed to be occupied early the next day. Vincenzo arrived at the market around 4:30 a.m. to begin baking and tending to the meats. On Mondays and Fridays, Vinny would join his father at that time to assist with the overhaul that came with the start of a new week and the beginning of a new weekend. Luella would arrive everyday at 5:30, and Elena would typically come right before open; a few minutes before 6:00. On the days when Vinny wasn't needed as an extra set of hands, he'd commute in with his wife.

As the day set into evening and the family was beginning to wrap up, Vincenzo and Luella sat outside on the front steps while the rest of the family was inside, gathering their things and saying their fifth goodbye.

"*Tesoro mio,*" Vincenzo grabbed his daughter's hand. "Is everything okay?"

"Everything's okay, *Papa*. Why do you ask?" Luella replied, but knew she had been giving off an energy of dismissiveness. Luella was twenty-two and nowhere near marriage, or even having a prospective partner. She wasn't sure if she wanted to continue in the market, or begin exploring her studies. She was starting to feel discouraged and unenthused about her days. Two things Luella was not; discouraged and unenthused.

"Luella," Vincenzo sighed, "I gave you that name because you're a warrior. You will always figure your way, and you are meant for greatness. Never doubt yourself and whatever it is that you're going through, even though you deny it to your own father, I am here for you."

Vincenzo always knew when something was off with his children. He had the parental instinct that Luella often questioned in herself. Her father knew when to say the most needed things, and when to offer advice.

"I just want to feel the spark, *Papa*. I'm not sure what spark that is. Love, work, life. Just… *a spark*! I'm feeling like I don't know why we're here." Vincenzo was quickly brought back to a conversation he had shared years earlier with his late wife. He saw Maria in Luella. He did not want to see the parts of her that were dark, depressed and unsure. He wanted to take whatever doubt his daughter may have been feeling and remove it from her immediately, except, he didn't know how to. He hadn't been sure with Maria, and he was not sure with Luella. The difference, though, was that Luella and Vincenzo spoke about everything. Luella was not afraid to talk about her feelings, nor was Vincenzo. He taught his children to be open with him and with themselves. This, however, was the first time he *felt* Maria's presence and uncertainty begin to bubble in his daughter.

"Luella, please. Don't think for one second your existence is in question. You are here to accomplish and see greatness. God created you to be a warrior, a survivor and a giver. You have the heart of a lion and will always find your way. You are here for all of the beauty life has to offer, and you have a gift. You will give people part of you, and that, *tesoro mio*, is what you will do. You will be a treasure to all."

Luella smiled, looked at her father and laid her head on his shoulder. There was nothing else to be said at that moment. Vincenzo did as he always does, offering up the most heartfelt response to one's emotions, making them feel secure in the time they needed it most. Luella was left with her father's words and her thoughts. As she rested her head on his shoulder, looking across the street, beyond the houses and towards the horizon, she imagined what a gift she could be to someone.

1951

The sound of Luella's alarm went off as it usually does, except this Monday morning, she was a bit slower in her reaction time. Typically, Luella jumps out of bed, nearly frightened, as if every morning is not the same expectation of the previous one. She's such a deep sleeper, that she cannot help but get startled at the sound of her consistent 5:00 a.m. alarm. This morning was different. She slowly arose from her lying position, sat up for a minute and looked out her window. She loved the smell of mornings, the sounds of the early risers humming in the distance and the birds welcoming the sun with their chirping melodies. She made it a point this morning to pause and soak it all in. Luella felt everything deeply, and her morning backdrop was no different. When she got out of bed and began arranging the sheets, comforter and pillows appropriately, her mind was fixated on what her father had said to her the night before. *He only said I'd be a gift because I'm his daughter. His gift, and his treasure. No one else will feel that way about me,* she thought. She held her arms above her head in a stretch, went to shower, and get herself together for the new week.

Elena was already in the office when Luella opened the back door of Greco's; this wasn't the norm, but also wasn't surprising. Sometimes when Vinny had to be at the market earlier than usual, Elena would start earlier too. No sense in waiting until 6:00 to head in if she were already up at 4:00.

"Hi Lu. I already have the coffee going, your cup is on the counter for you. Half a cup of sugar and a gallon of milk, with a drop of coffee." Luella liked her coffee light and sweet, but preferred it that way due to the strength of the blend she'd brew. She'd need the added sweetness to mask the dark, strong roast she'd so perfectly concoct.

"Thanks Elena. How'd you sleep?"

"Not bad. When Vinny gets up sometimes on the earlier days, you know how it is. I just couldn't fall back asleep. I also was thinking about some of the inventory lists, and wanted to get a head start on the Petrelli's for this week. I feel terrible about Umberto. I was thinking of offering to bring it down myself." Elena was thoughtful. She wholeheartedly wanted to make everyone around her comfortable and was happy to offer a hand where she could.

"I'm sure they'd appreciate that, and *Papa* would too." Luella turned to leave the office and headed down the hallway, only glimpsing quickly at the shelves that housed the linens to her right.

"*Ciao famiglia*!" she shouted as she made her way down the hallway. She figured her loud greeting would cover both her brother and father, regardless of where they were at the moment.

Luella went about her normal routine; opening the gate, securing the outdoor sign from behind the counter, and making her way towards the door with a minute left until 6:00. After placing the sign, she saw out of the corner of her eye, the large white and blue delivery truck turning the corner onto Lafayette Avenue a few blocks down. Luella rushed inside, ran behind the counter and straight to the bathroom.

"Lu! You okay?" Elena shouted from the office.

Luella was breathing heavily and began to shake slightly, overjoyed by the delivery that she had been waiting for since the Saturday before. But as she looked in the mirror, she thought, *Oh my God*. Not expecting Joe, she put no time into her appearance. She couldn't let him see her like this.

"El, I need your lipstick. Please, fix my hair. I look like a mess!" Luella exclaimed.

"What is this about? Calm down, you look beautiful as you always do. But what in the world are you getting ready for right now? I can't imagine anyone aside from the Patrowskis, Marco or the very pregnant Sarafina have even been in sight yet."

"Andriotta," was all Luella could say, and instantly, Elena jumped into action. She knew that the first interaction was one that drew Luella to act in her own way, flirtatious. She could sense when Joe Andriotta was in her sight, that Luella was nervous due to her undeniable attraction. Elena grabbed her leather satchel off the back of her chair and jolted the lipstick out of the side pocket, unscrewed the cap, and turned the tube.

"Here," Elena forced the lipstick into Luella's hand with very clear instructions. "Swipe, swipe, dab."

Elena reached for her hair brush and found a matching set of hairclips, pinning both sides of Luella's hair back, wiggling some pieces lightly until Luella's natural bangs fell in front of her face. In that instant, Luella realized that Elena had noticed the bangs from Saturday, when she'd expected to see Joe Andriotta.

"There. You look beautiful, and not too overdone for 6:00 a.m. on a Monday." Elena winked and returned to her desk as if the beauty drill had not just happened.

"Thank you." Luella grasped her hands tightly and embraced her sister-in-law with a grateful look.

"Go! Go pretend you're busy and *not* waiting for him. Act natural. He's going to be in love by the time he leaves our parking lot." Elena shooed her sister-in-law from the office and pretended to get back to work.

Luella went as hastily as she could to the front. Vinny was already there with the tray of fresh bread put into their proper baskets on the shelves. He was tending to Sarafina who couldn't kick her craving for Italian bread with apricot jam this morning. Sarafina looked a bit more presentable, wearing an oversized pajama top and light blue slacks, however her hair still remained in the rollers from the night before.

"Lu! I was hoping I'd see you this morning. I wanted to tell you about my dream. They're getting stranger and stranger the bigger this kid gets, I swear. We were all waiting for you and it was a birthday party. I just can't remember whose birthday it was. Anyway, there were talking dogs! Can you imagine? Talking dogs. I swear, this kid is going to come out and direct films if it's his brain that I'm starting to get."

Luella feigned interest and offered a nervous giggle, but she was preoccupied with wondering if Andriotta had any other stops before Greco's.

"That's it? No wise remark or response? You feeling okay?" Sarafina questioned.

"I'm fine. Sorry, just a little preoccupied, thinking about the order for the Petrellis. That is funny. If he comes out thinking the same way your dreams have been going, he'll have a unique perspective on the world, that's for sure!"

"*Ciao, Giuseppe*!" Luella's ears perked up as she heard her father's voice from the back of the store. She needed to handle the delivery.

"*Papa*! I got it! You finish up the work in the kitchen. Plus, I have extra linens in the front that I saw from Saturday." Luella took the door from her father and swiftly made her way between him and Joe.

Vincenzo raised his hands, patted Joe on the back, and made his way towards the kitchen, shouting on his way, "Tell your father I said hello, *Giuseppe*."

"Good morning," Luella said, making her best effort at flirting.

"Good morning, Luella Greco! I was hoping you'd be here this morning, and as fate would have it, here you are." Joe smiled and made his way past Luella through the doorway, heading towards the drop stop, admiring her as he moved.

"Fate, huh?" Luella laughed at the remark. "I wasn't sure if you'd be coming on Saturdays from now on; we weren't sure when to expect you." She looked down at the large cinder block they had used as a door stopper and decided against having it hold the door open.

"You said you had more dirty linens in the front, do you want to tell me where they are so I can get them?" Joe offered.

Luella had made that part up to try and get her father to vacate the area. She had to think quickly so Joe wouldn't catch her in a lie.

"No, no, I can run and check."

Luella quickly ran to the front of the store pretending to move things around looking for the make believe linens that she had mentioned. She returned to the back of the store and heard a throat being cleared as if to get her attention come from the office. Elena was peering up from her work to make eye contact with Luella. Once their eyes connected, Elena's quickly brought Luella's to the corner wall where there were a few clean linens that could quickly look as though they needed to be laundered with a bit of disheveling. Luella silently mouthed "thank you" as she put her hands in the praying pose and made her way to the linens. Roughly loosening them and gathering the pile in her arms, she returned to Joe.

She dumped the pile into the burlap bag Joe held out.

"Thanks. I'll swap these and get out of your hair." Joe winked and paused before trailing off his reply, "Your hair, by the way, looks very nice. Your eyes really stand out and you have really beautiful skin." As he left, he looked down for a door stopper, not wanting to have to bother the Grecos by ringing the buzzer again. Luella had to figuratively collect herself up off the floor that second in disbelief that Joe had acknowledged *and* appreciated her quick effort upon his arrival. Before she could think about what to do next, she just moved. Nearly skipping after Joe, she followed behind him, "No worries, I'll come out with you."

Joe looked at Luella: "You know, you're something Luella Greco. I wasn't sure what to make of you at first, but now I realize that you truly are something."

"Me? What do you mean, *I'm something*," as if mocking Joe. "You don't even know me." She laughed.

"You're right. I don't know you. But I know about you. I can tell I *want* to know you. Who you are. Who Luella Greco is." Joe climbed in the back of the delivery truck, unloaded the dirty linens into a bin, and hung the bag on a hook displayed from the ceiling. Before grabbing the clean linens, he said "Luella Greco, can I take you to dinner?"

Luella laughed nervously. "You want to take *me* to dinner?"

"I don't want to, I have to. I have to take you to dinner Luella Greco. I have to know who you are. Less of a question, more a demand." Joe looked back at her and winked. "So, what do you say? How about tonight? We both have early mornings, so I won't keep you out too late."

Joe picked up the clean burlap bag and jumped from the back of the truck to land standing directly in front of her.

Exhilarated, she responded: "Tonight is fine. I can be ready by 6:45?"

"6:45 is perfect." Joe made his way with the bag over his shoulder towards the back door.

Luella opened the door and as Joe walked past her, he grazed her body with his. Luella stood in the doorway admiring Joe's physique, every indent on his arm from the perfectly chiseled muscles. Joe turned around and grabbed the paper slip from his back pocket, handing it and a pen to Luella. As Luella grabbed the paper, their hands lightly touched, and their eyes connected. She pressed the paper against the wall to sign and handed it back to Joe.

"Thank you, Luella Greco. I'll see you tonight then. Should I pick you up here, or is somewhere else good?"

"You can pick me up here, that's fine. I only live a block away." Luella remarked.

Joe rolled up the signed invoice and waved it graciously at Luella before putting it back in his pocket.

"I'll see you tonight."

Joe headed out the back door and towards his truck, turning to smile and wave again at the wide-eyed, young Luella. The anticipation was apparent in both of them, and the energy was lively. Luella closed the door behind her and stopped at the doorway of the office, waiting to see if her sister-in-law had a response to the encounter. Elena looked up and before the two could say anything, they both squealed and laughed, jumping up and down where they stood. It was what everyone wanted; for Luella to find happiness and love.

Chapter 8

1951

It was 6:37 p.m. and Luella had decided she wanted to be outside already, waiting on the bench when Joe arrived. She turned to catch a glimpse of herself in the window's reflection. She was wearing her favorite outfit for a summer night - a blue and white striped, short sleeve blouse, tied in a knot at the bottom, with high-waisted, tapered red pants, and her hair in a high ponytail with a matching red ribbon in it, allowing her bangs to wisp freely. Luella loved fashion, and at the turn of the new decade, pants were acceptable for women to go out in, so she took full advantage. She played with vibrant colors and patterns, and mixed and matched where she could. She felt her shape was done much more justice in a more fitted shirt and pant combo than any drop-waist dress.

As Luella waited, she took her compact out of her handbag to snag one last glance of her lipstick and hair. Out of the corner of her eye, Luella noticed the 1947 Cadillac Series 62 Convertible Coupe with a fresh coat of wax that was pulling up. It glistened under the turning dusk sky, practically sparkling. In the driver's seat of the convertible, was Joe Andriotta. He fit so perfectly in the automobile that it looked as though the car were made for him, and he, made for the car. Joe cut the engine and smiled, his bright teeth perfectly displayed. As Luella stood up from the bench, Joe jumped out of the car to quickly grab Luella's hand. He held it up to his face, and planted a gentle kiss there. Just from this, Luella noticed that Joe had soft lips.

"Hi, Luella Greco. You look beautiful," he said, guiding her to the passenger door. As he got her situated, he leaned so far in, it was as if he were going to kiss her. He was ensuring she was securely and comfortably placed in the car before closing the door.

"Hi Joe Andriotta," she said, "Why do you always say my full name?" She didn't mention his chivalry, appearance, or effort.

Joe smiled. "I'm not sure. Perhaps it's because Greco's Market was the last place I ever expected to meet such a beautiful and intriguing woman. It's funny how things work out."

Luella smiled at the thought of Joe considering her beautiful *and* intriguing.

"You're not so bad yourself," she said. "But when you address me with my full name, it sounds so formal and my knee-jerk reaction is to also call you by yours." They smiled in silence for a few seconds.

"So, where are we headed? I hope what I'm wearing is alright. It's nothing fancy."

Joe admired Luella, her hair, and her outfit. He appreciated a woman who pulled herself together as Luella had.

"Well, I figured since we both have Italian food for just about every meal, we'd switch it up. Are you up for a trip to Rutherford? They just opened this Irish Pub and I figured we could have a pint and try something different. Then, I know this nice little walking path near an ice cream shop. That is, if you're not too tired and up for a stroll." Joe's plan was thoughtful. It *was* true; they both ate Italian food nearly every meal of every day.

Eager to get their date started, Luella settled into her co-pilot's seat and smiled at Joe.

"That sounds lovely."

They talked easily the near-thirty-minute drive to Rutherford. They found they had so much in common - music, movies and a shared culture. Their upbringings were so similar, it was as if they'd already met one another's family. The Italian roots that made them who they were bound them from the beginning. The familiarity in what they understood, expected and appreciated made conversation effortless; the lack of silence was, naturally, due to their ability to hold a conversation. *Italians.*

Four hours passed before realizing how late it was. They spent their time engaging at the Irish eatery; talking, laughing, and sharing a beer- a welcomed change from the daily consumption of wine. At an ice cream parlor, they shared a banana split, and then took a walk, just as Joe had envisioned.

As the black Cadillac convertible approached Cedar Avenue, Luella leaned back on the headrest and admired the open sky. The stars were as bright as white bulbs, and the blue of the night sky's backdrop looked as deep as the ocean. She had never before seen the night sky from within a car. This was her first time in a convertible.

As they pulled up to the Greco residence, Joe was about to go open her car door, but Luella grabbed his arm and pulled herself nearer to him, their faces only inches apart. She let out a sigh in his ear, and her breath hit his neck as if a small gust of wind had just sent shivers down his spine. He pulled back to admire her one last time.

"Thank you, Luella Greco, for a night that I knew needed to happen. Thank you for allowing me to quench my thirst by beginning to understand who you are."

The thought of Luella filling any desire that Joe Andriotta had made her feel full inside. She looked back at him and wanted nothing more than for him to kiss her.

"Thank you, Joe Andriotta. Thank you for a lovely evening, and what's to be an exhausting day tomorrow." Luella rolled her eyes and chuckled as she went to open the door.

Joe jumped out and ran to the passenger side; there was no way he was going to miss showcasing yet another example of his chivalrous character. He would walk her to the door. Joe shut the car door gently behind her, not to wake the neighbors, or Vincenzo. They walked arm-in-arm to the front door and stood under the porchlight. Joe slowly moved in and placed a sweet, soft kiss on Luella's cheek, and then kissed her hand just as he had earlier. Before opening the door, Luella turned back to admire Joe moving down the walkway and back towards the Cadillac, and then he turned too, looking back at her, grinning. He waited until she made it inside safely, then took off.

Luella closed the door behind her and placed her hands over her mouth, then remembering the kiss, over her cheek before pulling both hands together over her chest. Luella was floating and could not believe that just a week and a half prior, she had no idea Joe Andriotta was about to walk into her life and change it forever.

Chapter 9

1951

Holidays at Greco's Market were always bustling. Thanksgiving straight through to New Year's Day, the Greco clan expanded from a steady foursome to six or eight. Angelina, Sofia and Emilia would all help out, Dante too, when his work schedule allowed. Joe and Luella were an accepted item among Luella's family. The Grecos enjoyed seeing the pair together and Vincenzo loved having Joe around. During the holidays when he was done running his routes, Joe also came in as backup for the booming *Il Mercato de Greco*. He was an unofficial Greco. Vincenzo adored his father, and the entire Andriotta family. Although not from Sicily, they accepted one another because after all, the motherland was of the same roots.

Throughout the holiday season, bright red and green lights were strung around the large window in the front. Popcorn and cranberry garland draped from the ceiling and spread across the length of the store. Candy canes and angels were placed in nearly every open space on the counter without disrupting customers. A larger-than-life nativity scene sat above the bread shelves and glowed white underneath baby Jesus. Vinny had felt without the extra light, it wasn't angelic enough. The popularity of Greco's exploded during Christmastime; it was a true local attraction.

"*Ciao, ciao,*" Sarafina came in shouting over the sound of her wailing baby in her arms. "I need another panettone and a pound of *mozzarella di bufala*."

"You're not pregnant again, are you?" Emilia asked bluntly from behind the counter.

"Emilia!" Angelina nudged her daughter and gave her wide eyes so she knew what she said was inappropriate.

"What? Sorry, *sheesh*, I'm just curious." Emilia gritted her teeth.

Sarafina laughed, "God no. Marco's parents are going to come over and Angelo and I have eaten all of the panettone that we had so far." Sarafina winked at her infant while offering big smiles and air laughs, rocking her finger while he gripped it looking back at her. "And the cheese is for dinner."

"You give a three-month-old panettone? Is that normal?" Emilia interrogated judgingly.

"Emilia!" Angelina stood up from her stool and pushed her daughter out of the way.

"*Scusa*, Sarafina. Forgive my daughter, she shows no manners." Angelina made her way around the counter to admire the baby.

"Come, come," she said to Angelo as she extended her arms out and waved her hands.

Angelina was a sizable woman with thick black hair, beginning to gray, always pulled into a bun behind her head. She typically wore black and some type of house dress or apron covering her clothes, never really exposing her wardrobe.

"*Bambino, bambino*, you'll go to *sleep-o*." She began to sing as Sarafina passed off Angelo and Angelina took him in her arms, rocking back and forth.

"Do I hear baby Angelo?" Elena shouted from the back.

Since Sarafina had given birth, she brought Angelo down with her almost daily, if for no other reason than to say hello and escape the apartment for a bit. Marco was a mechanic, and spent a lot of time at work, so Sarafina got lonely, bored, or just wanted some attention for her perfectly plump newborn. Whatever the intention, it was always welcomed when she made her way downstairs. Everyone loved the baby.

Luella was waiting at the back door that led to the parking lot. It was just shy of 3:30 and Joe had enough time to drop off his truck back at Andriotta's plant, and make his way over to Greco's to help. If there weren't many customers and enough people to cover the front, when it was close to Joe's expected time, she'd run to the back to greet him.

"Hello, hon. How's the day going so far?" Joe asked.

"Okay. It's not too busy right now. This morning there was a line out the door and people were just piling in! It may pick back up in the next hour or so. We'll see."

Joe kissed Luella on the cheek and grabbed her hand. Having Joe work in her family store confirmed her feelings that this was right, and if it weren't, it would *not* be this easy. They'd work for a few hours together, and Joe would head back to the Greco residence most Saturdays, and enjoy an espresso with Vincenzo while Luella decided what they were going to do that night.

Joe hung up his coat before grabbing a clean apron and placing it over his head. "I should really just bring a clean one from the plant, rather than adding to your dirty inventory." Joe joked.

Luella rolled her eyes and laughed, tugging Joe along to the kitchen.

"*Ciao, Giuseppe!*" Vincenzo greeted as he always did.

Vincenzo rarely called him Joe. He liked his given name and the strength that the sound of *Giuseppe* had, how it matched the brawn of the man.

"Hey Vincenzo. How's today? How are you feeling?" Joe hugged and kissed Vincenzo, patting him on the back.

As Luella left Joe to tend in the kitchen with her father, she returned behind the counter. At this point, it was Angelina, Emilia, and Luella in the front, with Elena working in the office.

"*Zia* Angelina, do you guys want to head out for the day? I don't think it's going to get much busier, and if it does, it's nothing *Papa*, Vinny, Elena, Joe and I can't handle."

Emilia's eyes widened with excitement. She looked at her mother as if she were begging for her to take Luella's offer so she could meet up with her friends. Angelina looked at Luella and back at Emilia, hesitant, she replied. "If you think you're not going to need us, then okay. We'll go. I want to start cooking anyway. Tonight, I make veal!" She raised the piece of meat Vincenzo so meticulously wrapped for her with pride.

The family said their goodbyes with multiple kisses and hugs, knowing that they'd all be together again the next day for their Sunday ritual.

As they made their way out of the store, Luella could overhear her sweetheart and father's interaction, which made her happy. Then she drifted off, alone with her thoughts. When alone and in solace, she saw her life as big as she wanted it to be. She'd think about what was important to her, aside from her family, and what she'd want the ring of the new year to bring her. She and Joe were going steady at this point for five months, and still, Luella struggled to believe she was that *gift* that her father promised she would one day be for someone. She felt strongly about Joe, and knew that he cared deeply for her. It wasn't yet the love that she had witnessed the day of Vinny and Elena's wedding, but she was confident in their ability to grow into that. Still, in her silence, with Joe in the next room, she dreamed of the possibilities of a future. One, where she continued to be who she was, happy and content as Luella Greco, and the other, happy and progressing forward as Mrs. Andriotta.

1952

By the time spring rolled around, Luella had enrolled at Paterson State Teachers College for the fall. She felt she'd done all she could for her father and Greco's. Of course, just because she was going to start her schooling didn't mean she couldn't also assist with the market. She would never fully detach herself from the family business. After spending her entire life growing up in those four walls, around the food, preparing the shop for the day, and helping customers, the market was a part of her identity. By starting in the fall, there would be enough time for everyone to get comfortable with the idea of her not being there, full time. And it bought her a little time to make the adjustment, too.

"Wednesday, April 25th, 1952," Luella read aloud as she flipped the calendar in preparation for her day of work.

"Where is the year going, right sis?" Vinny asked as he stacked the loaves of fresh bread in their baskets. Vincenzo organized the meat neatly in the glass case.

"Hey, is Joe coming by today? I think I want to ask him to make me another one of those nice embroidered shirts."

"*Perche* Vinny? You have two of them already!" Vincenzo turned to his son in disapproval.

Joe had become such a constant at that point, that if the family hadn't seen him in a few days, they'd offer a question as such, just to make sure that Luella hadn't cut him loose or vice-versa. He'd come and go as he pleased and would willingly help out where he could. Whether it was continuing to step in at the market on a busy Saturday, help deliver orders, or just throw in a few additional linens on the house, he was always thoughtful.

"I don't know Vin, I think so. He'll be by this evening to pick me up. We're having dinner with his parents." Luella responded without making eye contact. She was fixated on the sound of sirens coming up the street. She made her way to the front of the market and looked out the large window to see what direction they were headed. She did the sign of the cross and said a silent prayer for whoever needed the assistance and similarly for the first responders.

It was just shy of 7:00 when the black Cadillac came down Cedar Avenue to escort Luella to Joe's house for dinner. Luella rarely ran late. She was always dressed and ready to go at least thirty minutes before Joe picked her up. She had time to spare and she'd use that time strategically; reviewing her outfit, fixing her hair, making sure her lipstick was applied perfectly. Nothing could be out of place when she went out with Joe.

Each time Joe picked her up was the same. He'd pull his car as close to the curb in front of the house as he could without scratching the rims. He'd quickly give himself a once over in the rearview mirror prior to heading in to say hello to Vincenzo before taking Luella for the evening. This time, however, was different. Luella was sitting on the front steps, with no indication that she was leaving the house that evening. She was presentable, but not dressed for a date. Joe didn't check his reflection. Instead, he rushed out of the car and nearly bolted towards Luella.

"Luella, what's wrong? Is everything okay?"

"Joe, can you sit with me for a minute?" Luella had been crying, Joe could tell.

"Lu, you're scaring me. What is it? Are you okay?" Joe grabbed her shoulders as he questioned before sitting down next to her. "Is your father okay? Your family? What?"

"I don't think I can do this anymore, Joe." The words leaving Luella's lips set off another stream of tears.

Joe couldn't register what was just said to him. He'd come to pick up his girlfriend to go have a nice supper with his parents as they so often did, and he was greeted with this? This was not at all what he'd expected to start his night off with.

"What?" Joe turned from consoling and caring to reserved and unclear as he pulled himself away from Luella to get a better look at her. "What can't you do, Lu?"

Luella stared straight ahead in silence with just the sound of muffled crying that she was trying so hard to hold in.

"What can't you *do*, Luella? Us?" Joe stood up and planted himself directly in front of Luella's line of sight, forcing her to look up at him. "Where is this coming from?"

Luella slowly lifted her gaze to connect with Joe, their eyes meeting while hers still looked as if she were in a daze.

"Joe, I think the world of you and one day, I'd maybe want to be your wife. I just don't know if that day is today, or tomorrow, or possibly a year from now. I can't commit to you the way you deserve until I commit to myself first. I'll be starting school in the fall and I have to continue to help *Papa* in the market. I don't know... It's just that I want to focus on Luella." As Luella finished her heartfelt answer to Joe's question, she looked back and forth between Joe, and somewhere across the street. It was apparent that she was torn.

"You want to focus on Luella Greco." Joe's response brought bittersweet reassurance to her; the words warmed her. He knew she needed time.

Her eyes focused back on Joe. She paused before saying, "Yeah, I do. I need to focus on Luella Greco."

Joe kneeled down in front of Luella, kissed her forehead before reaching for her hand, and placed one of his gentle kisses on top of it.

"Luella Greco," Joe said as he rested his other hand on top of hers, swallowing up her little hand in between his mitt-sized ones. "I will be here when you're ready."

Luella jumped from the step and threw herself in Joe's arms, embracing him for all that he was; strong, charismatic, understanding and empathetic. While they indulged in the sweet stillness of their embrace, they both let out a soft sigh. Tears continued for Luella, and Joe inhaled the largest breath he could, soaking in the smell of her. Joe was heavy-hearted, but he knew the type of woman Luella was. She was a force and he knew that if she wasn't filling herself first, she would be unable to fill anyone else, including him.

"Goodbye, Luella," he said.

Joe forced his shoulders back, placed his hands in his pockets and went back to his car, the engine still warm. As Joe turned the key and drove off, Luella began to wail. She sobbed with one arm crossed over her torso and the other up to her mouth, trying to muffle the sound of her hysterics. She closed her eyes and tried to calm herself down before heading back inside. She took in a deep breath, hoping it would help pull her together. She watched as the Cadillac turned onto Lafayette Avenue, and wondered if the choice she had just made was the right one, or a regrettable mistake.

Chapter 11

1952

By the following Sunday, the entire Greco clan knew what had happened between Luella and Joe and they were devastated. Vinny had hoped his kid sister would be happily on her way to wedding bells, and while Elena was disappointed, she stood by Luella's decision with no questions asked. Dante and Angelina were already chalking Luella up to join the convent or become an old maid. They couldn't fathom a perfectly fine young woman getting rid of a suitable bachelor like Giuseppe "Joe" Andirotta. Luella confided in Sofia on most things, so this was no news to her, and Emilia was too young to really care. Vincenzo, to Luella's surprise, seemed to understand the most. He consoled his daughter with an open heart and only asked questions that pertained to her happiness, comforting her with reassurance. Vincenzo's parental guidance confirmed that Luella had made the right choice.

Luella opted for a walk instead of attending mass before her family came over that Sunday. With no destination, she began to walk down the street, her legs taking her to wherever it was that her mind was going to stop her. She enjoyed the morning sun, the breeze and the smell of the spring air, welcoming all of the beauty that yet another turn of the season brought, without feeling guilty for spending time away and alone. The minutes turned into hours, the steps turned into miles. She'd been gone for about two hours and the long stretch of sidewalk she had covered felt like a victory. At a park overlooking town, she found a bench, positioned in a marvelous spot; she admired the openness the park had to offer, watched the children on the jungle gym to her right, and the greenery where couples had picnic blankets out to her left.

As Luella sat, she thought about what she wanted for herself. If she were really going to do the schooling, she needed to commit. Did she want to teach young children about art and literature, or did she want to explore new things for herself? Was she meant to travel the world, be an actress or perhaps an activist like former First Lady Eleanor Roosevelt? The future was uncertain, but she knew she wanted to spend the time with and for herself to figure it out. She had never been certain about motherhood, and felt confident in her faith that if that were to be a part of her path, God would make it happen as it was intended to. While Luella was deep in thought, she couldn't help but notice the tall, slender man playing with his golden retriever, throwing a tennis ball and engaging in a game of fetch. As she allowed herself to drift off with her thoughts, she closed her eyes for a moment to envision what it was she wanted to do, where she wanted to go and who she wanted to be. Luella, alone in her thoughts, imagining all of life's possibilities, was quickly disrupted by a ball hitting her forehead, and was immediately sucked back into the present.

"Miss, I am so sorry!" The tall man shouted as he ran over to make sure she was okay. "I'm so sorry, I totally misjudged that throw. Are you alright?"

Luella rubbed her head and looked up at the man now towering over her, struck by his bright blue eyes and thin face.

"Yeah, I'm okay. I don't think I've ever been hit in the head by a dog toy before." Luella laughed, holding her head with one eye squinted partially from the sun and partially from the pain.

The man laughed as he bent down to get a closer look at the forehead to ensure there was no damage. "Well, luckily it's not the dog's fault. I'm sorry again. Would you like me to get you some ice? It's the least I could do."

"I'm alright, really. Please, don't worry about it. I'll be okay."

The man took his hand from his pocket. "Well, I'm Mickey," he said before whistling for his dog, "and this here is Buster." The dog came running and jumped up on the bench, his tail wagging as he looked at Luella's face.

"Hi, Mickey." She laughed before she extended her hand for the dog to smell. "Hi, Buster." When Luella greeted the dog, he instantly gravitated towards her as if to share his love.

"Oh my! You are a friendly boy, huh?" Luella embraced the dog and laughed while he rested his front paws on her lap, panting heavily. "I'm Luella."

"Well, Luella, I'm sorry again. He really likes you."

"I always wanted a dog, but I think my father is afraid." Luella laughed as she said the words out loud, never really needing to explain that to anyone in her family since they all had the same sentiment toward animals.

"Afraid of dogs? Nah, you can't be afraid of dogs! Just look at him! They're harmless and just want to love and be loved." Mickey rubbed Buster's head and massaged his ear. "Do you live around here?"

Luella smiled at the dog and looked back at Mickey, admiring the combination of features that constructed his face; big, blue eyes, light freckles splattered across his nose and cheeks, the red hairs forming a bit of stubble around his mouth.

"I live in the next town over."

"Oh, Hawthorne or Wayne?" Mickey asked intently.

"Hawthorne. Do you live in Haledon?" Luella hadn't intended on walking as far as she did, in the direction she had gone or for as long as she had, but here she was. In another town, now in conversation with a stranger.

"I sure do. I live right up that road and to the left." Mickey pointed his arm in front of Luella.

They engaged in small talk for a few minutes before Luella stood up to leave.

"I'm really sorry again about the…" Mickey pointed to his head and scrunched up his nose before starting to smirk a bit. "I feel awful."

Luella couldn't help but laugh as she rubbed the lump already forming on her forehead.

"Please, don't worry about it. I've got a thick head. At least that's what my brother tells me."

Mickey smiled and laughed and when he did, his shoulders moved with his expression.

"Well, Luella. Would you like Buster and I to walk you home? You're quite a ways from Hawthorne and we have time to kill."

"I don't think that's necessary. I know where I'm going and will be just fine. I hadn't intended on coming this far actually."

"You didn't? Well look at that. As luck would have it, you don't plan on showing up to the park today, and when you do, you get clogged in the head with a tennis ball from an Irishman playing with his dog."

Luella, again, couldn't help but laugh. Mickey had a calming, sweet nature about him. He was unlike anyone Luella had ever met before. Unlike Joe, Mickey was tall and slender. His bright blue eyes, freckles and light reddish hair made it apparent he was Irish, whereas Joe carried his dark features as he carried his Italian pride; big brown eyes, thick black hair and olive skin. Mickey already looked as though he had gotten too much sun that morning, with his cheeks and arms already turning a slight pink from the exposure.

"Well, you know what, if you're up for the walk, how about taking me at least to the edge of town. That way I'm not putting you out too far and I get to learn more about Buster." Luella looked up at Mickey as she was petting Buster's head.

Mickey looked back down at Buster, "What do you say, boy? She wants to get to know you. You always do so well with the human race, huh?"

Mickey slightly pulled on the collar to put Buster's leash back on before allowing Luella to lead the way.

As they began to walk, Luella felt a sense of familiarity with Mickey. It was as if they'd already been acquainted many moons ago, and were catching up like old friends. There wasn't the nervous energy she had felt with Joe, or when she'd had other love interests before; this was different.

"I have to say, and I hope you don't think this is me trying to shmooze you, but you seem awfully familiar." Mickey walked alongside Luella with Buster guiding them down the sidewalk.

"Well, my father owns Greco's Market and I've been there every day since I was four years old. That may be where you've seen me?"

"Hm, no, never been there, but now I'll have to try." Mickey laughed and then went back to finishing his thought. "This is going to sound strange, but it's less about a familiar face and more about a familiar feeling. That's an odd thing to say to a stranger, isn't it?" Mickey turned to Luella as they continued to walk and scrunched his nose up again looking at her as if he, too, were questioning himself. Mickey's facial expressions were so distinct that Luella felt everything he said. They weren't just words coming out of his mouth, but there was emotion delivered right along with them.

"No, I don't think that's odd at all. I actually thought that you seemed familiar too, but I knew it wasn't your look. It was a *feeling* also." She emphasized the word feeling in air quotations with her fingers. Luella looked back at Mickey, while he shrugged his shoulders, unable to explain further.

"Maybe we met in another life." Mickey laughed and continued the conversation: "So, what do you do aside from the market?"

"Well, I actually registered for school in the fall. I'll be starting at Paterson State Teachers College, I think."

"Wow! A future educator. That's wonderful. Have you always wanted to teach?" Mickey's question struck Luella immediately.

"As a matter of fact, no. I hadn't ever really thought about it. I just want to do something for myself aside from the market, form my own identity, that sort of thing. I'm not even sure if I really want to do it, I'm just not sure what else I *would* do if it weren't school." Luella's realization came from saying her thoughts out loud to someone completely unbiased. "My goodness, I can't believe I just shared all of that with a stranger. I'm sorry, I'm sure you don't care about my unsure mindset and my schooling."

Mickey paused before responding, leaving Luella feeling embarrassed for a second from sharing such personal details with a mere stranger.

"I think you should take time to learn about what makes you happy. I believe we only have a short period of time before the good Lord calls us home. We have to chase the dreams we can and unbreak the chains we're in. If you're unsure about school, try it. And if you don't like it, quit." Mickey's matter-of-fact tone made Luella feel like she had the ability to do just that. Try school out, and if it doesn't work, it'll be okay. It was as if Mickey had just opened Luella's eyes to the possibility of exploring something new, not necessarily committing to it.

"What do you do, Mickey?"

"Me? I'm an ironworker by trade and a musician by night."

"A musician? That's lovely! What do you play?"

Mickey's eyes lit up from Luella's question.

"Well, not a professional musician. I get hired here and there at small local places. I write some music and sing. I play the guitar."

Luella loved music and admired Mickey for working his day job to provide and doing something that made him happy with the rest of his time.

"My, that's quite impressive. And your ironwork? Do you enjoy that too?" Mickey's eyes dulled as he chuckled.

"Not nearly as much as I love my music. See, that's the thing with art, though. It's a release that allows you to express all of your sorrows to the world while disguising it with beauty. I could be blue in all other aspects of my life, but somehow, all of that sadness turns into some beautiful music."

As Luella, Mickey and Buster continued to walk, their dialogue did not slow down. The conversation with the familiar stranger was therapeutic for Luella. As much as her father would offer a listening ear and heartfelt advice, it was different talking to someone completely impartial who, in their short meet, challenged Luella intellectually more than she'd ever been before. He asked her questions that expanded her mind and got her to think about the untapped world of possibilities for herself.

About three blocks from home, Luella had realized just how far they had walked.

"You don't have to take me any further," she said. "I only live a few blocks from here. I didn't even realize how far we'd gone. Buster must be exhausted." Without hesitation, Mickey replied. "That's quite alright. It was our pleasure. Wasn't it, boy?"

Luella extended her hand to shake Mickey's. Mickey took Luella's hand in his long, lanky fingers and squeezed it with just enough security.

"Thank you for the conversation. As for walking you home, it's the least we could do after that." Mickey pointed to Luella's forehead, highlighting the lump. "Sorry again."

Luella rubbed her forehead to see how much bigger the lump had gotten and quickly realized it nearly doubled in size in the time of their walk.

"I'll put some ice on it. It'll be fine. I told you, thick head."

Luella didn't want to say goodbye, but knew it was already after eleven and her family was probably wondering her whereabouts. She didn't know how to part from the conversation without making it obvious that she would welcome another chat.

"Okay then, Luella. It was lovely meeting you, even under such regrettable circumstances. Perhaps we'll see each other again one day." Mickey saluted Luella and whistled for Buster to take his lead towards home. Luella watched as Mickey walked away, wondering if she *would* ever see him again.

As Luella came through the front door, all of the calmness of her morning immediately faded into chaos when her family took one look at her head.

"Ah, Luella! *Quello che è successo?*" Vincenzo jumped up from the dining room table and ran towards his daughter, grabbing her face and examining her forehead.

Before she knew it, Elena, Vinny, Angelina, and Dante all came flooding over from where they were to get a closer look and console Luella for whatever it may have been she needed consoling from.

"I'm okay, really. I went to the park and a gentleman playing with his dog overthrew the ball."

"Yeah, and your big head was used as a wall for it to bounce off of!" Vinny shouted from behind the rest of the Grecos, laughing at himself. Elena lightly backhanded his stomach.

"Vinny, sh, please! She might be hurt!" Elena cried out, trying to make her way closer to Luella to inspect the damage.

"Everyone, please. I'm okay. I just need a little ice."

Luella barreled through her concerned family towards the kitchen. As she got herself some ice in a towel and held it against her head, she stared out the kitchen window thinking about Mickey and Buster. She hadn't intended on meeting anyone, feeling anyway or thinking of anything other than herself, but the conversation with Mickey left her wondering what she was really passionate about. She felt this itch starting to rise that needed to be scratched. Was it the effect a man had on her, or was it the feeling of still wondering who *she* was and what her purpose was? While unsure, Luella knew that there was something stirring inside of her again, and she couldn't dismiss it.

1952

Luella was skimming through the brochure of Paterson State School for Teachers, as she had multiple times, when Sarafina came through the door with Angelo on her hip, commanding the room.

"Did any of you hear about Maryann Higgins? James beat her real bad this time. Cops and everything were there. They said she *fell down the steps* and *took a nasty fall*." The apparent disbelief was evident in Sarafina's voice. "I know it was James. Apparently, the talk of the town and what came out of the cops' story was that she had broken ribs and a cracked face." Sarafina barely took a breath before continuing. "A cracked face! Can you imagine? I know my Marco has a temper, and he's slapped me around a time or two but it was warranted. I usually slapped him first or hit him after he hit me. A cracked face, though? Broken ribs?" Sarafina was talking in her usual fast-paced, high-pitched tone, walking around to channel her nervous energy and also to look at the inventory to see if she needed to bring anything back upstairs. Elena came from the back office.

"Oh my God. Is she alright? Is she in the hospital? Where are the boys and where is James?" Elena worried for her acquaintance who had confided in her about her husband's abuse.

Vinny overheard his wife asking and emerged from the kitchen.

"Where is he?" Vinny nearly demanded.

"I don't know, Vin. I have no idea. Apparently she was in the hospital for a few days. I think her mother came down from Boston to watch the boys." Sarafina said. "As for James? Who knows, probably comfortable on the couch with his feet up just waiting for her to be well enough to make him dinner and fix him up another drink." She bounced Angelo on her side, keeping him entertained. He was oblivious to the gravity of the conversation.

"I feel terrible. I wonder if…" Before Luella could finish her sentence, Vinny interrupted.

"If the sirens the other day were for her? Yeah, I'm thinking the same thing." Vinny took abuse towards a woman very personally. He never got to know his mother, but his father wasn't the type to raise his hands. He wanted to protect his father, sister and wife from harm, and as mad as he could get, he just couldn't imagine hitting a female, but sadly it wasn't uncommon. Women took nasty beatings from their disgruntled men and it was often thought they brought it on themselves. They must've done something to get the beating. Whether it was mouthing off, not having dinner ready in time, or looking at their men in an unappealing way, they had it coming. The Grecos, however, felt differently about this. Vincenzo had the mind of an immigrant and the women he loved in his life worked just as hard, if not harder, than the men. Holding jobs to contribute something towards the bills, cooking and cleaning, taking care of a family. The Italian women, and the Mexican woman he had shared his life with, all worked hard and he treated them as equally as he could. Vinny, having been raised this way, felt equally passionate about it. His younger sister had so quickly stepped into the role of a mother-like figure around the house as she became old enough. His wife was doting, caring and sweet, but also had a strong work ethic and loved to challenge him. He felt as though the men should be their guardians, warding off any pain that presented itself, not be the hand to deliver it.

"Vin, you can't get involved." Luella pleaded with her brother from behind the counter.

"Vin, it's not your battle, but this is why I love you," Elena said as she came around the corner to kiss her husband on the cheek and hug his torso. "We're all okay. I'm sure Maryann is okay. I'll ring her this evening and see if there's anything I can do."

Vinny dismissively got out of the hug that his wife had him in and re-tied his apron.

"It's not right. She doesn't have someone to defend her. If something happened to one of yous, I would kill him. You know that." Vinny, aggravated, marched back to the kitchen.

"*Madonna mia*, I hope she's okay." Elena grasped onto the cross around her neck as the worry lingered on her face.

Sarafina waltzed to the counter because as it turned out, she had found something else she needed. Angelo, perched on her hip, looked at Luella in the amazement that babies do while she rang her up and checked them out.

"Well, now that everyone's caught up on the Higgins' drama, tell me about you, Lu. I wanted to wait a few days before asking, but what the hell happened with you and Andriotta? He was a real looker… and nice too! You two made a real nice couple, I'm sad to see it didn't work out. What was he, a cheater? Did you find he was going steady with someone else all along?" Sarafina placed Angelo on the counter and held him up with one hand while leaning in as if she were about to get a juicy earful of gossip.

"No, no. Nothing like that. Joe's a great guy. He isn't the cheating type. I just felt it was the right thing to do at this point in my life." Luella's reply shocked Sarafina.

"The right thing to do at *this* point in your life? Lu, you're almost twenty-five years old. You have to settle down. Find a husband, have babies, make a family. You know, *that's* the right thing to do. What's the matter with you, what are you waiting for?" Sarafina's judgment didn't come from a place of anything other than ignorance. She meant no harm, Sarafina was never one to hold back, and quite frankly, that *was* how they were raised and a part of the societal standard.

"Sarafina, please," Elena interrupted. "Luella is a big girl with a good head on her shoulders. If she felt it was the right thing to do, let it be, would you?" Elena had her own thoughts about the breakup, but knew that her sister-in-law had her reasons and wanted to feel supported, not interrogated.

"Thank you, El," Luella said before looking back at Sarafina. "I have my reasons!"

Sarafina scooped Angelo back onto her hip and shrugged her shoulders.

"Well, I'm sorry Lu. I hope I didn't offend you. I just want you to have what I have." As she said that, she hoisted Angelo a bit and raised her hand up to the ceiling as if she were gesturing to her relationship with Marco and their home life.

"I know, Sarafina, I'm not offended." Luella smiled and waved. "We'll see you tomorrow."

Elena poked her head out from the office to confirm that they were gone, and came back up to the front of the store.

"Lu, are you alright? I haven't asked because I didn't want to pry, but if you want to talk, I'm here."

"I'm okay, El. I'm actually doing really well." Luella smiled from the depths of her. The conversation she'd had with the man in the park had brought her so much peace and helped validate that she made the right choice - to focus on what it was she wanted.

"Alright, as long as you know I'm here for you, always. Don't listen to Sarafina. You know she just loves to gossip because she gets bored with the baby and Marco never being home and all." Elena liked Sarafina, but had very little patience for stories if they were only being shared in the vein of spreading other people's business or making someone feel bad.

"Hey, El. Can I ask you something?"

"Sure, anything."

"How did you know you wanted to marry my brother? How did you know *this* was the life you wanted?" Luella was direct in her question, leaving no room for confusion.

"Well," Elena began, "When I met your brother, it was as if I was struck by lightning. Not in a harmful way, that is. It was as if I had been sleeping my whole life and finally woke up when we met. I'm not sure if it was love at first sight, but when he and I connected, I mean intellectually, he really made me feel as if I had just found my home." Elena looked towards the kitchen, beaming, imagining her and her husband's journey thus far. "It's something that I don't think I'll ever be able to put into words, but I hope that answers your question."

Luella couldn't help but to grin at her sister-in-law's heartfelt answer. "It absolutely does. Thanks El."

Luella thought back to her first meeting with Joe and remembered how she felt. The bit of nerves coupled with excitement. The conversations they shared were around things they both knew so well, their Italian families, food, music, family business. She knew Joe had brought her a sense of security, and in that moment, she could imagine herself as one day being Mrs. Andriotta. But once she was in the relationship, she couldn't deny something was missing. There *had* to be something missing or else she wouldn't have made the decision to leave. Luella wasn't sure if all she wanted to be was a wife and maybe, someday, a mother. What *was* the void she was trying to fill? When she thought about school, it didn't excite her as much as she'd hoped it would. She didn't wake up and jump out of bed in the morning counting down the days until her courses began. She continued to dream; to dream about all of the possibilities. The conversation with Mickey and his dog had opened her eyes to exploring some type of outlet that may bring her true happiness and add beauty to her life, just like music had done for him.

Chapter 13

1928

Vincenzo and Maria were successfully navigating life together, finally. They had gotten to a point where they leaned on each other for support, and looked forward to telling one another about their day. They still didn't have the deep intimacy either of them would've hoped for, but there was enough there to produce a child and get ready to welcome their second.

Maria was never sure about being a mother. She felt the world in which they lived was complicated and wavering; it could easily break a person. But when she found out she was pregnant, she was thrilled to be able to give birth to a baby in America and have it be part her and part Vincenzo. Maria's maternal instincts kicked in and she and Vincenzo were doing perfectly fine with two-year-old Vinny. Maria was happy with Vincenzo, especially after they became parents. She saw him for what and who he was as a father and a partner - attentive, caring and level-headed. Vincenzo, unlike many other men at the time, offered to get up with the baby in the middle of the night, and didn't mind taking over to calm him when he got fussy. Maria had a very difficult pregnancy with morning sickness for the whole nine months, and her second was much worse. She'd often wake up with night sweats and had fallen ill multiple times since carrying their second baby. Vincenzo did what he could to comfort Maria, and wanted to be a father who was present and made his children feel as though the world was their oyster. After all, they were birthing American citizens; the world *was* their oyster.

It was a few weeks before the due date and Vincenzo was with Francesco as he typically was on his Saturday afternoons. He and Francesco were going over the orders for both restaurant locations when Irma came storming in, panting from running from the automobile to where the two men sat in the kitchen.

"Vincenzo, you have to come, quick! It's Maria, something is wrong. The baby is coming and Maria is in and out. Hurry, please!"

Vincenzo sprung from his stool and looked at Francesco with complete shock on his face.

"Maria, my poor Maria! I have to go."

"*Dai*!" Francesco shot up with his friend and mentee. "I will take you. Let's go!"

The two followed Irma to the little apartment, only about ten minutes from where the restaurant was. The ten minutes felt eternal for Vincenzo as he sat in the passenger seat waiting to arrive at his home; his nerves and adrenaline made him feel as though he could've run there faster. He wasn't sure what to expect. Was his wife going to be alright? Was there going to be an issue with the baby? It was weeks early and this whole time Maria had been unwell. Was it a warning? Vincenzo's thoughts were scattering across his mind a million miles a minute. He didn't want to allow himself to think dark thoughts, but he couldn't help but feel as though he were about to walk into something unthinkable when he arrived home. How could it be, that he and his wife finally figured it out, finally had gotten to a place where they were building a life together, and now this? Vincenzo was silent with his thoughts, imagining a world without Maria, a world without a mother for their children. He looked out the window and felt tears rolling from his eyes. He didn't want to think the worst, but he couldn't help it. His mind was going to the darkest place.

As the car pulled up to the gravel driveway, the dust kicked up, but Vincenzo was able to make out what was behind the cloud of dirt. Angelina was holding Vinny, cradling him back and forth, crying. Vincenzo jumped out of the slowing car and ran towards Angelina, reaching for her abruptly, yet careful to not alarm his son.

"Angelina! Angelina, where is she? Is she alright? Is the baby okay?"

"Vincenzo, I'm sorry. I'm sorry, Vincenzo. I pray to God that the Lord welcomed her peacefully. I…" Angelina couldn't finish the rest of her sentence before wailing and hugging baby Vinny closer to her chest.

Vincenzo ran up the flight of wooden stairs and through the back door on the deck that led to their kitchen. The midwife was standing with the newborn, freshly cleaned off, crying. The midwife kissed the baby on the forehead and handed her over to Vincenzo.

"I'm so sorry, sir. It's a little girl. Your wife did the best she could; she fought terribly." The midwife was beside herself. Having seen this before, few and far between, it still shook her to her core. "I'm sorry I couldn't have done anything. She hemorrhaged and she was just too ill, she didn't make it."

The midwife pointed in the direction of the hallway which led past the bedroom and straight down to the bathroom, where Maria was. Vincenzo looked at the midwife, coddling his newborn. A baby girl. Vincenzo kissed the baby on the forehead and left her with the woman standing in his kitchen for another moment before making his way toward the bathroom. He braced himself as he began to walk, using the walls to hold him up. He was dizzy and felt his chest begin to tighten. Vincenzo wanted the two of them to continue to figure out life in America together, with their two children. He wanted them to continue to learn about one another and grow as individuals, to continue to see all of the beauty life had to offer them. Maria was only twenty-six years old. Vincenzo had imagined them living together, peacefully, until they were old and gray.

As Vincenzo neared the bathroom he saw the feet and blood that had been poorly cleaned up on the tile floor. He slowly made his way in, as if not to disturb her. He knew the outcome already and as he got closer, his knees began to buckle, his hands starting to shake. The gasp that came out of him rang throughout the entire apartment and could be heard by Angelina outside and downstairs. When Vincenzo saw all of Maria, lifeless, his cry was so deep it swallowed up every other sound that day. He slowly knelt down and took her resting head propped up on the wall into his arms.

"Maria! Oh, Maria, I'm so sorry. I'm so sorry I wasn't here and I couldn't save you. I'm sorry this is how you left this world. May God have mercy on your soul." Vincenzo's words came out in between his hysterics. "Maria, we were supposed to do this together! We were figuring it out. How am I to raise two children in this country alone?"

Vincenzo continued to rock back and forth, crying with Maria in his arms. He couldn't help but think of Maria coming to this country as he did- young and alone- with a family that he does not know still in Mexico. He couldn't help but to acknowledge the harsh reality that he will have to bury her without her knowing her daughter, or seeing her son grow up. In all of the loneliness that had surrounded their relationship, they were together. They were two people from different worlds trying to make it work, together. Now, Vincenzo was alone. He was alone in trying to raise his two children who would never know their mother. He was distraught over the fact that his daughter would not know a mother's love and that his son would never understand a maternal touch. He found himself, in that moment, needing to say goodbye to his partner and dig deep to find his strength. Because now he had two children that he had to live for. As Vincenzo calmed his cries, the medical examiner walked into the bathroom.

"Excuse me, sir. Mr. Greco, I'm here to record your...."

"My wife. My wife, Maria Greco." Vincenzo did not make eye contact with the medical examiner. Instead, as he gazed off past him and down the hallway, he heard the cry of his baby girl. He looked down at Maria, still in his arms, and laid a long, sweet kiss on her head as if it were to last through eternity. Vincenzo did not want to say goodbye. As he released his lips, he stayed with his head leaning on hers and the tears continued to fall. He gently began to remove himself from underneath her propped-up body and lightly rested her back onto the wall. "I love you, darling. I'm sorry we didn't say that more. I'll see you on the other side."

Vincenzo slowly got up and walked past the medical examiner

straight to the kitchen to his daughter. He did not say anything as he approached the midwife, still holding the baby, and eased his arms in between hers and the baby's body before effortlessly scooping her to his chest. As he looked down at the baby, admiring every bit of her, he noticed she had the shape of Maria's face, and would have dark features as they both did. He was soaking it all in, and he began to cry. These tears, however, were of joy. He brought the baby closer to his face and rested his cheek on the baby's arm, with his eyes closed.

"Thank you Heavenly Father for this gift, my daughter."

The midwife quietly interrupted, "She's perfect. A healthy baby girl with ten fingers and ten toes." She wiped the tears from her eyes, torn between delivering good news amongst such a dark and horrific time.

"Thank you", Vincenzo looked back at her and nodded before resuming his prayers.

"Thank you, Lord. Thank you for her, and my son. Please welcome Maria and watch over her soul. May she find eternal peace with you, Father. Thank you, Maria."

As Vincenzo concluded his prayer, balancing the baby in one hand to do the sign on the cross, he stared down at the baby girl and admired her for a moment.

"My daughter," Vincenzo said, "We will name you Luella. Luella, *warrior*. You fought, and your *mamma* did, too. I love you, Luella."

Chapter 14

1952

Elena appreciated the cooler breeze that graced her walk to the front door of the Higgins' house that Saturday morning. By focusing on the perfect weather, she could resist the eerie feeling growing inside of her, the vision of her mangled friend. Typically, the Higgins' residence echoed throughout the neighborhood with the playful shouts of the twin boys running around, but today, it was quiet. Elena had told Maryann after the news broke of her injuries that she'd drop off some food from the market for the week, if she wasn't up to cooking. Elena knocked and while she waited for an answer she roughed with the cloth towel covering the basket of goods from Greco's, ensuring it was presentable. She heard someone approaching from inside the house and her heart began to race. She could hear her husband's voice in her head, *"El, if James is there, you leave. I don't care how uncomfortable it is. I don't want you in the same house as that wife beating excuse of a man."* What was she to do if James answered the door? She knew Vinny would expect her to pay her respects, offer up the food and politely turn around and head back to the store, but she felt herself beginning to freeze in terror. The door opened, revealing Maryann.

"Thanks for stopping by, Elena," Maryann nearly whispered.

The left side of her face was badly bruised and still swollen, barely allowing the words to be heard, her mouth only able to open narrowly. Her eye was ballooned out from the swelling and she couldn't open it all the way; her body hunched towards the left from broken ribs and excruciating pain.

"Oh, Maryann." Elena placed her hand over her mouth as she examined her friend who usually looked so beautiful and put together, standing tall with Irish pride and her red, wavy hair. Now she looked defeated and mutilated.

She removed her hand from her mouth and leaned in to carefully hug her friend, holding back tears as she gently leaned in on the right side, not to hurt her left side.

"Come in. James isn't home and the boys are up the street at the Watson's. Thanks for bringing the food, I can't tell you how much it means. James will be glad that he doesn't have to pick anything up and that there will be a hot meal."

Maryann took the basket from Elena and hobbled backward into the foyer, making room for Elena to squeeze in, not wanting a neighbor to catch a glimpse of her.

"Maryann, I am so sorry this happened to you. I don't know what to say. How are you?"

"Well," Maryann lifted her right arm as if to show off her injuries and chuckled. "I'm as good as I'm going to be right now. The bruises will fade and the ribs will heal, but my pride won't. This time was bad, Elena. It was real bad."

As the women made their way to the kitchen table and sat down, Elena looked around to notice that the house had clearly been unkempt the last few days while Maryann was obviously out of commission and unable.

"Maryann, what brought this on? What could you have possibly done?"

Maryann laughed and looked past Elena and out the window as she responded.

"I didn't do a damn thing. I'm so sick of covering for him and saying that I brought it on. *I did this*, or *I did that*. I had myself ready, the boys bathed and his favorite meal on the table when he got home that evening and you wanna know what he said to me? He said 'bitch, get up'. In front of the boys. Clearly, he was gin-soaked." Maryann paused to reposition herself on the chair in discomfort. "In front of my boys, he addressed me like that. When I said no, he came storming in the kitchen and grabbed me by my hair. The boys were terrified. They didn't know what to do and I just remember the fear on their faces. Timmy started to scream and Tommy ran over and started beating on his leg. He pushed Tommy and he went flying. I was so mad I started punching his arms above me and he dragged me. He dragged me and I just yelled to the boys to run. I only remember a few punches to my head and then him kicking me in my stomach and that's all I can recall."

Elena could only respond with profanities at that point, heartbroken for her friend.

"We have to get you out of here. You and the boys have to leave." Elena meant *now*. "Where is James?"

"Who knows. He's been here since and has apologized, but I haven't answered him once and he comes and goes as he pleases. I have no idea if he's at work, with another woman, at a bar. I don't know. My parents want me to go stay with family in Haledon, since he's never met them before and maybe wouldn't think to look for me there. My father is too weak to fight, but my mother wanted to come here with a shotgun."

Elena envisioned what the parents felt and her anger rose.

"Let's get you there, today. What can I do to help?" Elena stood up ready to take action and pack the entire house if she needed to.

"My cousin is planning on coming by at some point to start to take some of my stuff over. He should be coming by shortly actually. I told the boys to go by the Watson's so that I could get some of their stuff out without them getting chaotic and being detrimental to our getaway."

Elena, still standing, understood that Maryann did not want her friend to go ripping through everything in her home to pack on her behalf. Instead, she channeled her nervous energy towards digging into the basket for some of the freshly cut prosciutto, four slices of bread, the cheese and the tomato spread to fix them a couple of sandwiches.

"You've got to eat. I can't imagine you have been eating." As Elena finished her statement and looked at Maryann and down at the sandwiches, she quickly realized Maryann would be unable to get the sandwich in her mouth and chew it. Her jaw was too swollen and she'd never be able to get her mouth to open wide enough. Elena felt deflated.

"I'm sorry, Maryann." She continued to pack back up the fixings and place them back in the basket. "I'll bring you something a bit easier to eat later today. We'll keep this for the boys."

"Thank you, Elena. You don't have to do that, though. They've got plenty to eat and so do I. I can't say I've got much of an appetite, but I certainly have food here that I can eat."

The women continued to talk about James, his temper and how Maryann found herself in the position she was in. She said that she had allowed it for too long and this instance was the straw that broke the camel's back. James had beaten her one too many times, but this time was different. This time, came from a dark, dark place inside of him. The anger he released on her was pure hatred and he didn't come to realize that he could've hurt one of his children. Maryann imagined a life of beatings here and there if she were to stay with her husband, but she never imagined he'd take it out on his kids. He never let the twins see his temper or his disdain for their mother when he was drinking. Instead, he'd hide it and if Maryann showed up one morning looking roughed up, he'd say she was clumsy and that she'd brought it on herself.

Footsteps approached the front door and Elena immediately ran to the window to make sure it wasn't James. To her relief, it was a tall, willowy man approaching the steps.

"Maryann, I'm not sure who this man is, but he looks like he knows you."

"Is he long-legged and skinny? Red hair like mine?" Maryann asked from the kitchen table, unable to turn around.

"Yes, yes that's right."

"That's my cousin. Do you mind letting him in?"

Elena opened the door and greeted the gentleman. "Hello, I'm Elena, Maryann's friend. She told me to let you in, she's at the kitchen table."

Elena followed him towards the kitchen where Maryann was still sitting and decided that now would be an appropriate time to leave.

She didn't want to intrude upon a family talking amongst themselves, understanding that there was a certain level of comfort there. Elena began collecting her things as the lanky man sadly looked at his cousin.

"Oh Maryann, this is it." The man said before acknowledging Elena, putting his hand on his cousin's shoulder. "I'm sorry, what did you say your name was?" The gentleman extended his hand, apologetically.

"Oh, that's quite alright. Elena. I'm Elena." They shook.

The man nodded and Maryann said, "This is my cousin, Mickey. He's the one who lives in Haledon with my aunt and uncle. The boys and I will be staying with them."

"Nice to meet you, Mickey. I've got to be getting back to the market, but you take care of this young lady, alright?"

Elena leaned down and kissed her friend on the cheek to say goodbye.

"Market?" Mickey asked out of curiosity.

"Elena's family owns Greco's on Lafayette Avenue. When I can eat again, we'll go there. The best fresh bread and cold cuts you could ever desire." Maryann blew a kiss and placed it on Elena's hand.

Mickey's realization was silent. "Huh, Greco's. I've heard good things."

The air felt lighter for a second as Mickey connected the dots. How small the world can be. The thought was fleeting as he quickly snapped back into reality and knew he had to act fast to collect some of Maryann's things before James got home. But all the while, he had something on the other side to look forward to.

Chapter 15

1952

By the following week, Maryann and her sons had gotten all of their necessary belongings out of their home and into her relative's house. Maryann was able to heal and regain her strength in peace with the help of her Aunt Kathleen and Uncle Tom, who were comforting and protective. They were a Godsend.

It took Mickey a few whiskey sours to muster up the courage to finally head towards Greco's. The coincidence of meeting Elena made him convinced that their paths were meant to cross. Mickey wore his usual, black, button-down shirt and his gray slacks, with a pair of saddle shoes as he walked into Greco's. The door opened and the bells on the top of the hinge rang. Luella was crouched behind the counter, with her arm in the glass case, reaching for the very specific piece of mortadella.

Luella lifted herself back up to eye level with the gentleman in front of her. "Will that be all?"

"That's it. Thank you."

As Luella turned back around, her smile took over her face. She beamed at the man from the park, who accidentally hit her in the head, now standing in her store.

"Well, if it isn't Mickey. The man with the arm and no aim." Luella laughed, as she folded her arms across her chest. "Where's Buster?"

"I thought I'd leave him home for this one, less chance of a tennis ball flying around," Mickey said.

"I'm glad you finally decided to try our food. What can I do you for?" Luella unfolded her arms and gestured towards the wall, housing the bread baskets.

"Well, I think I'll take a sandwich?"

"Alright, what'll you have? How about a prosciutto, fresh mozzarella, and roasted red peppers?" Luella suggested.

"Oh my, that sounds good. I was just thinking maybe a roast beef and cheese, but I like your idea better."

"I'll tell you what, I'll make one of each and I'll eat with you. We can split them in half; that way you still get your roast beef, and you'll try my specialty."

Mickey nodded, excited at the fact that they were about to share a meal. He had been hopeful to see Luella again since their only encounter, and it seemed to him that Luella felt the same. She came around the counter, and made her way towards the small table in the front, gesturing for Mickey to follow her.

"So Mickey, really, what made you finally come in?"

"Well, truth be told, I met Elena at my cousin, Maryann's. When she mentioned she worked here, I was reminded of you and how I needed to come and check Greco's out for myself."

"I'm glad you did. Elena gave me the update on Maryann. I had no idea she had family local. I'm happy you were able to help her." Luella took a bite of her sandwich and wiped her mouth before continuing. "Hey, listen, I've been thinking an awful lot about our conversation. About how you have the courage to work your job as an ironworker for a living, and make music in your time off for pleasure. You've inspired me." Luella blushed as she stammered through her sentence.

"*I* inspired you?" Mickey leaned in intently. "Alright, now I'm intrigued. How so?"

"This is going to sound so silly, but you're the only person I've ever met that made me think about adding beauty to my life. I'm not sure if I want to teach. It may be a good job, but it won't keep me happy for the rest of my days. At least, I don't think it will."

"Okay then, what will?" Mickey's gift for listening and hearing made Luella feel as if they were the only people in the world.

"I'm not sure, but I know that I want to find it, and once I find it, I don't want to let it go. Just like you and your music. I want to hold on to it and squeeze every ounce of beauty and happiness out of it that I can." Luella made a fist as she explained: "I want to jump out of bed every morning because I can't wait to feel the joy and explore more of whatever this *thing* is that I'm looking for."

Mickey sat back in his chair watching Luella as her eyes widened and lit up at the thought of something making her that exuberant. He was soaking her in, all of her.

"When you figure it out, I'd like to know what it is," Mickey said and smiled.

"Well, maybe you can help me find it." Luella poked at Mickey's shoulder and started to laugh. "I'm sorry, I know how truly crazy this must sound."

"It doesn't sound crazy, Luella. It sounds determined and exciting. I'd love to be a part of your journey, if you'd let me."

Despite how briefly they'd known each other, Luella wasn't hesitant, and didn't question the words that came out of her mouth. She knew that Mickey had been placed in her path for a reason, and in that moment, she felt more comfortable with him than she'd ever felt with anyone.

"Would you like to go for a walk with me later, Luella? Is that okay?"

"It's okay, as long as you bring Buster, but without any flying objects."

Mickey smiled teasingly. "Alright then. It's a date. Buster and I will be back here around 7 o'clock. Does that sound good?"

Luella smiled and nodded, not entirely sure of what she had just agreed to. Was this walk the start of Luella discovering a talent or hobby? Was it the start of a new love affair? So many questions, but she knew one thing for sure: she was excited.

Mickey and Buster were waiting outside Greco's by ten to seven. Buster patiently waited for his command to continue with his walk, while Mickey waited for Luella to be ready. Mickey had changed only his shoes and his red hair he had finessed a bit more than earlier.

"Luella, where to?"

"I'm not sure. This was your idea."

"Yes, but it's your neighborhood."

"Let's just see where our legs take us, shall we?"

Mickey laughed and tugged on Buster's leash to begin their route.

"Mickey, can I ask you something?" Luella began.

"Anything."

"Have you ever been with someone, and they make you feel connected?"

"Connected how?" Mickey responded.

"I'm not sure. I guess, connected to yourself. I know that sounds like a silly question."

"I feel like we have a lot of silly questions between you and me already, don't we?" Mickey smiled back at Luella. "But to answer your question, I have. I am. It's an unexplainable feeling, but I think I feel it with you, too."

"You do?" Luella asked. "I thought I was crazy for even saying it. I mean, I barely know you and here I am saying that you make me feel connected to myself."

"Not crazy at all. I think that life has these funny little mazes already mapped out. There are these roads that connect certain places to people and there are situations that connect other humans to each other. The unexplainable, like us." Mickey said.

"How did you know you wanted to do music? Was it something you did for *you* originally, or for someone else?"

"Ah, now that's a good question." Mickey put his hand in his pocket and readjusted Buster's leash on his other.

"I didn't know I wanted to do anything with music until one day, I just did. I went through a tough time as a boy, a real tough time. I've got skeletons in my closet, boy, don't we all? But music... music really helped me through. When I started to play guitar and sing, I felt lighter, even if only for a short song. It helps me lighten my load, at least temporarily. That's more than I can ask for." Mickey looked down at his feet.

Luella could tell that there was pain behind Mickey's eyes. There was hurt in the depths of him and she knew that there were demons he was trying to suppress from coming out.

"What happened? If you don't mind me asking. What was the rough time?"

Mickey walked for a few more steps silently before letting out a sigh. It was as if he were having an internal battle with himself, debating whether or not he should disclose such private history with someone. Luella could tell that he was conflicted.

"When I was a boy, about fifteen or so, my buddy and I got in with the wrong crowd. They were some real Irish mobsters, if you will. My buddy and I were trying to figure out our way, and trying to make a name for ourselves in the street. Well, turns out, you don't want a name anywhere near that type of association, not unless you want to be haunted by demons for the rest of your life." Mickey was visibly uncomfortable. "My buddy and I were sent to go find this guy who owed the head honcho some money and maybe some other stuff, who knows. We didn't really ask questions. Anyway, when we showed up to his house, he was waiting for us on the front porch and started to fire his revolver. My buddy ran straight for him and tackled him. He was fearless really. As he had him on the ground, he was yelling for me to come and help. As the man was trying to reach for his gun, I remember feeling like it was life or death, I went into a fight or flight response. At first, I felt flight. I wanted to run as soon as I could feel my legs. But then, while my friend was trying to wrestle with this man, I was watching from the porch steps, frozen. Until I saw the man get the gun. Then I saw black. I lunged at the two of them, and got my friend off of him. I began beating on this guy. I was landing so many punches that my hand was numb. I didn't kill him, but he died in the hospital a few days later from unrelated complications. I know I killed him. I take that with me everywhere. Everywhere, every day I think of this man. I think of his face and I think of his life. My hand was never the same and it's a constant reminder of what I did to someone else. I will never forgive myself, and often, I think about ending my own life. Sometimes, the guilt is just too unbearable."

Luella tried to wrap her head around the story. She could feel the weight of his burden and the cross he bore every minute of every hour. It was evident that Mickey was remorseful and felt a kind of guilt that a decent human being should never have to feel. She reached for his hand. Mickey's eyes looked into hers and captivated her with their sadness. At that moment, he was not seeing her, but through her. He was vacant and she realized that he was lost. She knew in that moment, that throughout his life, this seemingly gentle man would find himself lost in his adolescent mistake that would cause him terrible, continuous suffering.

"Mickey, you were just a kid. You didn't know any better." Luella reached up for his shoulder to offer a warm touch and genuine forgiveness for him. "I don't think you were responsible for his death at all."

"I did know better. I should've known better." Mickey's eyes hollowed. "That man would've never been in the hospital if it wasn't for me. He probably would've been strong enough to fight whatever *complications* they found had I not beat him to a pulp." Mickey removed Luella's hand from his shoulder. "It's something I live with and will live with for as long as I can stand it. It's taught me to be patient and be the best person I can be. For as long as I have left here, I made a pact to that man that I would pay it forward in treating every person I meet with kindness."

"Thank you for telling me." Luella didn't know what else to say. She did not investigate further. This was a man who made a mistake as a child. The death wasn't from the beating, but from something else. She wasn't in the company of a murderer. She was in the company of a soul who was in the wrong place at the wrong time.

They continued to walk in silence for the next few minutes before the conversation picked back up. Luella asked how he then discovered music and what he was good at. She asked about how he'd allow himself to be so vulnerable with his art and whether or not he felt judged for it at times. Mickey indulged in the conversation and asked questions about Luella's interests, trying to pull from her what she may want to do. Mickey had a natural, calm demeanor that made it hard to imagine a young Mickey snapping the way he had. Luella wasn't scared after Mickey had told her about his past. Instead, she felt honored that he trusted her so much to tell her something so private and difficult, and she felt that it was her responsibility to help him lighten his load, to help him remove the blame from himself. She wanted to be his fixer and help him heal the very dark, broken pieces of him.

Chapter 16

1952

Luella and Mickey spent every day together from that day forward. They were inseparable. Luella's strength complimented Mickey when he found himself weak and Mickey's assurance in Luella helped her when she was feeling self-doubt. Their insecurities and strengths were complementary, and fueled the love that was quickly growing. They did things that Luella had never done. He'd show her movies that were in foreign languages and had her listen to records that were outside of the classic Italian American artists that her father always played, or outside of what was regularly on the radio. He challenged her to read more, and to find beauty in everyday things. He told her that in doing so, she'd be able to unlock the beauty that was intended for her and that she'd know when she found it because it would speak to her.

Mickey took Luella to an art exhibit in New York City and introduced her to the idea of visual art. Luella had always gravitated towards music. Because her family were immigrants, she felt that music was a universal way for people to connect. She knew that no matter what they were saying, the melody or tune of a song could catch you and make you tap your foot, even if you had no idea what the lyrics meant.

Visual art, however, Luella had very little exposure to. Mickey made it his mission to expose Luella to all different avenues of beauty, he wanted her to find what made her happy because seeing Luella happy gave him purpose. She was filling voids in him that he never thought could feel whole.

"Well, Lu, what do you think?" Mickey asked at an art opening.

While Luella didn't have the language to discuss art, she didn't need to. All she knew was that she loved it. The colors, the shapes, the abstract creations, the mood of a painting. It was a whole world of its own.

"It's beautiful, Mick. All of it. I want to jump inside of a painting and spend the rest of my days there."

Luella rested her head on Mickey's chest and took in the art quietly. She was utterly appreciative of Mickey's encouragement to help her find things she could love. He spent countless hours thinking up ideas that might spark something inside of her. This, however, was different. Luella felt a sense of peace in the art gallery that she hadn't felt before. She felt inspiration beginning to bubble from her mind and began to itch with excitement.

"Mick, can we go? I think I want to try and paint. I think I can do this." She turned and looked up at Mickey, eager to get back to New Jersey to try out what she thought could be her calling.

"I thought you'd never ask!" Mickey grabbed Luella's hand and kissed her.

As the pair walked to the train station, Mickey started to laugh.

"What's so funny?" Luella squeezed his hand in hers.

"It's nothing. It's just that I knew this would be it for you. I just had this hunch." Mickey said laughing.

"Yeah, and…" Luella knew Mickey wasn't done with his thoughts yet.

"Well, and… Maybe I already bought you some art supplies. Solely going off of this hunch." Mickey looked at Luella to see her surprise and excitement. She was like a kid on Christmas morning.

Luella stopped them from walking and jumped into Mickey's arms. The way that Mickey knew Luella on the levels that he did amazed her. His ability to reach down into her soul and dig up her happiness was indescribable. She was ecstatic to get home and use the already-purchased art supplies.

Luella felt lucky to have a man like Mickey. He loved her with parts of him that she would never fully know. He loved her with all of his hurt and pain; he wanted to make her happy. Her happiness made him feel invincible. She knew that he loved her without him even needing to say it. It was hard, fast and heavy love. The kind of love that could swallow you up if you're not careful with it, and Luella was reckless. Luella wanted to be enamored with Mickey's love and she never wanted it to go away.

When the two arrived back in New Jersey, Mickey opened the trunk of his car to showcase the easel, canvas, paints and paint brushes he had purchased the day before.

"Mickey, I can't believe you did this for me. I can't believe you *knew* to do this for me." Luella said in awe. "What would you have done if I hated the art gallery, and said painting was stupid?" Luella smirked up at Mickey as she grazed the brush bristles through her fingers.

"Well, I'd be headed back to the store tomorrow to try and return all of this nonsense and I'd never speak a word of it to anyone!" Mickey grabbed Luella's waist and spun her around to face him. They stayed in the warmth of one another's arms.

"Luella, I want you to find what makes you happy and I hope this is it. I just want you to be happy. If this isn't it, we'll keep looking. I want you to find the beauty that you bring me every day."

Luella looked back in the eyes of the man she adored. He only ever wanted the best for her. She inspired him and he was her muse. Looking in his eyes, she felt she knew exactly what her hands would do when they were given the paint, the brushes and the ability to glide strokes across the blank canvas. Mickey made Luella feel like she could achieve anything and that she was destined to create something heavenly. He gave her the motivation that she needed to let go of her fear around needing to know whether or not Paterson State Teachers College was the right move for her. The pressure alleviated and she felt light and airy enough to be able to take a chance. She'd take a chance with art, with school and with anything else that she may have thought would be of interest to her. She was able to fully let go of the worry that surrounded all of her decisions because Mickey empowered her to do so. He made her feel secure and reminded her that regardless of the outcome, it would all be okay. It was okay to make mistakes. It was okay to try and fail. It was all part of the process and she couldn't wait to get started.

Chapter 17

1952

Luella spent all of her free time painting. She painted everything from nature, to people walking, and food in the market, she used her surroundings to steer her work. She'd find a tree outside of her bedroom window that, prior to tapping into her artistry, was just another tree. Now, however, that tree could be the focal point of her work. The big, wide stump with its roots buried deep into the ground, and branches that stretched out, covering nearly all of their yard and some of the roof. The leaves were big, bold and explosive, bright green during mid-July, and Luella would dip her brushes into the green and add whites and deeper greens to emphasize their beauty. She'd paint and Vincenzo would proudly hang her work in Greco's, telling everyone who walked in that he hadn't told before in his broken English, "My daughter did this!" Everyone was happy that Luella had found something that she was passionate about. Up until she started painting, she would have the eagerness in her eyes that wanted to be driven by something, she just didn't know what.

The other aspect of Luella's life that was new to her, was her relationship with Mickey, which was vastly different from what she'd had with Joe Andriotta. Mickey would rarely come to the market, not in avoidance, but because he, too, was busy with his job and working on his music. He wouldn't want to disrupt the family operation, and didn't believe in going in and just *hanging out,* waiting for Luella to be done with her day's work. Vincenzo, Vinny and Elena misinterpreted Mickey's absence as a lack of interest in getting acquainted with Luella's family. They did not see Mickey O'Rourke as a future for Luella. Mickey was a gentle, kind man, but had not embraced the rest of the Grecos. He hadn't been to a Sunday dinner yet because, to him, it felt foreign. In the O'Rourke household, Sundays were for church and chores, not for taking a break and relaxing over an extended meal. The purpose of the day was to realize God and prepare yourself and the home for the work week. Mickey's Sundays consisted of helping where he could, and using Buster as an excuse to get out for a walk, and have some time to himself. After all, the O'Rourke house was now full with Mickey, his parents, his cousin Maryann, and her twin boys. Mickey had given up his room and opted for the basement while the Higgins were staying at his house. He wanted the boys to have as normal a stay as possible. Luella admired Mickey and the way he supported his family. There was a part of her that did, in fact, want Mickey to make the effort with her family, yet there was this other part of her that was completely comfortable with how it was. She felt that her small, Italian family could get too involved and having Mickey just for herself and at a safe distance was a breath of fresh air. It allowed them to relieve some of the pressure that came along with new relationships and just focus on each other.

Mickey did not try to impress Luella with reservations at a new restaurant, or long drives to places that required them to be overdressed. Instead, once he felt he'd help Luella find what she was passionate about, they'd spend their time in the same park where they met. Mickey would bring his guitar on its strap so that he had free hands for Buster's leash, and holding Luella's hand. They'd lay out their blanket and enjoy a basket of food Luella brought, and the pureness and vision of the nature that was surrounding them. They felt most inspired when sitting together, not needing to say much. Mickey would strum his guitar and hum a new tune, writing in his small notebook some words that he'd string together to form a song, while Luella would quietly admire him and paint what she'd find inspiring.

"Lu, do you want to hear what I've got so far?"

Luella smiled and nodded as she continued to stroke the canvas with her brush to finish the spot she was working on before resting her hand on her leg to give Mickey her attention.

> *"The beauty that we see*
> *Not always what it seems,*
> *But I've got you and you've got me.*
> *When you take me there,*
> *I know that I am home,*
> *You're with me in my dreams,*
> *I'm no longer alone."*

As Mickey finished his melody, the guitar accompanying the tune, Luella reached for his shoulder and gave him a gentle rub.

"It's beautiful, Mick. I can't wait to hear the rest of it."

"You think so? I've still got work to do, but I think I like the direction it's headed. Maybe another hour or so, and I can create a smash hit! We can call it *'Park Song.'*"

Luella laughed as she picked her paintbrush back up to give her painting its finishing touches.

"I'm not sure about *'Park Song'*, but I do like it." Luella shook her head laughing.

"Alright, alright. I'll think of something catchier. Hey, what have you got so far? It's your turn." Mickey pointed to Luella's canvas, gesturing to turn it so he could see.

Luella blushed and smirked as she lifted the canvas off of the easel to showcase what she had been working on. In watercolors and in her own abstract way, it was a painting of Mickey with his guitar and a small, yellow dog that could be made out in the bottom corner. The painting of Mickey was charming and peaceful. His face focused intently while picking at the guitar strings, and the utter happiness in his eyes as he sat looking down at his instrument. It was a clear depiction of how Mickey had always wanted to see himself. Mickey was in amazement.

"Lu, this is beautiful. I can't believe you painted me. Here this whole time I thought you were painting that chump over there!" Mickey's joke was an attempt to cover up his tears of joy. "I'm really honored. It's beautiful."

"You're beautiful, Mick. All of you. I wanted to capture you, happy." Luella looked and admired her work, truly showcasing the man she knew that the rest of the world didn't always see.

"Capture me happy, huh? That's what the painting should be called." The smile slowly left Mickey's face.

Mickey's feelings of being flattered and cheerful quickly lost the battle to the harsh reality that set in. He had so much hurt in him realizing he couldn't always be the person Luella painted. In fact, he couldn't even be him most of the time. Mickey fought internally every single day, and punished himself regularly, never really knowing if he'd get better. With age came experience. The more Mickey experienced in life, the less he could enjoy it. Feeling as though he ripped the opportunity from someone, although arguably out of self-defense, he couldn't forgive himself. He couldn't move past it. Even with lovely Luella in his corner.

With age came experience, but with it also came angst. His feelings of sadness, shame and remorse would so often take over him. He'd get consumed.

"Mick? What's the matter?"

Mickey's gaze at Luella felt blank and empty. She knew he wasn't with her anymore. The painting she thought was going to bring him so much delight was paired with the jarring reality that the man in the picture was rarely Mickey.

"Let's get you home, Lu."

1947

Vinny came into the market singing after his delivery to the Petrelli's that Tuesday. He was gleaming and seemed lighter than normal.

"What do you sing?" Vincenzo asked in his broken English. "I want to sing too!" He said teasing his son.

Vinny grabbed the rolling pin from his father, "*Ciao, Papa*! Let's sing! Let's sing because I found my wife!"

"Your wife?" Vincenzo questioned with a laugh, confirming he heard right. "Let's hear it!"

Luella was setting up shop in the front of the market, getting ready for another day when she overheard the conversation between her father and brother.

"What's that?" She shouted from the front, "Did you say you found *your wife*?"

"Yes, sis, I did. *Papa*, Luella, I met *Elena Cutri*. And I know for a fact, one day, she will be my wife." Vinny said her name in what seemed to be his version of Italian. His eyes widened and he danced as he spoke her name aloud to his father and sister.

"How do you know she's going to be your wife?" Luella questioned. "Who is she?"

"Luella, *tesoro mio*, when you know, you know," Vincenzo said affirmatively to his daughter as he turned his attention back to Vinny, who was clearly enamored by this mystery woman.

Luella listened to her father and heard his words. She repeated them back to herself. *When you know, you know.* Luella thought for a moment. At nineteen years old, she hadn't known love yet, or at least she didn't *think* she knew love yet. She dated casually, as young adults do, but she never felt something electric, *magnetic*, with someone. Would she know it when the right person was there? Would she ever have the opportunity to experience that sense of certainty at all, she wondered.

"Come, son. Tell us about *Elena Cutri*."

Chapter 19

1952

Monday morning and Vinny was early to rise to assist his father with preparing the food for the week. As Vinny quietly plucked himself out of bed, not to disturb his wife, he felt a tug on his shirt.

"I'm sorry, hon. Did I wake you?" Vinny leaned back and moved the hair from Elena's face.

"I don't feel good, Vin. Something doesn't feel right. I'm exhausted and unbelievably nauseous. I've gotten up a few times already because I thought I was going to be sick. I'm surprised I didn't wake you."

"Oh, my love. Why *didn't* you wake me? Let's see." Vinny placed the back of his hand on Elena's forehead and then on her cheek to feel her temperature. "Well, no fever, or at least it doesn't appear to be. What else do you feel like?"

"Just queasy. Very uneasy stomach." Elena rested her hand over her eyes and rolled herself onto her back. Before she could get comfortable, she jolted to the bathroom with her hand covering her mouth and began to vomit. Vinny followed his wife to the bathroom and looked at her with a sly, knowing smile.

"El, you don't think…" Vinny gestured to his stomach.

Elena's face changed instantly from sick and displeased, her eyes widening with excitement and her mouth slowly opening. She had put on some weight, solely around her gut, over the last few weeks and she noticed that the smells that she once loved, such as pancetta frying on the stove, suddenly made her feel lightheaded and unsettled.

"You think? Vin, do you really think I could be?"

"Why don't you place a call to your doctor this morning and let's go find out. I'll just tell *Papa* that…"

"Don't say a word! I don't want anyone knowing a thing until we're sure."

"Alright, alright. I'll just tell *Papa* that…"

"You'll tell your father nothing!" Elena proclaimed.

Vinny crouched down next to his wife, still kneeling on the hard, cold tile of the bathroom floor and wrapped his arms around her.

"I love you, Elena Greco. No matter what the outcome is, it is exciting to think that a baby Greco could be inside of you. A little *bambino* just waiting to take on the namesake."

Vinny laughed and poked at Elena's face to tease her.

"I love you too, Vinny. It's a girl, though, if it is anything." Elena quickly mocked back, poking Vinny's cheek.

By midmorning, Elena had made it to work after she phoned her doctor and set an appointment for the following day. Trying not to get ahead of herself, she jumped right into her Monday morning responsibilities to stay occupied. A few minutes after ten, there was a knock at the back door. She knew it was Joe delivering early, as he had been doing as of lately, in hopes of seeing that Luella was upfront and busy handling customers. The midmornings were typically a bit slower. Elena steadily poked her head out the office door and to the left, hoping that Luella was distracted by some regulars. Once she confirmed there were enough people to keep Luella busy, Elena turned to the right to open the door and propped the cinderblock in front of it for Joe.

"*Ciao* Joe. How've you been?" Elena was fantastic at being diplomatic. Kind and welcoming, but extremely neutral.

"*Ciao* Elena. How are you doing?"

Joe draped the large, heavy sack full of linens over his shoulder and excused himself past Elena and to the shelves.

"I'm okay, Joe. We're busy, but everything is good."

Joe looked back at Elena to continue with formalities.

"Oh, are you…" Joe pointed to his stomach and then at Elena. She hadn't even realized she'd been holding her belly while the two were engaging in small talk.

"Oh, my! No, no. I'm not… We're not… No." Elena stammered and chuckled, trying to brush off the awkward encounter, and rushed her hands to her sides.

Before long, Elena heard Vincenzo coming up from the cellar with a box of fresh tomatoes. Vincenzo and Joe, as always, quickly began chatting about how the Andriotta family was doing. Vincenzo had a genuine interest in how Joe Andriotta's father was enjoying retirement - a state that Vincenzo could never quite picture himself in. The family did a nice job of keeping Luella and Joe's relationship out of the weekly business encounters that they had. Vincenzo, Vinny, and Elena all worked extremely hard not to make either one of them feel uncomfortable. Before they knew it, Joe had quickly done the exchange of swapping the dirties for the cleans and was on his way.

Elena practically ran to the kitchen to find her husband and share in their secret of what just happened.

"Vin! *Psst*, Vin!" Elena whispered, trying to get her husband to notice her while not drawing attention to herself.

Vinny was in front of the ovens kneading the fresh dough for the second round of bread to go out. Covered in flour, he dusted off his hands and walked over.

"What's up, hon?"

"You're never going to believe this. Andriotta was just here…"

"Yeah, I believe it. Every Monday…" Vinny smiled and winked.

"Vinny, stop it! Joe was here and we were talking, and, well, he caught me holding my belly! I was holding on to my stomach and I didn't even realize I was doing it! What do you think that means?"

"Well, I think it means that there's a baby Greco in there, but we're going to find out for sure tomorrow."

"Do you think I subconsciously know? Do you think my body is trying to tell me something?" Elena was genuinely surprised by her ability to potentially foresee her future baby and want to protect it, and hold on to it.

"Perhaps, hon. I think you should not think that much about it right now, and let's see what tomorrow brings."

Vinny placed a kiss on Elena's forehead and patted her on the back.

Vinny and Elena arrived at the doctor's office at 9:45 sharp for their 10:15 appointment. They wanted to have plenty of time to get settled, fill out the appropriate paperwork, and rehearse the questions they had, not to forget any. Vinny told Vincenzo and Luella that Elena had a dentist appointment and due to what the dentist may want to do, she would perhaps be unable to take herself home, so he promised he'd be in by noon.

After checking in, they took two open seats near a window. Elena quietly filled out the required forms while Vinny observed passersby outside the office. He noticed many women, round and seemingly uncomfortable. Coming or going, he recognized the emotions that he'd seen; ecstatic, scared, or heartbroken. He had never given much thought to what it must be like to become a mother. He hadn't remembered much of his own, and couldn't understand or empathize with the emotions that go along with finding out that you're growing a tiny human inside of you. He began to imagine how his mother must've felt finding out she was pregnant with him. Sure, he assumed she was happy to have the news, but he couldn't help but wonder if she was also met with immense fear. Fear that life in America wouldn't work out as she had hoped, or fear of her family in Mexico never meeting her children. Did she fear dying so young and not getting to know her own children? As he wondered about his mother, it made him appreciate his father, the man who raised him and his sister and made them into the people they had become. An immigrant from Sicily. An only child, with his parents who had stayed in their home country until their deaths. The only kin was his cousin, Dante. Vincenzo, in Vinny's mind, played the role of father and mother admirably. Vincenzo never made Vinny feel as though there was a void he had from not having a mother. Vinny appreciated everything his father had done for him and Luella since they were kids. While thinking about his parents, it struck Vinny like a lightning bolt: he, too, wanted to be a father.

"Mr. and Mrs. Greco?" The nurse called from the door, looking around the waiting room.

"Yes, right here." Elena quickly shot up and looked back at Vinny standing right alongside her, giving her a wink.

The two followed the nurse down the hall and into the exam room. The nurse gestured to the open chair for Vinny and looked at Elena.

"Weight, please." The nurse pointed to the scale.

Elena propped herself up on the scale and waited for the nurse to dismiss her.

"136 pounds. Please have a seat on the table. I'm going to take your blood pressure and have you change into a gown. Then I'll go get the doctor."

The nurse wrapped the velcro fabric tightly around Elena's arm and put the cold stethoscope underneath it, pumping to get a read.

"120 over 80." The nurse noted the intakes in her chart.

"Please change into the gown and the doctor will be right in."

She closed the curtain separating the bed from the chair that Vinny was sitting in. When the nurse shut the door, Vinny started laughing and peeled back the curtain.

"We wouldn't be here if it weren't for what she was trying to keep me from seeing."

"Sh, Vin. You really shouldn't even be in here!"

Elena laughed and undressed, slipping into the gown. She sat anxiously on the bed.

"Did you hear what she said? 136 pounds! That's ten pounds heavier than I was when I last checked. I can't believe I've gained ten pounds, I don't understand how that could even happen."

"It's going to be alright, hon. I promise." Vinny said assuringly.

Moments later, there was a knock on the door before it opened to reveal the doctor.

"Mr. and Mrs. Greco." The doctor nodded and extended his hand for a shake to Vinny.

"I'm Doctor Titulli. I can guess what brings you in today, but I never like to assume."

The doctor's friendly demeanor helped calm Elena's anxieties. She wasn't one to rush to doctors, nor did many people in 1952, but this situation was different. Elena couldn't live with just waiting and waiting until one day she popped and started to feel something moving inside of her. She needed to know immediately.

Doctor Titulli pulled the curtain back to separate Vinny again from the exam table. While he performed his routine check, he also finished by measuring her belly and listening closely with his stethoscope for a heartbeat. Once completed, the doctor opened the curtain and wheeled his chair back to look at both his patient, and her husband.

"Well, folks, I'm not sure if this was the plan or not, but you are certainly expecting. Congratulations."

Vinny immediately jumped up and over to his wife and began to kiss her.

"Did you hear that, El? We're going to have a baby!"

Before she knew it, Elena began to cry. She was overjoyed and nervous all at once. She couldn't believe that by the grace of God, she and her husband would be welcoming a baby into the family and into the world.

In Vinny and Elena's absence, Luella and Vincenzo were working the market with the help of Angelina. When Angelina was there, the store couldn't help but feel a bit more structured. Vincenzo ran his business extremely well and very thoroughly, but he treated everyone who came in like family. Angelina, on the other hand, played the role of a drill sergeant. She'd unintentionally bark customer's orders back at them, only to confirm she'd heard it correctly, but she was rough around the edges and had a stern demeanor. Luella liked it when Angelina was there because she would constantly reminisce about when she and Dante came to America and she'd share what they missed most about Sicily. Sharing stories of the beauty and the culture of both worlds, and how she did her best to collide the two.

"*Zia* Angelina, I got this one, why don't you take a seat. You've been on your feet all day."

Angelina was trying to bend down into the meat case to fix up the sandwich someone had just ordered when Luella noticed she looked visibly uncomfortable.

«*Grazie*, Luella. I'm an old woman now. I get tired fast." Angelina said in her broken English, hobbling over to the stool in the corner behind the counter, holding her back.

"*Zia*, you're sixty-five. You're not old."

Angelina scoffed and brushed off her niece while making herself comfortable on the chair.

"I'm old!" She exclaimed, propping her feet up.

Luella rolled her eyes and shook her head while finishing up the sandwich order. As the customer was leaving, the back door whipped open. Elena and Vinny came down the hall while Vinny shouted out for his father.

"*Papa! Papa*, come to the front, please. We want everyone here all at once!" Vinny expressed.

As the family gathered near the counter, Vincenzo was brushing the flour off of his face with a wet paper towel he had just used on his hands.

"*Che?*"

Vinny and Elena looked at each other before turning back to face their family.

"Elena and I are having a baby!"

Elena and Vinny stood holding hands waiting for the roar of the response. The family shouted in glee and ran to hug the couple. Chatter commenced about whether it would be a boy or a girl. Luella felt tremendous happiness for her brother and her sister-in-law, knowing how badly they wanted this and what good parents they'd be. They were a model of what a solid, healthy relationship could look like and Luella knew they'd raise lovely children. Luella would soon be an aunt! She'd be a *zia*, just like *Zia* Angelina, but better. There was about to be a new generation of Grecos joining the clan and paving the way for the family's destiny.

Chapter 20

1952

Luella was getting herself together for Mickey to pick her up and take her for ice cream. She had been floating since the day prior when Vinny and Elena shared their exciting baby news. Luella felt a niece or a nephew was coming at the most optimal time; Vincenzo was getting older, and Vinny and Elena had been married two years now. There was no need to wait any longer to welcome a baby. Plus, Luella selfishly anticipated the baby because she felt it would possibly help sway her one way or the other. Perhaps having a baby around would make her feel strongly about whether or not she, too, was meant to be a mother.

When Mickey arrived, Luella gathered her things; purse, jacket, lipstick, and an extra compact to check on herself throughout the night. Luella flew down the stairs and called for her father to say goodbye.

"Hey, Luella, where are you going?"

"*Papa*, I told you. Mickey and I are going for ice cream."

"Ahh, *che* Mickey. Mickey this and Mickey that," Vincenzo threw his hand up, brushing it off. "Mickey wants to make the time to see you, but never see the family. What do you do with this Mickey anyway?"

Luella wasn't in the mood for a lecture or a deep conversation. She'd had a long day at the market and painting, she just wanted to enjoy some ice cream with her date and not have the kind of pressure Vincenzo was looking to put on her.

"*Papa*, we're going steady. He's a good guy. What else do I want with him? I'm not sure, but he treats me well and helped me find my painting. You like my painting, *si*? Isn't that enough?" Luella looked at her father, displeased. She understood why he was asking the question, but she did not want to ruin her perfectly arranged evening by thinking so critically about what her relationship with Mickey could, or should be. Luella folded her arms across her chest and sighed. Above her father was a framed photograph of her mother. In the photo, Maria and Vincenzo stood firmly, Maria holding Vinny, just a few months old. Neither of her parents were smiling, as immigrants rarely did for photographs in those days. The photo was antique style, with hues of grays, browns, and blacks, darkening some areas of the setting. It had been taken by a professional, which cost her parents a fortune for back then. She knows that because her father had embedded it in her head throughout her childhood. They worked hard to make that photograph happen. Luella admired her family. She knew that her father wanted her to go on and start a family of her own, and she respected him asking about her intentions because he did not want her to waste her time. Luella knew that being a father was Vinenzo's greatest accomplishment and one that he did not take lightly. He'd challenge himself as a man, and his children, every day to be better than they were the day before. His lessons were invaluable, and the kind that only a parent could offer in the times when they're most needed, but hidden in subtleties that may sometimes take years to string together. Vincenzo wanted his children to experience being at the helm of that. Now knowing that Elena and Vinny were pregnant, he didn't want Luella wasting time with someone that he, or she, couldn't see a future with.

"*Papa, ti voglio bene.* I'll be back in a little bit." Luella kissed her father on the head and gave his thick, silver hair a run through her fingers.

Luella opened the door to find Mickey, the tall, slender Irishman, who was dedicated to making her happy. But she recognized just how much it bothered her that he did not make the effort to meet her family or get to understand her roots. His interest was solely in Luella, not about the family that helped make her.

"Hi, beautiful lady." Mickey extended his arm to escort Luella down the steps. "Shall we?"

She linked her arm with his as they walked to the ice cream parlor. "No Buster tonight?"

"Nah, I decided to leave him home. I figured we'd be out for a while. Plus, the boys enjoy playing with him so between the twins and the dog, they tire each other out."

Luella and Mickey spent the walk catching one another up on their days, swapping stories about their encounters, mishaps, and how they ended. Mickey asked Luella about what she had painted so far this week, since this was the first time they had seen each other since the weekend, and Luella posed the same question to Mickey, wondering if Mickey had written any new songs. At the ice cream parlor, they waited in line and continued their easy conversation.

The midsummer heat brought the crowds in during the week for an after-dinner treat that also doubled as a cooldown. Luella debated between the mint chip and vanilla bean, her two favorites. She typically opted for a cone but decided that night, she didn't want to have to deal with the ice cream melting on her hand.

"I'll take a small mint chip in a cup, please. Can you also add a few extra chips to it?"

"Sir?"

"I'll do the same."

Luella looked at Mickey. "Huh, you don't typically do the mint chip. What's with the change of heart?"

"I figured it's what you like, so I wanted to give it a try."

The words Mickey responded to her should've landed softly as he intended them to make her happy. Instead, they hit her in the face like a tractor-trailer. Luella never wanted anyone to do something for her if it wasn't done out of a genuine desire. Mickey intended to try it because he figured if she liked it, it would make her happy. And, in turn, his liking it would also result in her happiness. Mickey's devotion to pleasing her was masking the inability to please himself. Unable to ever truly fill his voids, he overcompensated in filling hers. Luella felt that her voids were hers alone. Mickey had helped guide her to fill one, but they were hers essentially, to fill. She wanted to respect the journey that God had planned for her, her faith strong, believing that she'd get there in due time. Mickey, however, was forcing nature. He was trying to fit into this mold of what he envisioned Luella wanted, and that was a burden Luella did not want to carry. She was responsible for her happiness, as Mickey was responsible for his.

"Mick, why don't you get something you like?"

"Well, it doesn't hurt to try. Plus, I know I'll like it because you do."

The response sounded like nails on a chalkboard to her. How foolish she felt she had been. All this time, she had blindly followed Mickey's lead, and she was feeding into his hunger to make her need him by relying solely on him for her happiness. Mickey had demons that Luella knew she could never fight. Reflecting on her father's question from earlier, she found her answer for herself. She wasn't sure what she was doing with Mickey. She hadn't even told him the news of Vinny and Elena expecting a baby. How could she be with someone and not want to share such enormous and exciting life-changing news?

Luella took her ice cream from the young kid from behind the window and thanked him quietly. She stepped back from the line while Mickey got his and paid. Luella found a bench near the gravel parking lot that was facing the road, away from the building. She opted for the seat on the left, feeling as though it offered the least exposure to other guests that evening. Mickey followed behind her and parked himself, seated closely up next to Luella with his mint chip ice cream.

"Mick, how come you spent so much time trying to find my hobby?"

Mickey, caught off guard by the question, continued with his lick of the ice cream and started to laugh.

"That's an odd question," he chuckled, "I did it because I want you to be happy. You're the most beautiful woman in the world and I knew something was missing. I wanted you to have every piece of you as you continue your path. I figured if I could help you find what made your life more beautiful, you'd thank me one day."

Luella was surprised by Mickey's response, having little to do with the dependability on one another, and more about him staying a memory in the future. Puzzled, she replied.

"I'd thank you one day? What do you mean by that? I thanked you when you first took me. I thank you still, today."

"I know that. But because of this, you'll remember me forever. Even when you and I are long over, and you're settled in your life with your family. When you're an old woman, talking about how you began painting, you'll think of me."

What came out of Mickey's mouth jolted to Luella's ears and through her head.

He wasn't selfishly trying to fill his own voids. He genuinely wants me to be happy, and he wants me to remember him. He already knows we're not going to be together forever.

Luella's thoughts raced and her mind scattered. They were both knowingly committed to one another, *for now*. Luella hadn't shared the news about the baby, or pushed Mickey to meet her family because she didn't see a future with him. Mickey loved Luella and she knew that because she felt it. She felt it deep in her bones without question, that he truly loved her. He'd express it in his own way, but Mickey was unable to commit to anyone long-term because he knew no one *could* ever fill his voids.

The pair had spent immense time together in their short tenure. Their time was full of life, love, and beauty. It was spent embracing the art around them, within them, and the unexplored. Mickey loved Luella and Luella knew Mickey was special. She was unsure why she couldn't picture a future with him. She had no idea what particularly disconnected her from him in that way, but she knew. Mickey and Luella enjoyed the rest of their evening, but Luella knew where their relationship was headed. The trajectory of her foreseeable future was changing. She knew, yet again, that it was time for her to move on.

Chapter 21

1952

Come fall, Luella decided to wait another semester to start school. It was obvious that she was avoiding the commitment of school as Elena was growing in size. The market was busy with mothers in the morning ordering fresh cold cuts and bread to make sandwiches for their children who were back in school. The ability to only be responsible for breakfast and dinner was a load off of the homemakers, so they opted for easy lunches that Greco's could offer them. Every time Elena would come to the front of the store, the other women would dote over her, asking how far along she was now. Every day, multiple times throughout, ladies would rub her belly and pat her shoulder, giving words of encouragement and saying things like "Hopefully the baby has your eyes" or "If it's a boy, let's hope it gets Vinny's stature." Elena would smile politely and accept the exchanges while looking over at Luella, resisting the urge to roll her eyes.

The midmorning rush had calmed much quicker than normal and Luella was cleaning up what mess was made from the slew of customers that had all needed to be served at once. Elena was on the phone with the bank, Vincenzo was in the kitchen singing and Vinny had stepped out. The loud knock on the door echoed to the front and paused Luella in her tracks. She looked up at the clock noticing it was a few minutes after ten. Luella stayed still to hear if Elena was going to answer the door, or if her father had stopped his singing to acknowledge the knock. Neither of them stopped what they were doing. Luella slowly made her way around the counter and waited quietly, confirming what she had heard. The loud bangs proceeded as if they were not heard to get the attention of someone inside. Luella jumped and walked towards the back door. She fixed her hair and peeked in the office to find Elena with her back turned rummaging through the filing cabinet looking for the appropriate papers the bank was asking for. Luella went to turn the handle and opened the door. As she did, the sack of linens fell into the doorway as Joe had leaned them up while he ran to the truck to fetch his clipboard.

"Oh, Luella," he shouted, running back to the door. "I'm sorry. I was knocking for a while and wasn't sure if anyone heard me. I figured I'd grab the paperwork to save everyone the time."

Joe hauled the sack over his shoulder and gestured for Luella to lead the way.

"That's alright. Sorry, everyone was a bit busy and the noise drowned out the knocking. How are you?"

Joe's eyes lit up, excited to have the ability to tell Luella about how he'd been. He'd waited for the moment to connect with her, one on one, but respected that he didn't want to force it.

"I'm doing good, Lu. The summer was busy. I took a lot of trips down to the shore and enjoyed more than enough sun. How are you? Did you start school? I've been so excited to find out."

Joe's eagerness to see Luella was contagious and filled her like a warm, spring breeze.

"I figured I'd start next semester," Luella smiled and shrugged. "I guess I just can't remove myself completely from here yet."

"That's okay, Luella. That's great." Joe stumbled over his words. "I mean, it's great that you've still got time, and that you'll still be here. I think it's all great."

While Joe exchanged the linens, Luella couldn't help but keep the conversation going. She was eager to learn whether or not Joe had been seeing anyone, and what he'd been spending his time on. She wanted to know if he was doing well, and she asked if he'd noticed Elena's growing belly. They fell right back into normal conversation. Luella undeniably felt at home with Joe. He was her family. He had been so familiar and safe to her, that she missed the fondness the two shared and she hadn't even noticed. She wanted to tell Joe about how she had been painting. Better yet, she wanted to show him. She wanted to share the beauty she had spent the summer creating and would continue to create. While Joe finished up, Luella followed him out to the parking lot.

"Joe, it was so great seeing you. I know we haven't spoken since, well, you know… But would you like to get together with me soon?"

Joe's eyes widened and his smile beamed.

"Luella Greco, I'd love nothing more."

1952

The holidays came rolling back around, and normalcy was restored with Luella Greco and Joe Andriotta, picking up where they left off, not having skipped a beat. Luella was able to share her newly discovered passion through her art and Joe was continuing to thrive and add more customers to his route, expanding the family business since he had taken over for his father.

The expected seasonal crowds rushed in and flocked around the store daily beginning two weeks before Thanksgiving and straight through New Year's Eve. Vinny's typical holiday display grew in size as his unborn baby did too. He spared no expense in creating additional miniature nativity scenes throughout the store, perfectly placing them amongst the crates that acted as shelves propped throughout the market holding inventory such as pasta, seasonings, and breadcrumbs. The homemade garland doubled in count, for every one strand, there were an additional two where Vinny could fit. There were mini Christmas trees and handmade paper snowflakes that Elena spent the time perfectly crafting. Vinny wanted the first official Christmas of him and Elena being parents-to-be to be filled with holiday cheer. After all, they had everything to celebrate, in addition to the birth of Jesus.

Joe was unable to regularly step in and offer a set of extra hands this year around Greco's. In his time apart from Luella, he had focused all of his energy on growing the Andriotta Linen business and had successfully achieved it. Joe decided for himself that if he was going to commit to carrying out his father's legacy through the business where his father spent the larger portion of his life building from nothing, it was his responsibility to take it to the next level. He added nearly a dozen new customer accounts and doubled their routes. Joe spent his time carefully selecting an additional driver to assist him in handling the accounts and once he found Antonio Pilio, he knew he was the right guy for the job. A *paisano* who understood the Italian-American lifestyle and knew hard work firsthand. Together, they were able to continue to deliver timely and exceptional service and exceed their customers' expectations. With Antonio, Joe could continue to service those accounts that needed the Andriotta touch, while also focusing on continuous growth.

With Luella and Joe being individually in places where they felt confident and happy with themselves, they were able to take their relationship to a new level. Luella, having found her passion and creative outlet, could now focus solely on Joe and being the best partner to him when they were together, not zeroing in on her uncertainties. Similarly, Joe felt he had the world on a string and could support Luella and one day, if they so choose, a family as well. They motivated one another to continue to follow their dreams. Luella rooted for Joe when he pitched the value of a linen service to a new restaurant, and Joe held Luella accountable to paint regularly when she got too busy with the market or helping Elena prepare for the baby. Because the couple could now inspire one another from a genuine place of happiness, it opened up a new pathway to explore their love and areas of each other in new ways. Ways that they were completely unaware of in their initial courtship.

Christmas Eve was always spent at Vincenzo's house. It was bigger than Christmas day and the family gathered around to indulge in multiple fish dishes, various assortments of pastas, and of course, *panettone* and *vino*. Dante, Angelina, and the girls were always present. The Petrellis would stop by to make their rounds and stay for an hour or two. Elena's parents would join and now, the Andriottas were in attendance. Presents were waiting for everyone, perfectly wrapped and displayed under the brightly lit and heavily tinseled, wide pine tree. The evening, however, was not nearly as focused on the material gifts as it was on the love that they all shared for one another, the celebration of the birth of their Lord, and of course, saluting their health.

Everyone was dispersed throughout the kitchen, dining room, and living room, casually grazing and picking at the larger-than-life display of food. Elena was happily refilling everyone's wine while sipping on her coffee and Vincenzo and Dante were sharing tales of their upbringing in Sicily. Angelina and Irma were exchanging stories, getting one another up to speed on their latest gossip, and all of the *extra* family members made themselves comfortable by settling in various places of the home. It was never quiet. There was music playing in the background, loud exchanges happening, and laughter filling the entire house. No one that was in the presence of the Grecos on Christmas Eve, wanted to be anywhere else.

Luella, having rarely stopped to sit down yet, was making her way from the living room back to the kitchen to refill the tray of cheeses and olives. Her apron was beginning to untie itself from the back, with her hands full, she wiggled her hips in an attempt to keep the strings from falling in front of her, causing her to trip. Joe gently grabbed her waist to stop her without causing her to be startled. He kissed her on the back of the neck and retied her apron.

"There you go, my love."

Luella turned around to thank Joe and kiss him. When she did, she realized the entire room had gone silent and as she turned to face Joe, she found him on one knee, holding up a ring box with it propped open. A small, perfectly cut diamond was sparkling from the box and Joe's eyes were beginning to fill up with tears.

"Luella Greco," Joe began, "It may have taken us some time, and possibly a longer road than we'd like, but there is no one in the world that I'd rather spend my days with. From the minute I saw you, I knew I wanted you to be my wife. Will you marry me and become Mrs. Joe Andriotta?"

The room was filled with eyes wide and hands covering mouths in anticipation. Angelina shouted from the background *"Madonna mia, Luella! Si, si!"*

Luella, still holding the tray of cheese and olives, stared at Joe, unable to close her mouth. Elena came and carefully took the tray from Luella's hands so that she could embrace the moment without needing any additional distractions or causing a mess.

Luella slowly placed her hands on Joe's face, not even yet able to admire the ring and its full beauty. She knelt down on the floor next to him before beginning to cry.

"Joe, I couldn't imagine a life without you either. I would love nothing more than to honor you and become Luella Greco." She smiled and kissed Joe before pulling back to correct herself. "I mean Mrs. Joe Andriotta!"

They embraced and the entire family roared with ecstatic cheers. Vincenzo, having known all along since he was called upon for his blessing, ran over to hug his daughter and congratulate Joe. Everyone gathered around the couple and continued to cry tears of joy and laugh and sing. The house rang with *"salute"* and *"cin cin"* as glasses clinked together to toast the newly engaged couple, congratulating them and sending blessings.

This was the love that Luella had hoped she'd find. After witnessing her brother and Elena's holy matrimony, she too, wanted to find love that felt like it could move an ocean. She realized that having spent time away from Joe was the best thing that could've happened to her and for their relationship. It allowed her to explore parts of herself and discover what it was she wanted out of life. Experiencing her short romance with Mickey confirmed that he was not the one for her, but allowed her to recognize just how special Joe Andriotta was. She now knew that she had found the love she'd been deeply and subconsciously aching for. She now felt near complete. She had her fiancé and her art, what more could she possibly want? Luella Greco was on her way to becoming her own woman, potentially starting her own family, and becoming Luella Andriotta.

1932

Vincenzo was four years without his wife and raising two children, ages four and six. His produce company, Greco Limited, was still staying afloat and successfully operating thanks to both of the Petrelli's restaurants being the main source of income. The bigger the restaurants got, the busier Vincenzo was. Having to support two young children, and having to travel as often as he did was becoming unrealistic. Vincenzo needed and wanted something more stable. He wanted to raise his children in a place he built. Vincenzo had always dreamt of owning a brick and mortar. He had dreams and visions of opening the doors to the most unique and authentic Italian delicatessen that one could find in Northern New Jersey in the 1930s. He envisioned himself welcoming customers and offering them the opportunity to look around, feel the nostalgia, smell the freshest scents, and provide them with the opportunity to experience the tastes of Italy. Instead of delivering and dropping off produce to them, they'd come in and he'd be able to bake fresh bread for them and have them indulge in a variety of the highest quality Italian meats, cheeses, and add-ons. He wanted to cater to his customers, but in a place he could call his own. He didn't want the bustle of a restaurant. He had never pictured himself in an environment where he had to have a wait staff and a more formal setting, with people sitting and waiting for their food. Instead, he pictured a home away from home, and with that, the idea of *Il Mercato de Greco* was born.

Vincenzo had never been quiet about his plans and after Maria died, he was sure to make it known to everyone he encountered while having business exchanges.

"Me? I'm Vincenzo Greco. Greco Limited is *limited*. We won't be around for much longer as we are because we're going to become Greco's Market! You'll have to come and see for yourself just how we do things in little Sicilian-America!" He'd tell people.

It was a normal Saturday morning, Vinny was riding alongside Vincenzo for his delivery down to the West New York location of Petrelli's, with Luella sandwiched closely in between her father and brother. Typically, Angelina would look after the kids when they didn't want to go to work with Vincenzo, but Vinny was at the point where he always wanted to tag along, and Luella was following suit of her big brother. Having it be the family's day out was becoming the norm.

When the trio arrived, they pulled up to the front of the restaurant and Vinny immediately jumped out of the 1929 Ford pickup. Vincenzo met Vinny around the back of the truck and lifted him up to grab from the bed of the truck, gated with wooden planks allowing the food to stay put. Vinny enjoyed his assumed duties, helping his father unload the crates of food for the restaurateurs and hand delivering it to people who he always thought were family. Luella sat antsy in the front, trying to turn herself around to get a glimpse of her brother and father from the front of the truck. She bobbed and fidgeted to try and see what exactly it was they were doing. Not before long, Vincenzo came back around to the front window.

"Luella, you stay here, *bambina*. Vinny and I will be right back. Don't you move!"

Vincenzo navigated his hand trolly full of the Petrelli's order, while Vinny followed with the clipboard holding the inventory list for Umberto to provide his sign-off. As they made their way around the back of the restaurant, they could smell the smoke from Umberto's cigar. It lingered around and created a visible cloud that filled the air they walked through. Umberto always had a cigar in his mouth, even while cooking at times, although he did his best to hide it from his guests. He'd say that the aromas helped him think clearly and added flair to his unique cuisine.

Umberto was shaking out his white chef coat out of the back door. He was anticipating Greco Limited's arrival and often looked forward to seeing Vincenzo's children. Umberto hadn't had children of his own but indulged in the young Italian-American children who would come around, acting as if they were family.

"*Ciao* Vincenzo! Little Vinny, you get so big! Every time I see you, you grow another three inches!" Umberto exclaimed, still standing in the doorway leading to the kitchen.

Vinny immediately lost all of his sense of responsibility when he saw one of the Petrellis and went flying around the corner to jump into Umberto's arms, careful not to get burned by the fat cigar hanging out of his mouth. Vincenzo and Umberto chatted for a few minutes while Vinny now clung to Umberto's leg, playing with the string on his pants. Before they even got to business, while spending the first few minutes catching up, the pitter-patter of small feet could be heard coming down the long alleyway and around the back of the restaurant. Vincenzo turned around to the sight of his four-year-old daughter, her knee slightly scratched from escaping from the truck and sliding out of the driver's side door.

"Luella! What are you doing? I told you to wait in the car, *tesoro mio*!" Vincenzo flew around the railing that was guarding the steps to the door, scooping up his daughter quickly. He brushed off her knee and kissed her several times on her head, causing her to giggle and squirm. Luella, in her innocent, growing mind, had decided she did not want to be left behind anymore when her father and brother did drops. She, too, wanted to be a part of the business engagements. Umberto let out a big belly laugh and teased Vincenzo that she'd be a handful for him and that he was raising two children who already had the work ethic of their father and the strength of their ancestors.

"Vincenzo, you can't continue to deliver with the children. It's safe when it's here or at my brother's location, but the small places you go in between, you can't do. Let us help you. You've been like a kid brother to us and I know Francesco feels the same. Let me talk to him, I have an idea."

Vincenzo couldn't deny the offer. Considering he had other dreams for himself and he trusted the Petrellis, he shrugged his shoulders, still holding Luella in his arms, and agreed to whatever it was Umberto was thinking.

About a week later, both Francesco and Umberto had a proposition for Vincenzo. They had owned property that housed some businesses and residential apartments. The tenants that were occupying one of their small storefronts were vacating because they had found a larger, more suitable place of occupancy. The Petrelli brothers called a meeting with Vincenzo, as they frequently did, sometimes for business and sometimes to shoot the breeze over a scotch. When the three began to converse and exchange ideas, the proposal was made that Vincenzo would be the perfect new tenant for the property.

"Vincenzo, you want a market, and we want to help you," Francesco said.

"We wouldn't want anyone in there other than you, and we know that it's a good location for you and what you think you want to do with it. A lot of *paisanos* around Hawthorne, they need a quick taste of home," Umberto chimed in.

Vincenzo's mind was moving a mile a minute. He had already thought of every way he could make his idea of a small eatery and market work. He now had the figurative, and literal, door in front of him, waiting to be opened, exposing the new land of opportunities.

"I don't know what to say aside from yes. Yes! Thank you! I promise I will pay my rent on time every month. In fact, I'll pay it early! I owe you both so much and to give me this chance, I promise, I won't let you down!" Vincenzo expressed.

They embraced in a hug and a *salute* to the new business that was about to become the staple in the Greco family for the foreseeable future and beyond.

Chapter 24

1953

Joe and Luella knew that they wanted a fast engagement. They spent little to no time deciding on where the festivities would be held because they had already discussed the hypothetical wedding while they were previously together. The two would wed in front of the Lord at a ceremony inside the walls of Saint Anthony's church on Diamond Bridge Avenue, the same church they attend on Sundays for mass, and where Vinny and Elena were married. That would be followed by a reception at Petrelli's in West New York, overlooking the skyline of New York City. Vincenzo was thrilled to have the people who had given him his chance host the wedding of his only daughter. The Petrellis knew Maria, had watched Vinny and Luella grow into adults, and had been considered family for as long as the Greco children could remember. Francesco, Umberto, and Irma were honored and assumed their duties welcomingly. Umberto called in the sous chef from the Paterson location so he could be in full attendance and not worry about the distraction that would require him to pay more attention to the food coming out and less attention to the wedding reception happening for his self-proclaimed niece.

By 11 o'clock, all of the Greco women were already present and helping Luella get ready. Elena, Sofia, and Emilia were Luella's bridal party, and Angelina took the role of an honorary mother, helping Luella step into her dress and buttoning up the back. Elena, nearly eight months pregnant, glowed in her blue chiffon Matron of Honor dress, waiting anxiously to help Luella with the final touches; a pearl studded bobby pin and her white lace gloves. Sofia and Emilia, in the same blue chiffon with slightly less tulle at the top, waited patiently to see their cousin walk out in white. Angelina opened the door of Vincenzo's bedroom and she and Luella stepped out. Elena, Sofia, and Emilia gasped and Elena began to cry. Holding her belly with the bobby pin and gloves in hand, she immediately put her other hand to her mouth and burst out into tears.

"Luella, you look absolutely stunning."

Luella's dress was timeless and pushed the envelope as she had always tried with her fashion. It was pearl satin and off the shoulders. The lining of the sweetheart neckline and sleeves were finished with lace. Her small waist showed off naturally through the fit of the bodice before tapering off into a wide skirt with a long, lace-detailed train. Her hair was pulled back into a perfectly placed curled bun, completely away from her neck, tastefully exposing her bare decollete. Her veil was attached to a lace cap that was pinned onto her head, waiting for the final pearl piece to add the additional detail she had hoped for. Angelina, standing behind her niece, tapped her shoulders in pride, holding back her tears. Luella stepped forward into the hallway and heard her father and Dante laughing downstairs as they were going back and forth in Sicilian. Luella smiled at the thought of what her wedding day meant. She had finally found what she loved and who she loved, and was now beginning to understand who *she* was. This was all her father ever wanted for her. She embraced each of the women in the hallway before Angelina shouted downstairs to prepare the men for her entrance.

"Come, look! We're coming down now!" When Angelina yelled, the brokenness of her English was much sharper and more prominent.

Sofia, Emilia, and Angelina walked down the stairs, Elena and Luella hand in hand following last. As the footsteps grew louder for Dante and Vincenzo, Vincenzo had already begun to cry. He was looking up at his daughter from as early as he could see her. The sight of Vinzenco's tears instantly filled Luella with great love. She, too, began to cry.

"*Papa*," she whispered.

"*Tesoro mio*," Vincenzo said as he put his hands out for his daughter.

"*Bellissima.*" He kissed Luella on the forehead and spun her around in front of him.

"You, my darling, are the most beautiful woman in the world. Today, you stand before me not as my little girl, but as a bride, and the most gorgeous one at that. *Ti voglio bene.*"

Luella allowed her father to admire her before jumping into his arms. The hug was strong and solid, just as their relationship had been. Vincenzo had always imagined he'd have his little girl forever. His little treasure, that had withstood the odds and survived coming into this world. It was she who gave his life additional purpose after his firstborn and the loss of his wife, and who would test him in every aspect one could be tested. Vincenzo, at that moment, realized he would have to step back from being the main male figure in her life. He was giving his daughter away and allowing her to pursue her own life and dreams. *This* was what it meant to be a father.

"I'm happy it's Giuseppe Andriotta I've got to meet on the other side of this. Lord knows that I wouldn't want anyone else to look after my only daughter!" Vincenzo expressed.

The church bells rang just as they had a few years prior when Elena and Vinny got married on that beautiful October day. However, this wedding was accompanied by the leftover snow from the day prior and the briskness that filled the air. Joe and Luella picked Valentine's Day intentionally. Joe had wanted a day that embodied all that love meant, and when he suggested the idea to Luella, she came to love it.

The nuptials were genuine and heartfelt. The vows that they so solemnly swore to keep to one another felt as true as the church stood firm. The journey they had taken to end up where they were, to have come back to one another and be ready, proved their ability and willingness to commit their lives to each other. It felt as though it was the most natural thing they could have done. There wasn't the slightest doubt for either Joe or Luella. They were confident in their holy matrimony and felt that God had brought them through their individual lessons to ensure they made their way back to each other. The love was present on that cold February day. The guests cheered and threw rice as they exited the church as Mr. and Mrs. Giuseppe Andriotta. The crowd shouted *"auguri"* and the American friends exclaimed their congratulations as they made their way to Joe's Cadillac with the "just married" sign hanging from the rear window.

The newlyweds, their families, and their friends danced and ate the night away at Petrelli's, overlooking Manhattan. The night was filled with love and well wishes. There wasn't a dry eye when the couple had their first dance to Perry Como's *"Till the End of Time"*. The way Joe moved Luella on the dance floor, pulling her so delicately, close enough to feel the loose hairs that had curled out of her tightly wound bun, tickle his nose when he leaned closer to kiss her or to whisper the lyrics in her ear. For those three and a half minutes, they were the only ones in the entire room.

Luella felt Joe's hands on her body and she felt the love pouring from him. She knew that he loved her deeply. He had waited, patiently, for her to find her way back to him. He had respected Luella enough as a person to understand that she was not the type to only be fulfilled by becoming a wife, but by becoming a person of her own. He loved her even more now than he had previously. He knew now that she was becoming her own woman, and while Luella was becoming her own woman, he was claiming her as his to the world. To the small, immediate world that was there to witness that day, on February 14th, 1953, Luella Greco became Luella Andriotta.

Part Two

1953

On April 17th, 1953, Vinny and Elena welcomed their baby boy into the world. The baby was paraded around the market at only a few weeks old as Vinny, the new, proud father, had been so eager to show him off. Dominic Antonino Greco entered the world almost three weeks late and Elena's labor went swimmingly. Dominic was the first of the next generation in the family. He'd make his father proud by being notably the longest baby the hospital had seen that year, and had a head of hair that you could tell was already thick and beautifully dark. Elena was undeniably exhausted from adjusting to motherhood, but still she gloried in it day after day. She took some time off from the market, but that didn't stop her from popping in almost daily. She and Sarafina would talk about their experiences from birth and Sarafina would share insights that she experienced with Angelo at that age. Elena would pass off Dominic to Luella and the proud aunt and the new baby would share seconds of their eyes locked in on one another. Luella would stare and admire Dominic as he slept in her arms. She didn't feel nervous or anxious to hold her nephew. She wasn't hesitant. The fierce and immense love for her brother's son was so innate that it took over any other feelings of doubt or angst that she had prior to him arriving in the world. Luella Andriotta was a proud aunt to Dominic Greco, the first of the new generation.

Joe had purchased a small home in Hawthorne, only a few blocks from Vincenzo. They started to host Sundays by their house a few times, not wanting to break the traditional clan spending hours eating and laughing at Vincenzo's. Only two months after being married, the Andirottas were settling into their new life together seamlessly. Luella loved her new role as a wife. She took it on willingly and ensured the house was tidy and neat. She did Joe's laundry, had dinner ready for him every night once she returned home from the market, and always tried to keep herself looking polished. Neither Joe nor Luella brought up responsibilities; they were just assumed. Joe was responsible for the bills, and Luella did the upkeep of the house. The couple felt like a partnership, however. Luella wasn't told to do anything, so she did it voluntarily. She did not have a mother to exemplify. She knew Elena and how she kept the home that she and her brother lived in with their new baby. Joe did not tell Luella what to do or not do. He helped in the kitchen and sometimes took over the laundry. There was, however, one thing that Joe felt he wanted to address with Luella.

"Lu, how's work been?" Joe asked, leaning against the doorway while Luella was standing over the sink, rinsing the tomatoes.

"Work? Well, busy with Elena out. I'm not sure if *it's* gotten busier, or just me having taken on the back office tasks." Luella shrugged her shoulders and chuckled.

"Have you given school any more thought? The last we spoke, you were unsure."

"Well." Luella lifted her eyes from the tomatoes up to the window directly in front of her before glancing back at Joe. Luella let out a sigh. "I don't think I want to go to school anymore. I want to be around to help Elena with Dominic. I want to be around for you now, too. I don't think school is important enough for me to put my family to the side. I've got you, I've got my art and now I've got a nephew. I don't think I need anything else right now."

Luella waited for Joe's response, unsure what it would be.

"That's good, Lu. I'm happy to hear that."

Joe brought himself closer to Luella, stopping behind her and wrapping his arms around her waist, resting his head between her shoulder and neck.

"It is? How come?"

"Because I don't think I wanted you to go to school. I don't think I want you to do something that you're not over the moon about. Plus, now that Dominic's here, maybe he needs a cousin." Joe let the suggestion settle in Luella's mind.

Luella looked at him sheepishly.

"Joe, are you saying what I think you're saying?"

"I don't know, hon. I'm just thinking that we've both been so excited since Dominic has come into our lives and I think that we, too, would make excellent parents. I think our children would be beautiful. I mean just look at you! Look at this hair I've got. If we had a son, he'd have my build and if the Lord gave us a daughter, she'd be your twin."

"Joe, there's no guarantee who the baby would look like." Luella laughed and dried her hands before turning around to face her husband. She put her hands around his neck.

"I wasn't sure about motherhood, ever. I never knew how I'd feel about a baby. I never knew if I'd be good at it, or if I'd have enough love outside of myself to love a baby more than anything. I questioned my maternal instincts all my life." Luella paused before continuing, looking directly into Joe's eyes. "But with you, and how I feel with Dominic, I don't question it anymore. I haven't once thought that I wouldn't be able to do this. In fact, I only think about the love I have for the baby when I'm holding him, and how I'd protect him from anything in the world. I look at you holding him, and have thoughts, even if they're momentary, of you holding a child of our own."

"Lu, I want us to try. If you're ready."

"I don't know if I'm *ready*, but I don't know if you're ever really *ready*."

"Well, you're probably right." Joe laughed. "They always say, 'you're never ready', you just figure it out."

"Are you? You know, *ready*?"

"Luella Andriotta, I am ready for all that life has in store for us. I will welcome everything with open arms and I would love nothing more than for me and the woman I love to have a baby."

Luella did not respond, she did not need to. Instead, she threw herself deeper into Joe's arms and kissed him. Joe moved his hands up and down Luella's back, feeling every inch of her through her dress and apron. He untied her apron and she pulled it over her head. He scooped her up and carried her to the couch. They made love while the tomatoes sat in the sink, the bread in the oven. The breeze from the open windows filled the house as Luella and Joe allowed themselves to get lost in one another. Gone were any past worries about a potential future, and they let the outcome be up to fate. They knew that if a baby were to be in their future, then a baby would soon come.

Chapter 26

1935

Vincenzo was proud to have the only Italian-American market on Lafayette Avenue with the biggest picture window. The rest of what lined the streets were smaller, paned windows. But Greco's stood out with the nearly floor-to-ceiling gallery view. It allowed him to strategically place a table in the front which he hoped would attract the people walking by and immediately draw them to the counter where the shelves had only the freshest of breads. He tried to leave the door open when he had the ovens fired up to allow the scent of the yeasty, slightly sweet aroma to drift out into the world, inviting people in. He'd learn that the doors could only be open before the days got too hot, or else he'd have to put five-year-old Luella on fly-swatting duty. He'd never want to see an insect in his place of business, so he'd make a game for his daughter to go around and kill any living bug that could interfere with the cleanliness of his sanctuary.

While Vinny was in school, Luella and Vincenzo would spend the days in the market. Dante almost immediately recruited Angelina to help out while he was at work, and Vincenzo was looking for reliable help. But typically, early in the morning and until their tenure would provide them a steady clientele, it was just Vincenzo and Luella.

"*Papa*," Luella was in the kitchen with her father, barely able to reach the counter he was working on. "Why do we make bread for other people?"

"Luella, *che*? You know why we do this. You forget why we have this market?" Vincenzo teasingly pinched his daughter's cheek before finishing his response. "We do this because everybody in the state of New Jersey… No, everybody in the United States should know what Italy tastes like! We do this for the *'medigans* who don't know what Italy feels like. We do this for the *paisan* who left their home. To give them the gift of memory through smell and taste. We do this, Luella, because this is our gift to the world."

Vincenzo gathered the loaves and placed them on top of the countertop, letting them cool before dropping them in the front of the store for the guests to shop. This was Vincenzo's routine with his daughter while Vinny was beginning his academic adventure.

"Come, Luella." Vincenzo gestured to his daughter to grab the remaining loaves and she took her assistant duties seriously.

"*Papa*," Luella's mind still wandered as a five-year-old's does. "Why did God take *Mamma* home?"

Vincenzo slowed his pace and put the last of the loaves in its assigned place before turning to his daughter. As all children do, Luella questioned everything. The world was just starting to make sense, and while Vincenzo could only hope he was doing a good job in explaining the unexplainable to his children, this question would sting him time and time again.

"Luella," Vincenzo wiped his hands on his apron and bent down to be eye level with his daughter, grabbing her hands. "We have our faith. We believe in the *Madonna*, the Father, the Son, and the Holy Ghost. We know that when people go to be with them in the Kingdom we call Heaven, it's for a reason." Vincenzo paused before continuing, allowing the consistency of the message to register. "Your mother was sick. She was sick and we didn't know until it was too late. She couldn't be in this world anymore, her body was too weak. So the Lord took her home."

Luella's little eyes wandered across Vincenzo's face, noticing his expression change as he looked back at her. He went from strong to hurt. Her tiny nose began to scrunch and her eyebrows pinched with curiosity.

"*Papa*, how come she got sick and I didn't?"

"Well," Vincenzo paused. He knew the story he had ingrained in his children and while he'd never have answers until he, too, made it to Heaven, *this* was the story he told them and *this* was what he believed. "Your mother gave you all of her strength so that you could be tough and be healthy. She knew that she had to give you everything that she had and she did, willingly! She loved you and she still does. She watches you grow up and grow bigger and stronger and she knows that she gave that to you. She wanted nothing more than for you to be here and live a big enough life for the both of you." Vincenzo's grip grew tighter around Luella's little hands and his eyes began to fill with tears. "Luella, this is why you're *tesoro mio*. You are a gift, a treasure. *My* treasure. This is why I chose Luella as your name. It means warrior. You are a warrior and you were put on this earth to do great things, and you will. You will be a strong woman with children of your own and you will know exactly why your *mamma* gave you her strength and it will all make sense." Vincenzo pulled his daughter closer to him and squeezed her tightly. She threw herself into her father's arms and wrapped her little arms around his neck. She got distracted by the pieces of hair that were slightly longer than the others and began to run her fingers over them before realizing her father's breathing became faster. His gasps for air trying to soften his cry were not working as well as he'd hoped. Luella pulled back from her father's hug and looked at his face. She wiped the tears from his eyes so gently.

"*Papa*, don't cry, I'm here. Me and Vinny are strong, *Papa*, and we're going to be strong like you. *Mamma* did that. *Mamma* made us strong to take care of you, too."

The innocence and genuineness behind the child's explanation made such sense to Vincenzo. He smiled at his daughter and couldn't help but think to himself how proud he was. How proud he was of Maria, of himself, and of his children. Even without his wife, he was raising his children exactly as they had both planned. They were inquisitive and curious, questioning everything to try and make sense of the world, but they were gentle and kind. Their strength would show through at such young ages in moments like this. Their empathy shone brightly and their resilience rose up from the depths of their small bodies. They *were* warriors.

Chapter 27

1954

"Joe!" Luella shouted from the top of the stairs. "Can you bring me a clean washcloth? She's fussy and I can't put her down but I don't want this to stain." Luella tried to wipe the vomit from the crib's sheets, covering nearly the entire top half.

It was May of 1954, and Carla Regina Andriotta was just five months old. Luella and Joe had welcomed a baby girl in December and their lives were fuller than they could've ever imagined.

Joe ran up the stairs, skipping every other to quicken his pace. He barreled through the doorway and into the nursery.

"Here!" He shouted as he raised the washcloth in victory before heading to the crib.

Luella was rocking Carla near her chest. The baby was crying and whimpering while robotically moving her tiny arms as babies do.

"Thanks, hon, it's at the top." Luella gestured her head towards the crib. She widened her eyes and raised her eyebrows in the direction where the cleaning was needed.

"I can't believe she's still not feeling well. I don't understand our poor little *bombolina*." Joe kissed his daughter's soft head and rubbed it before making his way to the bed.

"I don't know. Elena said Dominic was colicky and would have these fits too. Perhaps I should try a new formula."

Luella had taken to motherhood beautifully. It was as natural a transition as day to night. From the moment she and Joe found out they were expecting, Luella's entire life changed. She stopped painting because she didn't want to inhale the paint fumes. She tried not to allow the fear of her own mother dying at childbirth cloud her head, so she took as many precautions as she could to welcome a healthy pregnancy and a healthy birth. The Andriottas had gotten so much preparation in spending such a significant amount of time with Dominic, that they seamlessly fell into their new roles as parents. Luella doted over Carla. She was growing to be the perfect mix between Luella and Joe. Joe's heart expanded when Carla was born. The newlyweds were model parents.

"Whatever it is, we did a good job, sweetheart," Joe said to Luella wrapping up the cloth he had just used to clean the crib.

"We sure did. She is something, huh?"

Joe stood in front of Luella admiring the baby before turning his admiration to his wife.

"I love you, Lu. I love what we've got and I love what we're building."

"I love you too, hon. We've got to get a move on though, it's already 11:30 and you know how my father gets if we arrive late these days."

Luella rocked Carla for a few more minutes before placing her in her crib as she quieted down.

"I just don't know what's wrong with her. I hate that I can't figure it out." Luella stood above the baby, running her finger across Carla's red cheek.

"I'm sure she's okay, Lu. Babies are tough."

Luella smiled, not moving her eyes from Carla. The adoration she had for her child was so deep that she couldn't even begin to describe it. Carla had made Luella a mother. She had tested and pushed Luella in ways she'd never even imagined possible, but that was motherhood. Luella was finally at peace with her life, knowing now that she was complete.

The Grecos and Andriottas gathered for Sunday dinner as they routinely did. Dominic was fascinated by Carla at his young age and was drawn to his baby *cugina*. He'd smile and laugh if she'd move a bit and he'd try and figure out just what it was that she was doing as he was figuring life out himself at thirteen months. Elena and Luella were ecstatic to have had children near enough in age that they'd truly grow up together. They knew that no matter the age difference, they'd instill a closeness in their offspring to ensure the family dynamic didn't waiver, but due to them being just eight months apart, it was a given.

"*Domenico, ciao bello*!" Vincenzo proudly tossed Dominic up and down on his leg, looking for his favorite reaction, baby Dominic's smile that took up his whole face, just like his mother.

"Look at your *sorella*!" Vincenzo pointed at Carla on the play mat on the floor in the living room.

"*Papa*," Luella said. "You don't need to keep referring to Carla as his sister. We know that Vinny and Elena will have more, and Dominic will have siblings of his own."

"And you? What about you, Luella? Giuseppe? *Un*? You can't only have one. You have to have another, too." Vincenzo already knew the response that was coming from his daughter and son-in-law. "*When you're ready*, I know." Mocking the unsaid objection he knew his daughter would respond with, gesturing his hands in aggravation.

"There it is again! El, did you hear that?" Luella swept Carla from the mat and took her in her arms. Carla had made what seemed to be a coughing noise, but it was evident that it was causing her discomfort.

"Yeah, I heard it. Let me see?" Elena took the baby from her sister-in-law's arms and tried to listen to Carla's chest.

"One time, Dominic sounded like he could barely breathe and I remember the doctor told me to listen closely to hear if it sounded anything fluid-like."

"Fluid-like?" Luella questioned.

"Yeah, you know, sounding like mucus or something is building up." She pulled back from listening to Carla's chest. "I can't hear anything though."

"That's because you're not a doctor, sweetheart!" Vinny shouted from the kitchen to his wife.

Elena rolled her eyes at her husband's sarcasm.

"Men. They'll never understand a woman's ability. Better yet, a *mother's* ability."

"I understand it just fine!" Vinny shouted back at Elena.

"We love our pediatrician, Lu. You guys should take Carla there. Doctor LaBrizza, he's wonderful."

Luella thought about what Elena had said. She hadn't even thought to listen to Carla's chest. Should she have? She wasn't a doctor. Hell, she was a first-time mother who had absolutely no clue what she was doing. Motherhood, so far, was flying by the seat of her pants.

Joe could see on Luella's face that she was thinking and that her wheels were spinning. He came up behind her and sat down on the mat, reaching for Carla and his wife's hand.

"Come here, my two ladies. It's going to be alright, hon. You're overthinking. Carla's just got a little cough, that's all."

Luella and Carla moved closer to Joe and Luella placed the baby into his arms. Her eyes fixated on Carla the entire time.

"I know she'll be alright. I just hate worrying about her."

Luella kissed Carla on the head and felt herself getting lost in her baby's eyes. Her sweet baby girl was truly a blessing. She felt that her own mother had conjured up her pregnancy and had helped her manage through the crux of being a parent. Because of this, she couldn't ignore her maternal instinct that something was bothering her about Carla's mysterious ailment.

By the time they had put Carla down to sleep that night, Luella and Joe were exhausted. Luella felt emotionally depleted because she couldn't quite put her finger on what was wrong with her daughter, and Joe was drained from tending to the baby and reassuring his wife. They slept deeply that Sunday evening. The feeling of their tired bodies together, wrapped up in each other allowed them to drift off with ease. The night breeze flew through the open window and rearranged the stacks of papers on the desk in their bedroom. The stillness of the night moved through the house and crept up and down the hallway. What felt like Luella's deepest of nights of sleep, was disrupted by an indescribable feeling.

Luella quietly rose from bed and made her way down the hall to Carla's nursery. It wasn't uncommon for her to wake up and check in on her daughter in the middle of the night, but this was a unique instance. Typically, that would come from Luella being unable to sleep because the baby was fussy, or she heard her crying. This particular evening, it was the silence that caused her to wake. Luella pulled the sheet down to the most painstaking realization she ever could've uncovered.

The immediate wailing came so loudly from within the deepest part of her as she scooped up her lifeless child, praying that she was in a dream. Joe came running down the hallway and into the nursery to find his wife who had collapsed onto the floor with Carla in her arms, screaming. Joe immediately ran down the hall and phoned the operator.

"It's an emergency! I need an ambulance! It's my baby!" His shouting over the phone permeated the house, but Luella couldn't hear a thing. Everything was a blur. She sat screaming her daughter's name in between performing her best mouth-to-mouth, trying to breathe life back into her baby. Joe's voice being transferred to the police department faded into the background as a faint muffle while she continued on.

When the ambulance arrived, they tried to revive the baby, but soon after, they pronounced the five-month-old dead. When Luella heard those words, she was inconsolable and shortly after, went vacant. Up until then, she did not let go of her daughter. Her screams had turned silent and her tears continued to fall, quietly. It was as if she had turned off. She completely shut down. Her motor still running, but no one was home.

It was 2:30 in the morning when the unthinkable happened and Joe called Vincenzo. He immediately came over, trying to console his daughter, stricken by the unimaginable loss himself, he was trying to be strong as his worry for his daughter and son-in-law overtook him.

"Luella," Vincenzo started to make out his words through his cries. "Please, look at me. Look at your husband. We are here."

"She hasn't moved," Joe responded to his father-in-law. "The ambulance just left, and she hasn't moved." Joe had tears in his eyes.

Luella's slow gaze looked up from the floor at her husband standing over her and back down to her father kneeling next to her. She could see them but was not looking *at* them. She was looking through them. She was in a state of shock.

"Let's get her some water," Vincenzo suggested. "And call Vinny, *now*."

Joe was unable to process what had just happened as he made his way back down to the bedroom. He had just lost his daughter, and his wife had left her physical form as far as he could tell. He felt his knees begin to buckle and his chest start to tighten. He collapsed next to the bed, grabbing his shirt. He began to weep and roll himself on the floor, pulling his knees closer to his chest, he began to rock. Everything that had just unfolded had hit him, all at once like a ton of bricks. The Andriottas had just lost the biggest and best part of them. The smallest part in size and the biggest love in their lives was now gone.

The sadness and heartbreak filled every room in the house like rising floodwaters. The family stayed together, occupying their separate spaces, getting through the night. Nobody slept. They sat somberly until the sun came up on a painful day they'd now have to face, and the start of a painful new forever.

Chapter 28

1954

Luella was unable to plan anything. She barely spoke as she and Joe went to the funeral home, picked out the tiny casket, and planned the arrangements to say goodbye to their baby girl. She was unable to think or face the harsh reality of what happened. How could she let this happen? She knew something was wrong, but the sadness overrode the guilt and she had no room to blame herself. Every waking moment was torture without her baby, and when sleep came, allowing her to briefly forget, the waking brought the situation back anew.

On the day leading up to the services, family members did not leave Joe or Luella's side. Vincenzo, Vinny, and Elena, as well as Joe's parents, stayed with them in their home until the late hours of the evening. Joe was unable to care for Luella alone and did not know how to help her. He was mourning the loss of their daughter on his own; there was no sharing the grief with Luella. She was an island unto herself.

"*Giuseppe*, I think she should have medicine for the service. I don't think she can handle it. I don't think it's going to be good." Joe's mother quietly recommended to her son.

"Ma, I can't tell my wife she needs medication to bury our only child. What are you saying? There's no right way to do this. Of course, it's not going to be good." Joe snarked back at his mother.

"*Giuseppe*, please," She pleaded with him. "I'm trying to help. Of course, there's no right way. I'm just afraid Luella is still in shock. I'm afraid for her. I'm afraid for both of you." Joe's mother's voice broke as she held back her tears. "My beautiful *bambina*. She's gone now, and I just worry that Luella may end up in the hospital." She put her handkerchief to her mouth as she began to weep. Before waving her arm to try and stop herself from crying she said, "I am going to get medication. I have been taking the Valium that your father had. I can't cope with this."

Joe did not respond to his mother because he had nothing to say. He had nothing to give anyone at that instant. He could not be a husband to his wife, or a son to his mother. He could only be a father in mourning. Grieving the loss of his daughter.

It was raining as they pulled up to the funeral parlor and Luella could barely get out of the car. Dressed in a black mid-length, drop-waist dress and a black bonnet with lace covering her face, Luella sat in the passenger seat. Joe made his way around his car to open the passenger side door and help her out and onto the pavement. Luella grabbed Joe's arm and looked up at him as he bent down to assist.

"Joe, I can't do this. I can't do this. I can't say goodbye." Luella's eyes, even from behind the lace, brimmed with tears. "Please Joe, I want to go home."

The figurative knife that Joe felt in his heart was unbearable. He knelt down on the wet pavement of the parking lot and grabbed both of Luella's hands in his.

"I know, hon. I know. I love you and I'm sorry. I don't know why this happened to us. To *her*. We have to go inside *amore*. We have to say goodbye." Joe kissed Luella's hands through his cries.

Luella rested her head back on the seat and closed her eyes. She thought of nothing other than her daughter. The beautiful five months that she had with her and the gift she was in that short time. She began to bawl. She cried so hard that she was short of breath. Joe, still kneeling in the rain outside of the car, began to sob, too. Finally, as husband and wife, and as parents, they felt the intensity of the minutes leading up to the saddest day of their lives. They began to grieve together. They had each other.

Luella remained inconsolable as the service went on. She howled from the front row, unable to hear what the priest had to say. Her emotions took over the room and the entire crowd grieved with her. To bury a child is unthinkable. To bury a five-month-old is what feels to be the cruelest punishment one could endure. Joe held Luella the entire time, crying steadily with her. He knew he needed to be strong for both of them, but his strength had left his body. He was unable to think of a path forward. A few days prior, with his wife and Carla, having fought through everything they had to get to where they finally were, he never would've imagined having it all ripped from them. He never would've imagined this.

For two weeks after the funeral, Luella could not go to work. She was an empty vessel. But on the third week, she had the intense urge to paint. She threw herself into her art. She painted things that were indescribable and could barely be made out to be anything other than abstract thoughts. Painting became her outlet, her escape from her very harsh reality. She and Joe barely spoke and she felt herself lean deeper into that outlet she had uncovered a few years before. When she was painting, she was able to control her thoughts, to channel all of her pain into creating something. She was numb most of the time, but felt the littlest *something* when she was painting.

"Lu, hon, what can I do for you?" Joe asked quietly from the door of her studio room.

"Nothing." Luella's response was direct and she did not look up from her canvas.

"Lu, I think we should get you out of the house. Even if it's only for a few minutes. I don't think you've left since Tuesday and I think fresh air will do you some good. What do you say? You haven't eaten much. We can take a walk to Pazzo."

"I'm not hungry."

It had been eighteen days.

"Can I get you something to drink at least?" Joe bargained.

"I'm not thirsty."

"Lu, I'm trying here. I know that you're hurting and I know the pain that you can't describe. I feel it too. She was my daughter too. Please, talk to me."

Luella's gaze slowly moved from her canvas to Joe, still standing in the doorway.

"I know, Joe. I'm sorry. I don't want to talk. I don't want to eat. I just want to be left alone."

Their relationship would remain this way for nearly two months after Carla died. Luella practically locking herself in her studio room alone with her paint brushes, barely speaking to anyone. Joe pleading with his wife to eat, talk, or breathe fresh air, but the only thing Luella wanted to do was to shut out the world, and everything aside from the memory of her baby's smell, her face, and the softness of her skin. She wanted to be left alone to imagine the vision of Carla and see her in her thoughts and dreams. Joe didn't know how to handle their situation. He didn't know what was right or what was wrong. He began to go back to work after the first few weeks because he needed normalcy. He coped by honoring Carla's life. He'd talk about her often, admire her memory, and think of the things he did when she was still with them. His grief looked vastly different than Luella's. He needed his life to continue without losing the memory of their daughter, while Luella couldn't fathom life without her. She didn't want to allow herself to forget anything about their child. So instead, she sat in her studio, painting whatever it was that popped into her head or her heart and she allowed her hands to do the rest of the work for her.

Chapter 29

1954

After weeks, Luella felt ready to return to Greco's only part-time. She couldn't work full-time because it meant being away from her painting. Her grieving vehicle was allowing herself to paint, and she needed to be close enough to her supplies so that if she felt an immense pain taking over her, she could channel it into her art. Vincenzo, Vinny, and Elena all slowly understood and respected what Luella needed. Vincenzo set up an easel, canvas, and paintbrushes in the basement in case Luella needed her escape while she was at the market and couldn't make it home. Elena knew that sometimes, Luella couldn't tend to customers, but didn't want to be home, so she'd gladly trade places with her and have her cover the back office while Elena tended to the front counter. Vinny struggled with watching his sister go through the loss of a child. Everyone did, but Vinny took it the hardest.

"Lu, I told *Papa* that I'd take the Petrelli's order out today. Do you want to take the ride with me?"

Luella looked up at her brother and then out the window before quietly nodding yes. She untied her apron and hooked it on the wall behind the counter.

"Let me just tell Elena so she can cover the front."

"I told her already." Her brother responded with a warm smile and a wink, reassuring his sister that he had everything covered.

The siblings sat quietly in the car for the first few minutes of their drive before Vinny reached his hand over to pat his sister's leg.

"Lu, how are you doing?" Vinny asked reluctantly, afraid of the possibility that Luella could be doing worse than he thought.

"I don't know. I'm as good as I can be, I suppose." Luella looked straight ahead, seemingly uninterested.

"Is the market helping?"

"I think so. I only want to be painting or lying on the floor of Carla's bedroom when I'm home, so yes, the market helps. Joe tries, but instead, it drives me further away when he makes suggestions."

"Well, Lu, Joe's trying to be supportive and a good husband. He's trying to help you in the only way he knows how. " Vinny paused before his follow-up. "How are you *two* doing?"

"I don't know. He's my partner and my best friend. I love him, but I have no desire to interact with him right now. I want him to just let me be. I don't get how he can just move on but I try to be respectful of his process too, you know?" Luella finally looked over at her brother to make a quick second of eye contact.

"Everyone's grief looks different, Lu. He's not moving on. This is the way he can serve her memory. This is the way he still feels close to her, and that's okay. Are you two speaking normally?"

"Nothing's normal, Vin." Luella scoffed. "Nothing's been normal and nothing ever will be normal again, I can promise you that."

"Lu, I am not telling you how to mourn, or what's right and what's not. But what I don't want to see happen, is a wedge begin to take place between you and Joe. You two are husband and wife, life partners. That's the *somebody* that you face the best and worst times of your life with, holding hands, together. I can't say I know how I'd react if I were you, I can't. The loss that we're all facing, but the loss that *you're* facing, is unthinkable, sis. I know that. But I'd like to think that Elena would be my rock. I don't know if Joe is your rock right now, but he's trying. What could he do differently for you?" Vinny felt himself practically vomit the words that he'd been so nervous to say. Luella moved her gaze back from her brother out her window.

Luella, allowing the words that Vinny spoke to sink in, couldn't help but think of Mickey in that instant. She couldn't help but imagine that someone who also dealt with grief, with pain, the way she did, was out there facing his demons still. If Mickey were her husband, she was sure he'd understand. He knew hurt. He knew *her*. He would just get it. Luella continued to allow herself and her thoughts to drift off before responding to her brother.

"What could he do differently?" Luella questioned aloud. "I'm not sure I know. I don't think I have an answer, but I think if he were supporting me in a way that worked for me, I would know that much. I want him to understand that I'm not ready to move on. I'm not ready to just pick up where we left off and carry on. I don't think I'll ever be." Luella's eyes began to fill with tears, becoming glossy from what Vinny could see as he quickly glanced over.

"I'm sorry, Lu. I just want to help you." Vinny grabbed his sister's hand and continued to drive, silently.

Later that evening, when Joe and Luella were both home, in separate rooms, Luella decided to try and talk to Joe. The conversation with her brother, and the thoughts of Mickey perhaps left her feeling like maybe she, too, was not being the wife that her husband needed just as she felt he was not being for her. Luella plopped herself on the couch next to Joe, and slowly lifted her hand to his head, running her fingers through his hair as she so frequently used to do.

"Hi," She said as the two locked eyes.

"Hi, hon." Joe's head fell back on the couch as he looked at his wife.

"I'm sorry that I've been distant and making this even more difficult for you. I don't know what I need right now, I just make my way through each day and figure it out, minute by minute, step by step, you know?"

Joe nodded and his gaze did not break from Luella. "I know," he said softly.

The feeling of her touch on his head made him feel relaxed and light. The couple had barely touched each other since their loss. They hadn't kissed or even had any type of skin contact in the past two months, so the intimate gesture was welcomed. Joe's eyes slowly closed and a tear fell from his left eye, the far side from Luella's line of sight. He turned his head back toward her as she remained looking at him.

"I love you, Luella. I always have and I always will. We will get through this." Joe took Luella's hand from his head and pulled her in closer to his chest, holding her tightly.

"I love you too." Luella pulled herself back to look up at Joe before kissing him. "I need you."

"Luella, let's go somewhere. Let's escape our world for a few days, what do you say?" Joe knew it was a long shot, and hadn't been thinking much about this. In fact, his proposal was spontaneous and just felt right.

"Okay," Luella smiled as she and Joe held their gaze, "Let's go."

1963

"*Nonno! Nonno!*" The little voices shouted as children jumped and reached for Vincenzo in the kitchen of Greco's.

It was almost ten years since their firstborn daughter had passed, and Joe and Luella now had a full house. The couple fought through navigating their loss and each other's grieving processes. They worked on themselves and with one another, knowing that they made a conscious vow in front of God to love and adore one another through sickness and in health, through good times and bad. Joe and Luella Andriotta welcomed three healthy babies who were all growing and taking steps in their lives and filling space in their hearts, helping mend the wounds and fill the voids that they knew could never be filled, but their children were their world. They did not replace Carla; no one could. But they brought joy back to the house and color back to their world.

Vincenzo swooped down, still covered in flour, leaving a cloud of it as he moved so quickly to grab his four grandchildren.

"*Nipoti mia!*" Vincenzo squeezed each one tighter than the next.

Maria was Joe and Luella's first surviving daughter, born in 1955, just under two years after Carla. Maria, named after her grandmother and at just eight years old, was wise beyond her years and had a knack for understanding exactly what people needed and when. She was truly what pulled Luella out of the darkness that was her reality and offered light when there was none. Maria was a spitting image of Joe and had big brown eyes and dark, chiseled features. In September of

1958, they welcomed Anna, who was a fiery little girl with a desire to know everything. Ironically enough, it was Anna's appearance that resembled Luella's mother, Maria, and not her other daughter who was her namesake. Anna was giving the family a run for their money. Lastly, in 1962, they welcomed their one and only son, the now one-year-old, Giuseppe Andriotta II, who was the ray of sunshine in everyone's eyes and the last of their children. Joey, as they called him, was shaping up to be a little mini Luella. His infant features looked as Luella's had when she was born, and he had similarities to Carla. Life had purpose again for the Andriottas. It would never be the same, and the memory of Carla lived throughout all of the happiness and sadness over the years, but the parents felt it was she who brought in the three blessings at a time when she knew they needed them most.

The other half of the family, Vinny and Elena, also welcomed another child. Their second son, Michael, was nine years old and Dominic was now eleven. Vincenzo was the proudest grandfather, and while Luella was no longer a Greco by name, the Grecos were a full and mighty family, just as the market remained.

Dominic, Michael, Maria, and Anna routinely flew through the back door of Greco's after school and raced to the kitchen to see their grandfather. Typically Luella or Elena would pick the children up, and baby Joey usually stayed asleep in the back office where they had a bassinet that had been recycled through many times at this point. The children marveled at Vincenzo making bread, and kneading the dough. His artistry in everything he did in that kitchen mesmerized them. They were growing up as their parents did, in the market daily, but it was less responsibility for the new generation than it had been for Vinny and Luella when they were kids. The excitement and anticipation of what would come that day from being in the market, be it from customers, the food, or the deliveries, the cousins made a game out of it all. Their relationship was close and while the siblings typically sided with one another, the banter that little boys and little girls would so often encounter turned their experience at the market into a game. It kept them all close.

"Lu, let me see the baby," Elena said, following the children in with the youngest's book bag over her shoulder.

"El, you can make Anna carry her own bag, it's alright." Luella laughed as she bounced baby Joey on her hip in the office.

"It's alright. You know that one, she can sucker anyone into anything! You've got a firecracker on your hands, that's for sure." Elena placed the bag down on the shelf where the rest of them were all tossed in a rush, disheveled across the floor, spilling out of the shelf.

"Vinny and Joe are going to the city tonight to see that man about the space."

"Oh, I forgot about that." Elena brushed herself off before offering to take the baby from Luella.

"Should we bring the children to *Papa's* for dinner?"

"I suppose." Elena leaned in closer to Luella. "Did they tell him about the expansion plan?" she whispered.

Luella rose to her tippy toes to see beyond Elena, hoping her father was not in sight.

"No, I don't think so yet. I don't think he's going to go for it. This is what my father always wanted. This. His market in a small town, close to home and his family, serving his community and doing what he loves. Not expanding to the other side of the Hudson and getting so big it'd be hard to handle."

"I know, Lu. Perhaps *Papa* would be happy about the idea though. He's getting older and now that we've got another generation, I think it'd be good for the guys to explore expanding so that we can secure a future for the kids."

"I don't know, El. I grew up in this market and I wouldn't change that. But because of my upbringing, it's all I know. It took me until my twenties to realize I even had talent and a passion outside of Greco's Market. I don't want to subject our children to that. I don't want them to feel bound to something because their parents did it for them when they don't even know what they want for themselves."

"That's what your twenties are for, Lu," Elena responded. "Figuring yourself out."

"You don't understand. I didn't feel I had the choice to explore anything of my own or for myself. Not because my father *made* me work here, or gave me some ultimatum. It was because I felt a child-parent obligation, a responsibility, that I couldn't focus on anything other than being here, with him, all of the time. Making sure he was okay, that the market was running smoothly, and that if he needed anything, *ever*, I'd always be there."

Elena shrugged and nodded in agreement with Luella.

Vinny and Joe had decided that it'd be a good idea to explore vacant locations for rent in New York City. Andriotta's Linens was practically running itself at this point. Joe had gotten it to such a solid place with regular clients and a reliable staff, that it allowed him time to work on the administrative duties and spend time with his family, while also conjuring up other business ventures he could dabble in. Once time had passed and everyone felt secure again, Vinny and Joe discussed how they could do something together, for the children. And so, the idea of a Greco's expansion across the Hudson River was at the forefront of their minds.

Vinny and Joe were crossing the George Washington Bridge while they exchanged ideas of how, logistically, this could work.

"Well, I'm just saying, I think we both have to be here daily, at least while we're building our clientele," Vinny said as Joe was weaving in and out of traffic.

"I know, Vin, I get it. We'll figure out the logistics. I don't know if leaving your father, the women, and all the children every day, while we build the business here, is fair though. That's all." Joe's genuine response caused Vinny to pause and toy with the idea of only one of them being in the New York location.

"Well, I guess we can figure that all out after we see whether or not this is the right space. This guy was a real asshole on the phone, so he better not get wise when we get there."

"What's up with you, Vin? You seem a little tense."

"Ah, I'm not sure. I guess the whole thought of this, while it's exciting to think about and plan for, going behind my father's back makes me uneasy. I don't want him to think that we're doing something sneakily or out of spite."

"You know, we *can* tell him." Joe turned for a quick glance at his brother-in-law to gauge the response to his suggestion.

"I know we can. Maybe after this meeting. Let's see how this goes first." Vinny answered and looked out the window, his eyes drawn to the skyline. He always admired the skyline from when he was a boy. Like any young kid growing up in New Jersey, there was something about looking across the river and seeing the view that looked as though it held the key to endless possibilities. Its apparent closeness made everything seem so achievable, yet the crossing of the Hudson River made it feel far enough away to remain unattainable. He was eager to learn about the reality of that possibility, and how close it truly was for him and his family.

Vincenzo, Elena, and Luella sat at the dining room table finishing wine and entertaining baby Joey as the rest of the children played throughout the house.

"*Papa*, how are you doing? Can I get you more of anything?" Luella asked as she passed baby Joey off to her father to stand up and begin to clear off the table.

"No, Luella. I'm okay right now." Vincenzo sipped his wine while admiring his grandson's sweet face.

"When is your brother and husband coming home?" Vincenzo pointed at each of the women in question.

Luella and Elena shot each other a look, unsure which angle to play and how exactly to respond.

"They'll be here soon," Luella said.

"*Papa*, do you want espresso?" Elena asked as she quickly rose from the table.

Vincenzo waved her off and went back to entertaining baby Joey in his arms.

"Where are they? They've been gone for hours and I'm not sure how much longer I can keep this front up," Elena said privately to Luella in the kitchen.

"I don't know. They should be here soon."

Just as Luella responded, a car pulled in front of the house, and the two men got out and made their way up the front steps.

"Oh, thank God," Elena said, relieved.

In came the duo and their attitudes seemed positive. Unsure what the outcome was, the women waited for them to give any indication of what decision had been made. The men went straight for Vincenzo after greeting their wives.

"*Papa*," Vinny started as he pulled the chair out to sit next to his father. Joe followed quickly behind. "Joe and I have something we want to discuss with you."

Vincenzo's face seemed perplexed, unsure of what to expect from his son and son-in-law.

"*Che?*" Vincenzo asked.

"Listen, you started Greco's with your two hands and your big heart. God, it's *your heart* that's woven into the walls of that place, and I know that it's your pride and joy. Joe and I have been discussing that we, too, want to weave our hearts into it. Even more so than they already are. We want to build something that extends on the foundation that you've laid for us, and continue to pave the way for your grandchildren." Vinny paused for a moment, trying to read his father's poker face. "We want to open a Greco's in New York City. Joe and I have been looking at spaces to rent, but today, we decided that if you're on board, we want you to be a part of that decision."

Luella and Elena quietly listened on from the kitchen, relieved that the decision had been made to involve Vincenzo.

"You want to take Greco's and make another one? In the city?" Vincenzo repeated back, summarizing what he had just heard to clarify.

"That's right. What do you say?" Vinny replied.

Vincenzo looked down at baby Joey in his arms and listened as the rest of his grandchildren's voices echoed in the background.

"If that's what you want, then that's okay with me."

"Really?" Joe jumped in and questioned, making sure he heard correctly.

"Why not? I built the first, and you two can build the rest. If that's what you want, why wouldn't I support that?" Vinny shook his brother-in-law's shoulders and then pulled him in for a hug before the two men hugged Vincenzo, and kissed baby Joey on the head.

"Lu, El, pour the wine! We've got a lot to celebrate!"

Joe called for the kids and the entire family gathered around the dining room table and raised a glass.

"To the next chapter of Greco's!" shouted Vinny.

"And to the next generation!" Joe added.

Chapter 31

1963

The plans for the city location were coming along swimmingly and everyone seemed to play a part in deciding how it would be run. All of the children had special requests and spent most of their weekends heading over the George Washington Bridge with their fathers and occasionally, their grandfather, to see the progress that *Il Mercato de Greco, NYC* was making. Elena and Luella typically worked and covered the Hawthorne store to ensure Vincenzo could spend the time seeing the progression unfold from what he started.

"Do you know who I ran into the other day, Lu?"

"El, you always do have the strangest run-ins." Luella laughed. "Who did you see?"

"I saw Maryann Higgins. I haven't seen her in years. I remember after Jimmy really did a number on her, she went to live with family in Haledon and I hadn't seen her since. I ran into her at the jewelry store over in Midland Park, turns out she divorced Jimmy and has been with this guy for the past five, or six years. She looks great!" Luella went still for a moment. She would think about Mickey occasionally, and imagine what it would be like having him by her side when she had gone through the hardest days of her life. She wondered where he'd be now. Just as Maryann Higgins had moved on, just as *she* had moved on, what had Mickey been doing? Who was he with? All of life's questions entered her mind and she thought back to the days they spent together in the park. On a picnic blanket, they would marvel at each other and get lost in their passions, together.

"Lu? Did you hear me?"

Luella's mouth rested slightly open as she looked back at her sister-in-law.

"Oh," Elena put it together as she watched Luella compute. "Oh, that's right. I forgot about that connection for you."

"Yeah, sorry, it's not a big deal. I just got distracted for a second." She tried to bring herself back to the moment they were in. "Wow, I'm glad she's doing well. That's great. Did she say anything else?"

"No, not really. Aside from the fact that Jimmy's a drunk and doesn't see the boys, but other than that, no. It was nice to see her," Elena responded.

Luella allowed her thoughts to drift from her beautiful, full life with her husband and children to what she experienced with Mickey. Never in a million years did she think she and Mickey were meant for each other, forever. But, the thought of what he might've been able to do for her when she was grieving overtook her. She wondered about what he was doing at exactly that moment and prayed for him silently. Hoping that he had healed his demons and was living a happy life, with much of the good that he didn't believe he deserved.

Later that evening, when Luella was preparing dinner for her family, she couldn't avoid the strong desire that she had to paint. She stopped painting after she was pregnant with Maria, and while she'd dabble in it here and there, the reality of motherhood, running a household, being a wife, and tending to the market, left her little time to get lost in her art as she so often did when she was younger, or in the months after Carla died. Back then, painting saved her.

"Hey hon, do you remember Jimmy and Maryann Higgins?" Luella asked as she set the table.

"That's a random question to ask me." Joe's response was uncharacteristically sharp.

"Whoa, what's that about?"

"I don't know, hon. I'm sorry, I'm tired." Joe quickly tried redeeming himself. "Yeah, I think I remember them." Joe hurried into the kitchen and began fiddling with the steak that was ready to be cooked. "Why are you asking me about them?"

"It's just been a really long time since I've last seen them. Maryann in particular, and Elena ran into her a few days ago in Midland Park. I don't know, I guess it's just been on my mind. I haven't seen her since right before she decided to leave Jimmy."

Joe mumbled under his breath before turning to exit the kitchen and head towards the back door.

"I'm going to fire up the grill."

Joe sat down on the patio chair and rested his head and shoulders back, looking up at the sky. Inhaling through his nose and exhaling through his mouth to slow the beating of his heart as unnoticeably as possible, he closed his eyes for a few seconds before hearing Luella call for the kids to help set the table. Before he was able to bring himself to stand up and walk back inside, he shook his head as if to push the memory of his guilt back down. Joe was unexpectedly reliving one of the biggest regrets of his life for those few minutes.

Over the course of the next few days, Joe was busy with the New York City location planning and Luella was distracted with her normal routine; the couple didn't make much time for one another. They fought with themselves falling into their routines that overrode their need to please each other. The distance felt wider and the inability to connect felt prominent. Luella noticed that Joe was spending more time outside alone when he was home after a long day in the city rather than inside catching up with her and the children as he so normally did.

"Joe, hon, I miss you these last few days," Luella said from the kitchen while she was getting the last few things together for supper. The seasonal produce from the market and the thinly sliced pieces of poultry or beef made for the perfect dishes. The summer months often brought spectacular evening temperatures to grill outside and the barbecued meats from the market were a part of the seasonal routine.

"Me too," Joe responded vacantly from the back patio through the screen door.

The flames of the grill and the sound of crackling were distracting. Joe forked the food off of the grates and into a dish.

"How's everything in the city?" Luella asked as Joe came in through the kitchen door.

"It's alright," Joe said. He didn't make eye contact or conversation with Luella as he placed the plate on the counter. Luella went from the kitchen to the dining room, arranging each place setting as she rounded the table.

"What about my father? How's *Papa* doing with it?"

Joe thought of his wife, his children, and his father-in-law. He pictured Vincenzo and Luella and the life that they had all collectively built together, weaving every part of one another into their shared existence. Joe's heart began to race and he felt a tightness build up in his chest. The guilt began to overtake him and he started breathing heavily, standing over the counter. *Her father*, he thought. He didn't respond to Luella's question, causing her to head into the kitchen to see what he was doing.

"Joe? Is everything alright?"

Joe's hands gripped the edges of the counter as he leaned over it, staring down at the plate.

"Joe?" Luella made her way from the entryway over to her husband and put a hand on his shoulder.

Joe slowly turned around with tears in his eyes, connecting his with Luella's.

"Joe, what's the matter? What's wrong?" Luella grabbed her husband's face and began wiping the streaming tears from his eyes. "You're scaring me, what is it?"

"Lu," Joe's voice cracked and it took him a minute to compose himself. "Lu, I've got to tell you something."

"Joe, you're really scaring me, now." Luella's hands slowly fell from Joe's face as she pulled them closer to her chest.

"Luella, I love you more than anything in this world. You have always been it for me."

"Joe..."

"Lu," Joe paused. "After we lost Carla, we weren't connecting, you and I. We were both grieving. You were so far away, I didn't know if I'd ever get you back and all I needed, all I *wanted*, was you."

Luella's face remained puzzled as she began to step back from her husband.

"Joe, what are you saying?"

"Lu, I slept with Maryann. She comforted me when you couldn't. We were both two broken people, alone..."

Before Joe could finish, Luella interrupted him.

"You *what*?" Her voice remained even-toned. "She *comforted* you? You were *alone*?" Luella, trying to process what she had just heard, began to shake.

"Luella, it was only one time. Sorry doesn't even begin to cut it, I know. I just... We just moved on with our lives and things are so, so great now. I don't think about her, ever. I never did. She was never anything other than a body that comforted me. I buried what I did and I haven't even heard her name until you said it a few days ago." Joe pleaded.

"Is that why you've been acting so weird? You're telling me that you slept with another woman? Ten years ago, you slept with someone outside of our marriage, with Maryann, because you were *alone*?" Luella's rage began to rise. "You slept with another woman after we lost our daughter. Why, Joe? Was I not giving you enough attention?" Her tone began to sharpen and the sarcastic response was cold. "Was I not spending enough time on *you*?"

"Lu, no. Please, stop that. It's just..."

"Oh, I'm sorry, Joe. I was grieving the loss of our five-month-old daughter! You are disgraceful! You're a pig!" Luella screamed at Joe and raised her hands to hit his chest.

"Luella! Please, stop! Talk to me! I'm sorry!" Joe grappled with Luella's arms flailing back and forth, trying to calm her down. "The kids are going to hear you!"

Luella thought of her children and immediately rested her hands to her sides as their little voices got closer and the sounds of their feet running to see what was going on made their way nearer to the kitchen.

"Get out," Luella's voice leveled. "Get out, now."

"Luella, please," Joe started to cry.

"Get out, Joe. I don't care where you go. I don't care what you do. I need you away from me and away from my children."

Luella picked up the plate of food and left Joe standing in the kitchen, crying. Joe listened as she immediately snapped back into being a mother and ensuring her children felt comfortable, not to realize what was happening.

"Mommy, what was all of that noise?" Maria asked.

"Nothing, sweetheart. Daddy is going to go back to the store in the city. It's all okay. He's got to go though, tonight. So he won't be eating dinner with us and probably won't be home for the next few days." Her sureness left no room for questions from her kids and Joe knew that she was tactfully planting the seed of their father not being around the house for the foreseeable future. His heart sank as he made his way around the dining room and kissed each one of them on the forehead.

"Daddy loves you guys. I'll see you soon." He said as he embraced them, one by one.

"Daddy, are you crying?" Anna asked from her seat.

Before Joe could respond, Luella replied, "Daddy is not feeling well. He's alright." She kept the interaction moving.

Joe went upstairs to pack a bag and left before the family began eating. He got in his car and let everything release from him in the sounds of his wails. The guilt that he felt for what he had done to his wife, and his family, all came out when he shut the driver's side door. The thoughts of losing his daughter and the emotion attached to that timeframe that this all brought up for him came to the surface. As he allowed himself to cry and feel every emotion he ever possibly could, he turned the key in the ignition. The engine fired up and the sound purred as he let the car idle for a minute. With no destination in mind, he began to drive down their street for whatever it was that his future may look like.

The days passed and Luella had been so overtaken by the infidelity and betrayal she had completely forgotten about her own connection to Maryann Higgins. She allowed herself to think of Mickey. She drifted back to a place where she and Mickey were together. She thought back to him being completely enamored when it came to her. He would never have allowed her to face such a terrible loss, the loss of a child, alone. He would've stayed dedicated to figuring out what she needed from him and he would've supported her through the entire process. He would've never even thought of another woman. How could anyone do that? She'd ask herself, how could your life partner, the one you vowed to love, respect, and honor, go behind your back and do such a horrific thing to you? Especially while you were both mourning the loss of your child.

She allowed herself to sit with her thoughts and she made a conscious decision that she was not going to mention a word of the infidelity to anyone. Not until, at least, she had a chance to get off of the emotional roller coaster that she was unwillingly on.

While Joe was out of the house, Luella climbed up into the attic and sifted through all of what used to stay stationary in her studio, now baby Joey's nursery. She rummaged through boxes to get to the white sheet that was covering her paintings. She pulled the sheet off as dust filled the air and uncovered years of her work. She sifted through her art and as she touched each piece, she was taken back to the places she was in when she had first painted them. She found canvases from when she had first started painting and was with Mickey. She found paintings when she and Joe got back together. Her style was seemingly consistent, but the details varied as she placed herself back into the frame of mind she was in. In the corner behind the majority of what she had already gone through, was a gray sheet pierced with pointed edges of canvases stacked under it. She slowly pulled back the gray sheet, knowing exactly what she was going to uncover. Under the gray sheet, rested all of the work she had done when she was grieving. The style was angry and harsh. It was sad and broken and some were almost not even worthy of keeping because you could barely make anything out of them. She moved through the paintings and allowed herself to fall into them. As she journeyed through her past, she felt each painstaking minute that she had lived through just as vividly now as she did when it all happened. She began to cry.

In her uncovering of those paintings, in between the anger, grief, and sadness that she was feeling all at this moment, she felt forgiveness. She remembered how hard that time was. She remembered the feelings of distance between her and Joe, and she recalled how the two of them had very different processes that she learned to respect. She was not happy with her husband, but she knew that the time they had made it through could've very easily destroyed many couples. She began to feel guilt accompanied by heartache. She emotionally abandoned her husband during the time he needed her most. Unbeknownst to her, he needed her more than arguably ever. While Luella needed silence and to make her own solace in her art, Joe needed the closeness of his wife and she didn't read that. She couldn't. The two of them were on different wavelengths and in different universes. Luella held one of the canvases and began to weep. She and Joe had barely made it, but here they were. Ten years and three kids later, they withstood the hardest of God's challenges.

She was angry, hurt, and displaced, but she wasn't about to allow those temporary emotions to overtake the life she and Joe had built and the future they had to look forward to.

1963

The phone rang three times before Joe picked up.

"Yeah, hello?" He answered.

"It's me," Luella said on the other end. The silence that fell after her response permeated for what felt like an eternity to them both.

"Lu, hi. I, I wasn't expecting you. How are you? How are the kids? God, I miss you guys." Joe took a breath before continuing, "Lu, I'm so sorry. Sorry for everything. Please…"

"Joe," Luella interrupted. "Joe, please. It's alright."

"It's not Luella. I betrayed you when you needed me most and I let you and our family down. I let Carla down."

Luella moved the phone from her mouth to underneath her chin as she looked up at the ceiling trying to hold back tears and muffle the sound of her cry over the phone.

"Joe, honey, it's okay. I forgive you." Luella's sureness comforted Joe and made him, too, feel like he was going to cry. "*You* needed me, too. I want you to come home. We all want you to come home. The kids miss you."

"I'll leave the city right now, if you mean it, Lu. I'll come right home to you. To my wife, my family."

Luella had figured he was staying at the new Greco's since Vinny and Elena were away with the boys and Vincenzo would never cross the river without being invited to do so. As Luella agreed to welcome Joe back home and the two hung up the phone, she scooped up baby Joey from his crib and brought him outside on the back porch as Maria and Anna played on the swing set.

Luella, alone with just her children for three whole days without her husband, found herself imagining what it would have been like to have been a mother of four. To have had her eldest daughter survive and lead the way for her two younger sisters and of course, her baby brother. Luella closed her eyes and envisioned what Carla would look like now, running and laughing with Maria and Anna. She pictured her sweet, full face with her dark curly hair and her big brown eyes. She imagined Carla pushing Anna and showing Maria how to gently play with Joey. She wondered if she would have Joe or Luella's personality. Then she thought about what she would be like as a daughter to Joe. She would've grounded him when he needed grounding. She would've been his reasoning when he needed to be reasoned with. Only having been ten years old if she were still with them, Luella dreamt up a Carla that was wiser beyond her years and a kind soul that was bigger than life.

"Maria! Not so high! I don't want you to get hurt, please." Luella shouted to her daughter. She rocked Joey in her arms.

In the time that Joe was away, the hours of the late nights and the early mornings allowed her mind to drift and her anger to soften. She thought through varying scenarios in which her life could've played out. She thought of a life with Mickey. Her and an Irish husband, having connected over things that made their dreams feel limitless. The thoughts were passing with him. The life she envisioned them having felt boisterous, narrowly focused on only the two of them, not able to fit her children anywhere into the frame. She couldn't picture any life with Mickey O'Rourke aside from them staying immortally twenty-something. Because of this, each time it passed, it felt unnatural, muddled, and unfulfilling.

She imagined a life where she didn't take Joe back. A life where the resentment was too big a burden to carry, so she'd put it on her children. She thought of divorce, and the impacts of her children being raised separately from their father. Each time they'd meet to switch off with the kids, she wouldn't make eye contact, and she'd hear stories of what they did with Joe while she was home alone. The emptiness would quickly consume her as this thought penetrated her imagination. She didn't want any of that.

The thought that so regularly took up space in her mind, was envisioning Joe coming home. She'd flashback to early in their relationship when Joe proposed on Christmas Eve. How so many years later, she still felt the same ground shake beneath her feet from the overwhelming love she had for her husband. The life she and Joe already planned was at the forefront. They had dreams and ideas of what growing old together looked like, and she realized that's still all she ever wanted. Greater than any anger, or feelings of animosity, was the love she had for Joe.

She navigated through her feelings surrounding the infidelity. Luella allowed herself to sit with the emotions, and was surprised by the little jealousy she had in learning the news from the past. She knew the reason for Joe's cheating was not caused by any dissatisfaction with his wife. It was because both of them were so lost and consumed by grief, they didn't know the way out. The darkness that surrounded their lives after Carla's death left little room for light to guide the way through. Luella knew this, and she wanted Joe to know it was okay, that she forgave him.

"Girls, come. Daddy will be home soon and we've got to get supper ready."

"Daddy!" Maria and Anna shouted in sync, jumping off of their swings and running towards the house.

Luella opened the door with her left hand, allowing the little girls to run underneath her and inside to the kitchen while juggling Joey on her right hip. Before stepping inside, she turned to look back at the yard. The swings now vacant, slowing their swinging. She looked around before looking up to the sky.

"Thank you, my baby girl," she whispered as she closed her eyes and felt the warmth that the sun had cast onto her face.

The wind, coupled with the spirit that she felt around her, engulfed her in that moment. She allowed the sins of her and her husband to wash away with the breeze. She was making a conscious decision to forgive her husband. This would mean not holding it over his head in future arguments or allowing for it to come up later. She was confident in her ability to do just that, and it was through the strength of her daughter. Her Carla.

By the time Joe got home, dinner was ready and on the table. The final touches were Anna moving the bread to the table and Maria putting wine glasses out for her parents and milk for her siblings. The car door closed and was heard from the street all the way through to the kitchen. Anna ran to the couch, climbing the mountain of pillows, and making her way to the top to reach the bay window.

"Daddy's home! Daddy's home!" She announced as toppled back down, running to the front door.

Maria quickly hurried behind to greet her father with her sister. Luella placed Joey in his high chair and pressed down on her apron, making sure she looked presentable but also trying to calm her nerves. She took a deep breath in before turning around to see Joe walking up the steps and towards the front door.

"My girls!" He shouted as he dropped his duffel bag and scooped both Maria and Anna into his arms. Joe covered them in kisses and put them down before hugging each one tighter than the next.

"My girls, I missed you so much. Have you been good for your mommy?" Joe questioned, giving his daughters a side-eye.

"Yes!" The girls exclaimed in unison.

Luella walked over to the reunion and waited for Joe to stand up.

"Lu," Joe placed Luella's hand in his and reached for her face with his other. "You look so beautiful."

"Thank you, hon." Luella looked at Joe. Not needing to say anything more, they smiled, both of their eyes welling up. Their tears displayed the relief they felt.

"I'm glad you're home."

"I'm happy to be home. Come here."

Joe pulled Luella in to hug her and kiss her. The kiss was long and sweet, genuine and heartfelt. The Andriottas had gone through immense pain and suffering, but together, they've gone through growth and good fortune. Luella and Joe loved each other and wanted to be with one another, regardless of what had just surfaced from the past.

"Oh my God, it smells delicious in here. What did you make? Not my…"

Before Joe could finish Luella completed his sentence.

"Yes, Joe. I made your favorite." She laughed, "*Pasta alla Norma* with chicken saltimbocca."

"And we have *ch-ant-ee,* Daddy!" Anna yelled, pointing to the bottle of wine on the table.

"It's *key*-anti, banana!" Maria corrected her sister.

"Anna banana, you silly girl. Maria, why do you know so much about wine?" Joe rubbed his daughter's head before kissing it.

"Because you taught me, Daddy!"

As the family took their places and Luella moved around the table, filling each plate as she went, her heart felt full. She was exactly where she wanted to be and she was immensely grateful to have her children and Joe. She looked at all of them, soaking in every inch of each of their faces. When she got to Joe's plate, before filling it, she stopped in front of him and bent over to kiss him. Another gentle, long, warm kiss. When they separated and opened their eyes, they were greeted by little girls "ewing" and giggling.

"It sure does feel good to be home."

"It's good to have you home, honey."

Chapter 33

1963

It was a Sunday in July and the Grecos and Andriottas had just arrived at Monmouth Racetrack. Occasionally, over the summer, they'd swap their ritual Sunday dinners for the horse races down the shore. The racetrack had something that everyone enjoyed. Vincenzo loved betting on the horses, although he usually wasn't the betting type. He didn't believe in gambling one's hard-earned money away on something that was completely based on luck and out of your control. When it came to those horses, however, he would wager and enjoy, allowing himself to take the chance on the beautiful thoroughbreds that spoke to him. Vinny and Joe enjoyed it as well. The brothers-in-law would discuss who they thought would win and more often than not, argue on why they felt that way, causing them to bet on different horses every single time. Luella and Elena enjoyed it just as much. On occasion, they'd bet themselves, but typically they were watching the kids and mesmerized by the horses and all of their beauty.

Luella always felt lighter at the racetrack. She admired the majestic creatures and enjoyed watching the way they moved. She felt sorry for them when she'd allowed herself to, hoping they were doing something they were intended to do and not just what others wanted for them. She taught her girls that that kind of beauty came from God, and that they should appreciate it.

The men led the way down from the grandstand to get a closer look at the next race that was gearing up to start. Elena was holding baby Joey and pushing Dominic and Michael forward in front of her.

"Boys, please! Don't goof around on these stairs! You're going to bump into people and fall and get hurt. I'm going to get your father!" She exclaimed as she gritted her teeth. "Better yet, I'm going to get your father, your *zio,* and your *nonno*! Then what!" The boys looked at each other in childish fear and immediately fell in line.

"Sorry, Ma!" Dominic shouted as he playfully hit his brother.

"Good grief. You two are going to give me a heart attack, you know that?" Elena shook her head and pinched Michael's ear from behind him.

"Hey, Lu," she said, "Remember when I used to be so mellow? *Madonna, mia*! What I wouldn't give!"

Luella chuckled as she shook her head, holding each of her daughters' hands, guiding them in front of her while trying to keep herself from falling on top of them as they descended the stairs.

"Boys! Give your mother a break, would you? Quit being a *camurria*!" Luella tried to instill some level of seriousness as the two women managed their small army of children. She couldn't help but find the humor in the situation. "I just can't believe sometimes that these are all ours!"

Elena turned back to roll her eyes and laugh with Luella.

Finally, they made it down onto the dirt to stand near the fence, getting a closer look at all of the action that was taking place. Vincenzo muttered Sicilian curse words under his breath while trying to read the program, clearly irritated.

"*Papa*, what's the matter? I thought you wanted to be down here," Luella said.

"*Ahh*," Vincenzo waved her off, displeased. "I thought I bet on number five, but he placed my bet on number nine!" Vincenzo rolled up his program and smacked his palm with it.

"*Papa*, maybe number nine will surprise you," Elena offered.

As the horses came onto the dirt, the jockeys rode them around slowly, showing them to the crowd before making their way to the gate for the race to begin. Dominic, Maria, Michael, and Anna all stood right up on the fence, trying to climb as much as they could to get a better view. Elena handed Joey back to Luella so she could hurry over to Vinny before the race began. The children all stood marveling at the beauty of the gigantic animals. Luella scooted her way between Vincenzo and Joe, nudging Joe's arm with her shoulder, sending him a wink and a smile.

"Hey, you." Joe wrapped his arm around Luella and his son and kissed her. "Do you want me to hold the baby so you can get a break?"

"That's alright. Elena just carried him down, I'm okay right now. Plus, you've been waiting all day to see this race, I want you to enjoy it."

Joe smiled at Luella, pushing her in front of him so he could stand behind her, resting his arm on her hip that held Joey.

A small man with a black hat and red coat came to the center of the dirt and raised his long, silver trumpet, ready to sound off the inaugural tune that started every race. Maria turned to look back at her parents, wanting to make sure her mother and father were there to witness it all, too. Excitement had taken over and her smile was enormous and giddy. Just as Maria turned around, Luella smelt a familiar smell. It reminded her of something, but she couldn't quite place it. A man's cologne, but not Joe's. She thought for a moment that it could have been a smell that Vinny or Vincenzo had worn before. She slowly and inconspicuously turned to her left to glance over her shoulder. The trumpet began to sound and everyone was staring straight ahead as she was looking beyond her husband. While she quietly investigated, she heard a shout from the stands, "Nicky!"

Luella jerked her head from left to right and up to where it was coming from. She saw an older, chubby man standing and waving to someone in the crowd about five feet from where they were. Her heart began to race as she surveilled the group of young men, wondering who would respond.

"Nicky! Over here!" The voice shouted again.

Finally, the young man came forward, waving back up at the man in the stands.

She calmed her nerves and brought herself back to the moment with her family. She had allowed her mind to take her elsewhere; she took a deep breath in. It was not what she had thought. It was not someone calling out *Mickey*. But the scent she had picked up a few minutes before, *was* from him. That's where she remembered it from: Mickey wore that cologne.

"Everything alright?" Joe asked. His wife had been looking around distracted.

"Oh, yeah, yeah. I'm fine. It was just a bug."

A shot exploded into the air and the horses were off. The quiet wave of cheers quickly progressed into loud, vibrating energy that overtook the stadium. The horses were rounding out speedily and the announcers were narrating everything that they were watching over the loudspeaker.

"SnickerDoodle in the lead! Oh, it's quick and it's tight!" The pace of his voice was fast and upbeat, at times difficult to follow, but when focusing on what was there for the crowd to watch, his statements made sense.

"Number Seven, Nightingale is gaining! Oh, oh my, now here comes Moonstruck! Red, Number Nine, Moonstruck is hauling around quickly! Oh my God, it's Nightingale and Moonstruck! Nightingale has a small lead. No, now Moonstruck!"

"*Papa*! Moonstruck is you, *Papa*!" Vinny grabbed Vincenzo's shoulders and started to jump. "*Papa*, you could win it!"

The family waited as the vigor and roar of the crowd grew inside them all and throughout the entire racetrack. The children began to shout. Luella squeezed on tighter to baby Joey and began bouncing him with her excitement.

"*Papa*! Oh my God, Moonstruck is going to win!"

Vincenzo ripped off his black skipper cap and squeezed it in his hand with the program.

"Oh my God!"

"And Moonstruck did it! What a race! Moonstruck just beat Nightingale in the most anticipated race of the season and what an underdog story!" The announcer concluded as the bursts of cheers radiated.

"Unbelievable!" Vincenzo shouted in glee. "I am a lucky son of a bitch today, huh!"

It was rare that Vincenzo cursed in English and to hear it made his children and their spouses laugh.

"That you are, *Papa*! That you are!" Vinny grabbed his father's cheeks and kissed his forehead. "You lucky son of a bitch!"

"Son of a bitch!" Dominic shouted as he jumped up and tugged at his father and grandfather's pant leg.

"Dominic Vincenzo!" Elena shouted and lightly smacked his head, trying to hide her laughs. "You do not speak like that. You hear me?" Elena looked at Vinny for reinforcement.

"Son, you don't speak like that. But today, your *nonno* just won a lot of money so we won't punish you any more than your mother already did." Vinny winked at Elena and brought Dominic into the hug.

"*Salute!*" Joe joined in and pulled the Andriotta girls and baby Joey into the mix. "To family and Moonstruck!"

"*Salute!*" They all shouted together and raised whatever drinks they had.

Luella felt the rush of the race and the energy from her father winning. As her family celebrated, she couldn't deny the anxiety still sitting in her belly. She tried to convince herself that it was the adrenaline of all that was going on around her, but she knew deep down that it was the thought of running into Mickey.

Part Three

Chapter 34

1980

"Ma!" Joey's voice shouted down to his mother from upstairs, traveling through the house. "Ma, where's my belt?"

"Joey, please. I told you! I hung it up in your closet, to the right."

Luella was in the living room with Joe after dinner, having a glass of wine.

The year was 1980 and the Andriottas were as stable as they'd ever imagined they could be. *Il Mercato de Greco, NYC* was established and practically running itself. Vinny and Joe would go in two to three days a week each to ensure that at least one of them was there making sure everything was okay. Vincenzo still solely owned and operated the original *Il Mercato de Greco* in Hawthorne and had just celebrated his eightieth birthday. Elena and Luella would still get there daily, if not for the whole day, at least to drop in and make sure no one needed anything from them. Elena spent more time there than Luella these days, but Vincenzo had full-time help from Nick, Sofia's husband who really took a liking to the market and quickly stepped in when the opportunity arose.

Maria had married a young man, John, two years earlier. John came from a nice family from Bogota. John's mother was Sicilian and worked in fashion, and his father was Polish and owned his own construction business. John and Maria quickly fell for each other upon meeting through a mutual friend, married, and had been flourishing together since. They started a tile business of their own that was slowly taking off, luckily due to the relationships that John's father had established throughout his own career.

Anna and Joey still lived with Luella and Joe. Joey was an eighteen-year-old who had the world in his hands. He was a mama's boy, at best, but Luella tried not to spoil him too much. She didn't want to create a man who would quickly turn a woman off due to his helplessness. She was trying to raise him to be sensitive and empathetic, but strong and resilient, just as Joe was. Joey was in school and helped at both markets with his father, uncle, and grandfather.

Anna, similar to Luella at the exact age of twenty-two, felt lost. She often wondered what her purpose was, or if she'd find her calling, just as her mother once had. She'd dabble in the market, and she was in school for teaching, but she too, wanted more. Luella and Joe had created an apartment in the basement for her, allowing her the opportunity to feel as though she was independent of her parents and her brother.

"He's your son when he doesn't know where anything is and needs your help," Joe said facetiously as he looked up from the paper he was reading.

"Oh, right. Because my husband knows where his socks are all the time, too, huh?" Luella joked back with him, putting her glass of wine down.

"Did you find it?" She yelled to her son.

"Yeah!" A distant response seemed to be moving back and forth as Joe and Luella could hear Joey's footsteps move from his bedroom to the bathroom down the hall.

"Ma, can you make me an espresso?"

Luella looked at Joe as she rolled her eyes and pushed herself off the couch. Joe put the newspaper down and picked up his wine, watching his wife as she walked to the kitchen.

"You want one too?" She looked back at him.

"No thanks, hon. I'm okay with the wine for now. Why don't we watch *M*A*S*H** tonight?"

"That sounds nice. Is Anna still sleeping? I'm worried about her."

Luella unscrewed the bottom of the metal demitasse and filled it with water. She removed the holder and packed it with fine espresso grinds, reassembled it, put it on the stove, and turned the burner on. Luella went to the basement door to call down to her daughter just as Anna appeared at the middle of the stairs.

"Oh! Anna, you scared me. You've been so quiet. How are you feeling? Do you want espresso? I'm putting it on for your brother."

"I'm okay, Ma. Thanks." Anna walked past her mother and to the refrigerator, opening it slowly and blankly staring inside. "Do we have any cola?"

Luella bent down and retrieved an unopened liter of Coca-Cola.

"Sweetheart, do you want to talk about it yet?" Luella patted her daughter's back softly and flipped a piece of her long, blonde curls.

"I don't think right now, Ma. Maybe later." Anna didn't make much eye contact as she walked over to pour herself a glass of soda before heading back into the basement.

"*Banan*, Daddy and I are going to watch *M*A*S*H* later. Do you want to watch too?"

Anna Banana had been her nickname since she was a girl. Sometimes, the nickname got abbreviated and even replaced her actual name. Banana, *Banan'... Ban*, sometimes even when her father or brother were too lazy to finish the rest.

"Maybe." Anna walked back downstairs and left the door slightly ajar.

Joey came downstairs, dressed sharply. His thick, black hair was combed back and his windbreaker jacket unzipped a quarter of the way. He took his espresso already assembled from the coffee table in front of the couch.

"Thanks, Ma." He took a sip and licked his lips. "Pop, I'll come to the city with you tomorrow if you'd like. I won't be home that late tonight."

"Sure, okay. Where are you going?" Joe asked his son. "I don't want you hanging around with that Demitri fella tonight. You hear?"

"Ma, please. Tell him not to nag me like this." Joey whined.

"Oh, yo! I'm sitting right here. Don't look at your mother when I'm talking to you."

"Sorry, pop. It's just that I told you a bunch of times that I haven't seen him in weeks since you told me not to." Joey looked at his father, trying to gauge whether or not he believed him.

"Alright," Joe said, "Come here."

Joey leaned over and kissed his father on both cheeks and then proceeded to do the same to his mother.

"We're leaving at 7 o'clock tomorrow. I got coverage in the morning and the new meat supplier said he'd be there by 10. So that'll give us enough time to get in and get situated. I want you to meet with him."

"Okay, pop. That sounds good."

Joe picked his paper back up before looking at his son again as he walked out the front door.

"We're leaving no later than 7 o'clock, son. Don't be out too late."

Joey looked back and nodded before smiling and winking at his mother and closing the door.

Luella and Joe were on their elongated sofa with a blanket covering them, watching their television show. When they watched television, they typically did not come to a choice or agreement quickly. But, they enjoyed the show *M*A*S*H** together and hadn't been able to catch it in quite a while.

Anna walked into the living room from the kitchen and turned the light up, disturbing her parents.

"Anna, what's wrong?" Luella said, sitting up. Joe searched for the remote to lower the volume.

Anna stood in front of them crying softly.

"I just didn't think Tommy would ever break up with me." Anna put her hands to her face and wept.

Joe and Luella quickly parted, making way for their grown daughter to come snuggle in between them.

"Come," Luella said, patting the spot they just made. "Come here.

Anna, you know you don't deserve someone who ever doubts that they want to be with you." Luella held her daughter in her arms.

"I'll kill him," Joe said, half joking and half serious.

Anna laughed as she leaned into her mother's chest.

"I just," she paused, "I just really thought he was *the one*. You know?"

"Banana, do you want me to make you an espresso?" Joe asked as he rubbed her arm. "Or, or how about some ice cream? I think we actually have some in the freezer. Will that make you feel better?"

Anna looked over at her father and nodded.

"Okay then." Joe kissed her forehead when he got up.

"Honey, do you want to talk about it?" Luella pulled herself back from resting her chin on Anna's head to look at her.

"I don't know, Ma. I just don't know if I'll ever find someone to have like you have Daddy. Like Maria has John or like *Zia* Elena has *Zio* Vinny. Why don't I have somebody to love?"

Luella knew the exact questions her daughter was enacting on herself. She knew the frustration she was feeling and the uncertainty that could consume her.

"Anna," Luella paused. "Do you know it took me until I was your age to really start to know what I wanted?" Luella thought about if she wanted to tell her daughter about her and Joe, about the break in between, and her time with Mickey. About how if she hadn't found Mickey in between all of that, she's not certain she and Joe would have made it. She wasn't sure if she wanted to lay all of what her life had been to get her to where she was today, with Joe.

"Anna, you deserve the sun, the moon, and the stars. If someone can't give that to you, then they aren't meant for you. Perhaps that's why Tommy ended things. Maybe…" Luella let out a sigh, "Maybe he knew he couldn't give you what you deserved. You've got to find peace in what's meant to be, will be. You have to find out who *you* are. The rest will follow, I promise."

Just as Luella finished, Anna wiped the last of her tears away and Joe came back with spumoni ice cream and fresh, homemade whipped cream on top.

"Here you go, baby." He said, handing the bowl to Anna. "You'll never be too old to be my baby, or too old to say that ice cream can't make things better."

"Thanks, Dad." She sat up and moved over, making more room for her father to join.

Anna took a bite, looked at her mom, and smiled. "Thanks, Ma. I love you guys."

As the three of them repositioned on the couch, Joe turned, laughing. "Who cares if we miss this show again, right?"

Luella laughed, "Who cares is right." She kissed Anna on her head, and breathed in her daughter's hair.

Chapter 35

1980

The holidays had gone through stages for Luella throughout her life. When she was young, she spent every Thanksgiving and Christmas Eve with her father, Vinny, Dante and Angelina and their girls, and occasionally the Petrellis. Then, when their family started to expand, it was the Greco clan in addition to the significant others, Elena and Joe. Then came the children. Some of the most enjoyable Christmases were when all of the children were young. When Dominic and Michael would taunt Maria and Anna, and Joey was just learning to walk and talk. Luella held onto those memories, the innocence of them all. She remembered how their little hands would softly touch the Christmas tree branches, or how their eyes would widen with surprise and excitement at the sight of their collective mountain of gifts. The warmth of her memories, however, were always met with the background of grief.

Now, Christmas looked different. Her children were older, and their excitement had shifted to what they wanted out of life. Maria was the only one who had a husband who joined in with his parents for the Christmas Eve festivities. John Kowalski and his parents were a lovely addition. His mother, being Sicilian, always offered to come and set up the seven fish feast that was going to be taking place at the Andriotta's.

Maria, Anna, Elena, and Luella spent their time in the kitchen the day before Christmas Eve, making sure everything was prepared for the next day and would just need to be cooked. Vinny and Joe were in the New York City location since it was the busiest time for both markets, while Vincenzo, Joey, and Sofia's husband Nick were the steady hands in addition to a few staff members in the New Jersey market. The house was filled with the women laughing and sharing stories over the Dean Martin Christmas Album that Luella had been playing every year since it came out in 1966.

"So," Maria nudged her sister as the two of them stood in an assembly line cutting up eggplant into perfectly thin slices. "What's going on? Mommy told me about Tommy. Why didn't you call?"

Anna looked over her shoulder rolling her eyes at the thought of her mother telling her older sister about her breakup.

"Don't be annoyed with her. She was just worried about you, that's all." Maria affirmed.

"I didn't want to talk about it," Anna replied.

"Do you want to talk about it now?"

Anna looked at her sister and shrugged. "I guess," she said. "There's not much to talk about. He broke up with me because he knows he doesn't deserve me. He knows that I need more than he could ever give to me." Anna's voice shook a bit, but her statement came out confident as though she had been rehearsing those lines to herself.

"You're right," Maria winked. "He doesn't deserve you. John has this really nice friend who I just recently met. His name is Paul and he works in the car business. I brought Daddy to him when he was looking for the new Cadillac and John just brought him up the other day. He said that he was really tired of the same scene and was ready to find a nice girl and settle down." Maria smirked at her sister before finishing her thought. "What do you say?"

Anna laughed and shook her head, returning to slicing before Elena overheard.

"What's that?" She asked from behind her nieces. "Lu, did you hear that?"

"*Zia*, please!" Anna laughed and pushed her elbow jokingly into her aunt.

"Oh no, your *Zia* is approving everyone that wants to see you, now. *Zio* Vinny wanted to drive to that Tommy's house with your father when he told Vinny that he broke your heart. You know how protective he gets over you girls. It's like you have two fathers." Elena shook her head and laughed. "So, I decided I'd vet the next prospect."

"What about the mother? I don't get to be a part of the vetting process?" Luella barked.

"No." An affirmative response came out simultaneously from Maria and Anna. They started to laugh at the fact that it wasn't planned, but felt like a scene out of a sitcom.

"Hey! Why not?" Luella laughed.

"Ma, you're my *mother*. You just... you just can't. You and Daddy would scare them all away!" Anna said.

"Fine. Have your *Zia* Elena do it." Luella shrugged it off, pretending to be annoyed. "But don't come crying to me when she scares them off first. She only has boys. She's been practicing her speeches for girls since you two were born. Just wait!"

They all laughed and continued with their tasks.

"Alright, maybe next weekend. After the holidays." Anna quietly said to her sister.

"After the holidays," Maria confirmed.

"Hey Ma, can I help with anything?" Joey asked as he came to greet his mother.

"Oh, hi honey," Luella was vigorously cleaning the floor. "Do you mind getting me another *mapeen*?"

Joey returned with the kitchen towel and handed it to his mother before sitting on the couch.

"Hey Ma, so I wanted to talk to you about something," Joey hesitated before continuing. Luella stopped her arms from the back-and-forth motion and looked at Joey.

"Okay..." Luella said.

"Donna's family..." Joey inhaled and exhaled loudly. "They, they invited me for Christmas Eve. I told Donna that I don't think so, but Ma, I want to go. I just didn't know how to tell you and Daddy. I don't want to disappoint you or *Nonno*. I don't want anyone to feel like I don't want to be with my family on Christmas."

Luella sat back on top of her legs underneath her, wiping the hair falling from her face with her forearm. Her hands were still gloved and wet from scrubbing the hardwood floors.

"Joey," Luella sighed. "You're eighteen years old, I can't keep you home forever. I'm upset and your father will be upset, but if that's what you want to do, I'll talk to him." Luella continued. "But did you mention having Donna by us on Christmas Eve? She can bring the family. We'll have Daddy and *Zio* get extra food from the market, and *Nonno* too. Then you guys can spend Christmas day with her family. How's that sound?" Luella bargained with her son. Her eyes were wide and anticipatory, already knowing what it was that her son wanted to do.

"You know what, it's okay, Ma. Don't even worry about it. I don't have to go, maybe next year."

Joey stood from the couch and walked up the stairs. Luella felt herself crumble inside. She knew her son's heart was being secured by a lovely young woman, and that one day he'd have a family of his own. She just wanted so badly to hold on to her children as she felt the time disappearing, minute by minute. Each day that rolled by was like sand slipping through her fingers and traveling with the wind. She just couldn't control it. She wanted so desperately to freeze time, to stop her children from growing. Hell, if it were up to her, she'd turn the clock back to when they were young and only wanted to be with one another and with her. Luella dreaded the days that her children would leave the nest. She felt lucky that she still had Anna and Joey living at home, but she knew it was borrowed time. Luella *also* knew that she did not want to be the mother who guilted her children into spending time with her. She hadn't wanted her children to experience that. She wanted them to feel as though they were free to make their own choices with no ramifications of a parent's judgment, only their support and guidance. She was failing at this moment. She knew what she'd done and felt herself begin to tear up. She quickly stood, brushed herself off, and collected her cleaning supplies. Luella stood at the foot of the stairs and called to her son.

"I'll talk to your father. Did you already say yes to Donna?"

Joey quickly appeared from around the top of the stairs, elated.

"Thanks, Ma. Yeah, I told her that I'd probably be there."

"You told her that you'd *probably* be there? Joey, Christmas Eve is tomorrow. That makes you sound flakey." Luella's voice was stern. "Did you really say that?"

Luella and Joe had met Donna when they started dating in the eleventh grade. She was a beautiful young woman with ambition and came from a nice family on the other side of town. Luella did not want her son to come across as inconsistent or lackluster to Donna, or her family.

"*Ugh*, fine. I said yes already." Joey shrugged his shoulders at his mother.

Luella rolled her eyes and tapped her foot.

"Your room better be tidy for this entire year when I go in there."

Joey flew down the stairs and grabbed his mother, embracing her in one of his big bear hugs, towering over her at only eighteen years old.

"I'm serious, Joey. Not a thing on that floor. I'm not picking it up."

Joey kissed Luella on the cheek.

"Your father will be home soon. I'm going to need some wine."

Everyone poured into the Andriotta's around 2 o'clock for the holiday celebration. The Andriotta residence was by far the most well-dressed house for Christmas. Joe spared no expense at hanging lights and decorating every bush and tree outside. Giant red bows hung from the peaks of the Cape Cod and one above the garage. The wreath that hung in between the storm door and the wooden front door was a replica of a handmade one by Luella and Maria when Maria was just a little girl. Luella loved looking around her table and seeing all of her children, her father, her brother and sister-in-law, and her nephews. Alongside her the entire day, was her husband. Joe and Luella embraced the duties of hosting and happily waited on their family.

Vincenzo, at the opposite end of the head of the table, proudly stood and raised a glass.

"My family," he started, "*mia famiglia*. I look around and am so proud of each one of you. I can't express how happy my heart feels when I look at all of you and how far you've all come. I love you all very, very much. *Buon Natale!*"

"*Buon Natale!*" The family saluted in unison.

"We'd also like to say something." Maria quickly stood. She looked down at John and tugged on his shoulder to stand with her. "We love you, *Nonno* and *Buon Natale*, my beautiful family. John and I have some news."

As the couple glanced at each other, their sheepish smirks gave away that they were ready to share something big. Luella grabbed Joe's hand, already anticipating what the announcement would be. She squeezed it tightly.

"John and I are expecting!" She grabbed her belly. "We're pregnant!"

The family jumped and cheered. Luella ran to her daughter and grabbed her face, her eyes filling with tears.

"I love you, Maria. I'm so proud of you!" Luella kissed her daughter on the cheek and they shared a long hug, rocking back and forth. As Maria pulled back, she held her mother's arms.

"You're going to be a grandma!"

The family roared again with excitement at the thought, all of them making their way to the expectant couple.

"And me! I'm going to be a great-grandfather!" Vincenzo shouted in his broken English from where he stood. "*Cin cin!*"

As Luella stepped back from her daughter and son-in-law, allowing the rest of the family to give them their love and well wishes, she felt the utmost peace. In the middle of the loud, chaotic celebration, she felt calm. She embraced the wave of stillness that washed over her as she watched her world spin in slow motion. *This* is exactly what she'd been waiting for. A new generation was beginning, and her children entering the next phase of their lives confirmed that she, too, was entering the next phase of hers. She was going to supersede the role that she's played for so long of a mother and graduate to becoming a grandmother. Where the responsibility lightened in the mundane tasks of the day-to-day, but widened in the spoiling of the children and the lessons that she could teach them, the wisdom she could cast upon her grandchildren. But along with the happiness, peace, and excitement, she felt the slightest bit of remorse. Her family, as well as herself, were moving on. They were arm in arm moving ahead in life, and her firstborn's soul was somewhere in the ether. While she felt Carla's presence in all that she did and all that she was, she knew she was experiencing this with them, she couldn't help but feel guilt and a touch of sadness. Just as the wave washed over her, Joe came up around her and placed his arm around her waist, kissing her cheek.

"Hey Grandma," he whispered in her ear. "You doing okay?"

Joe had a way of reading his wife in all of their years together at this point, knowing just what she needed at just the right time.

"I'm okay, Grandpa," she teased.

"Let's go celebrate our new titles." Joe guided Luella to the kitchen where just the two of them raised a glass and toasted.

"To becoming grandparents," Joe pronounced, raising his glass.

"To becoming grandparents."

Chapter 36

1981

It was shaping up to be quite a year for the Andriotta family. Maria, nearly nine months pregnant, was rarely left to tend to anything by herself. Between her husband and the rest of her family, there was no shortage of people to step in and help get ready for the baby. Joey had proposed to Donna, and Anna had been going steady with the friend of John's that Maria had introduced her to since the New Year. Typical Saturdays were now spent quite differently. With Maria due in only a few short weeks, Luella, Anna, Elena, and John's mother, Rosanna, all tended to her while the men, when not at the markets, helped John prepare the nursery.

Luella, her daughters, and Elena were sorting through gifts from the shower the week prior and writing out thank you cards when there was a knock on the door.

"Who's here, Ma?" Anna asked, looking over at her mother curiously.

"I'm not sure, we're not expecting anybody else," Luella replied. She placed the clothes that she had neatly stacked on her lap on the floor next to her before getting up and heading to the door.

Luella was greeted by a young man she did not know, but had recognized.

"Luella?" The man said, questioning her intently. "Luella Greco?"

"Yes, that's me. Greco is my maiden name. I'm sorry, who… who are you?" Luella was taken aback by the greeting she was just met with. She was obviously confused by the man in her doorway who referred to her by Greco instead of Andriotta. He was clearly not a delivery man carrying a package, nor was he someone she was waiting to see on the other side of the door. The rest of the women stayed quiet, overhearing the conversation from just inside. Maria grabbed her back and tried to lift herself off of the couch to see who her mother was talking to.

"Ma, who is it?" She pulled the door back a bit more, standing behind her mother.

"My name is Noah. Noah O'Rourke. My father was Mickey."

Luella's head tilted slightly, her eyebrows pointing downward in confusion.

"I'm sorry, what?" Luella could not compute what was happening.

Elena, overhearing the name *Mickey*, knew immediately to go to the door.

Now, the young man claiming to be Mickey's son was faced with three women with whom he had no familiarity.

"What's going on here?" Elena asked abruptly.

"You're Luella Greco?" He again asked intentionally. "My father was Mickey. My father wrote about you. I've been trying to find you. My Aunt Maryann said I may be able to find you here."

"You said your father wrote about me? What do you mean?" Luella asked.

"My father passed away last week. I…" There was hesitation in the young man's voice, unsure how to proceed. "I found journals he kept, and letters he wrote. Many of them, addressed to *you*."

Noah's words hung in the air as Luella remained still. Tears slowly began to fill her eyes.

"Ma, who is Mickey? What is going on?" Maria was trying to piece together the encounter that was unfolding in front of her with her mother and this stranger.

"Maria, honey, can you give me and your mother a minute with Noah," Elena said, pushing herself in between Maria and Luella.

"*Zia, what* is going on?"

"Mickey had a son?" Luella looked Noah in the eyes. "Mickey is *dead*?"

"I can come back another time. I'm sorry to just show up like this, I'm just hoping you can help me unscramble parts of my father." Noah sighed defeatedly. " I shouldn't have come." Noah turned to leave and as he did, Luella noticed letters folded in his back pocket. She quickly hurried down the front steps and onto the walkway to follow him.

"Noah, wait," she reached for his shoulder. As Noah turned back to look at Luella, she saw it- Mickey. The shape of his nose, the stature of his build, and the look in his eyes. It was as if she were back twenty-something years ago looking directly at Mickey. The feelings of being young, in lust, and unsure of herself flooded over her. The uncertainty weighed heavily in the air around her.

"I'm sorry. I'm chasing ghosts. I just…" Noah paused, tears now forming behind his eyes. "I just want to know why."

Luella was completely beside herself and utterly confused. She began to think back. *Was Mickey having an affair? Is Noah here to wonder why his father cheated? Could he have had a secret life all along?* Her mind raced.

"Noah, I'm sorry. I'm so sorry for your loss, I truly am. But why on earth are you looking to me to help answer questions about your father dying? How old are you?"

"I'm nineteen. It was stupid of me to come." Noah reached back into his pocket before pulling out stacks of letters rubber-banded together. "Here."

"What are these? Honey, maybe you can help me understand. Why did you come to see me?"

"My father killed himself. He killed himself and I don't know why. I don't know what I did or didn't do. He left me a letter, too. He told me about something that happened when he was a kid, but I don't care. I don't know if I, or anyone, for that matter, could've saved him. All I know is that when he wrote about you, he seemed to be… *free. Happy.*"

"Your father *killed* himself?" Luella was in shock. *Mickey had taken his own life.* Her brain could not comprehend what she was hearing.

"I'm sorry, I should go." Noah turned and began to run to his car parked down the street. Luella couldn't bring herself to say anything else. She stood there, on her walkway, looking down at the letters in her hand.

"Ma, what the hell!" Anna, now in the archway, shouted from the door as Elena ran past her to Luella, having watched the whole encounter.

"Oh, Luella," Elena grabbed her sister-in-law's shoulders and turned her to the front of the house, consoling her as best she could. "Come on, let's get you inside."

"So, let me get this straight," Anna asked as the group of ladies returned back to the living room, trying to sort out what had just happened. "You loved some guy named Mickey before Daddy. He committed suicide. You haven't seen him in God only knows how long and he wrote you letters?" Anna facetiously tried to calculate. "Oh, and his son just came to deliver the news with a bow."

"Anna!" Maria gritted her teeth at her sister, smacking her leg.

"What? You don't think this is weird?" Anna asked the room. "It's weird!"

"Ma, are you okay? Do you want to talk about it?" Maria asked from the far side of the couch, leaning over to rub her mother's knee.

"I didn't love him before your father," Luella said. "I loved him in between your father."

"You *cheated* on Daddy?" Anna exclaimed.

"No, God, no. I didn't cheat on your father. I dated him, then we broke up and I dated Mickey, and then your father and I got back together."

"Okay, so Daddy knows," Anna confirmed, sighing relief.

Luella and Elena exchanged a look that said otherwise.

"Okay, so…" Anna knew what the look between her aunt and mother had symbolized. "Daddy does not know about this *Mickey*."

"Well, we never really talked about what we did in between. Then when we got back together, things happened so fast, and then…" Luella's eyes started to drift, "Then you know… Your sister."

"It's okay, Ma." Maria, grew visibly uncomfortable, scrunching her nose in discomfort while consoling her mother. "We understand. It's okay, let's not even ta…" Maria could not finish her sentence as she wailed in pain grabbing the arm of the couch and squeezing her mother's knee.

"Maria, honey?" Elena looked at her niece and back and Luella. "I think you're having contractions."

Before the women could discuss anything any further, Maria's water broke and they were phoning John to let them know it was time and to meet them at the hospital. They piled as comfortably as they could into Luella's car and drove off. Luella sat in the backseat with Maria while Elena drove and Anna rode shotgun. Luella guided her daughter through breathing. And as she did, her mind and all of its thoughts and questions were now fleeing and the only thing that she could think about was that she was about to become a grandmother.

1981

The steam from the coffee filled the immediate space in front of Luella's line of sight, temporarily obstructing her clear view of Joe sitting in front of her. As she sat and stared through the smokey ora clouding above her cup, she allowed her thoughts to run. She thought of her granddaughter, so new and pure entering a world of so much pain and confusion. She knew, however, that it was her duty as her grandmother to teach her about life's blessings and the heartaches that may accompany them at times. She'd tell her about her experiences and she'd teach her about how to take time to figure out what it is that makes her eyes glow, just as she had with her own daughters, but different. Being a grandma gave her a different level of responsibility. She could offer maternal advice without parenting. She'll tell her about Mickey, she decided, when she was old enough. She'll make sure that she tells her about love, what she thinks love is, and how sometimes it's okay to not know. Luella was deep in thought about the lessons she'd grace upon her granddaughter before the silence was broken.

"Hon?" Joe interrupted Luella's racing mind. "Do you want me to make you some eggs? You haven't eaten much."

Shit, Luella thought. Her loss in appetite was a telltale sign that something was wrong. She hadn't wanted to tell Joe about the letters or news she had gotten from Noah. She wasn't sure how to tell him that her heart was breaking without breaking his.

"Sure," she responded. "I'll make them." Luella superseded Joe slowly making his way to the stove.

"What else do you want?" she questioned as she pulled the pan from the cupboard and retrieved the eggs from the fridge. "How about some sausage?"

"That sounds great. Thanks, hon. But my intention wasn't for *you* to cook breakfast. I know there's a lot going on with the baby being here now and I know how excited you are, but I just can't help but feel something's bothering you. Is it Carla? Are you thinking about her?"

Luella paused for a second before continuing what she was doing and answering Joe's question.

"I think about her every day, Joe. Everyday." Luella looked intently at the eggs cracking over the side of the pan, sizzling as they hit the heated middle. "I'm just taking it all in. I want to make sure Maria is okay and the baby. I want to make sure Luanna has what she needs and that everyone is settled."

Maria had named her daughter after both her mother and her living sister. *Luanna* paid tribute to the women who made Maria who she was. The women who were alive and strong. Those who were present figures throughout her entire existence. She'd felt there was so much honoring the past and talk of who *was,* that she wanted her daughter to pay homage to those who *are.* Those who were with her every step of every way.

Luanna came into the world a few weeks early, so they held both Maria and the baby for a few extra nights in the hospital. Luella spent every day with Maria in the hospital until the day when John had told his mother-in-law to get some rest and take care of what she needed to. He assured Luella that he, Maria, and baby Luanna would be heading home that afternoon. Until Luella received the call that they were home, she couldn't stop her mind from wandering. She had an innate reaction wanting to protect her daughter and her granddaughter, and would often find herself raising her voice with the hospital staff if she didn't have an answer she was satisfied with. While she couldn't control fate, she sure as hell tried to control the circumstances around her.

Joe came up behind Luella as she retrieved the eggs from the pan.

"Grandma," he whispered in her ear, causing the hair on her neck to stand. "Please, relax. Everything is going to be just fine, my love. Both of our girls will be home before we know it."

Luella turned to face her husband and let out a sly smile.

"I feel old with my new title." Luella playfully smacked Joe's chest with the towel she had over her shoulder. "How are you doing, *Grandpa*?"

Joe kissed his wife and as he did, he moved his hands up to her cheeks, holding her face in his palms.

"You're beautiful, Grandma. You know that?" Joe planted another sweet kiss on Luella's lips. "And, you're not old," he paused. "Because, if *you're* old, I'm old. And I just won't accept that."

Luella loved the way her life had turned out. She loved being a mother. She loved leading her children through their time on earth. She loved embracing them. She loved teaching them every lesson possible. She even found herself loving the tough moments of discipline because she knew it would result in well-behaved, polite children with strong morals, unlikely to waver. Luella loved being a wife. She adored Joe. Even through the turbulence they'd had at times, she adored him and the way he loved her. She loved the way he knew her and the way she knew him, and how after all their years together, the love had only grown stronger, the roots maneuvering more deeply. As a hundred-year-old tree's roots would grow and move through the ground, unsure where they begin and end, so did the roots of Joe and Luella's love. She loved, already, being a grandmother. She felt blessed to have healthy children who could have children of their own. And she felt grateful that her daughter used her as inspiration for her child's name. She loved her firstborn daughter, and the gift she'd been in her short time. But arguably, above all of this, she loved the sureness she had about herself. Luella had fought long and hard to figure out who she was as a person. At fifty-four years old, Luella was confident in herself down to her core. She believed in who she was, what she stood for, and what her purpose was. She attributed everything else, her ability to be a loving mother, grandmother, and wife, to that. She welcomed this next chapter willingly and she decided at that moment, that it was time to dedicate herself to painting again.

Chapter 38

1938

Vincenzo had taken his children to New York City to meet with an old friend who recently came over from Italy. Anytime the Greco children went to the city, they were overjoyed with the selection of buildings to look up at. They were awed at the fact that they, themselves, were these tiny people who could walk up flights of stairs, or take a ride on an elevator, and be as tall as the tallest building they could find, overlooking Manhattan.

Vincenzo swiftly moved through the crowd, holding Vinny's left hand, Vinny's right hand gripping onto Luella's. The three of them formed a chain. Vincenzo excused himself through the waves of bustles of people, protecting his children who were too small to be seen in the crowd. 7:15 p.m. on a Saturday and the city had significantly more people than would be seen in their small, quiet town of Hawthorne, New Jersey. Luella noticed all of the strangers as she looked up at them as their quick faces breezed past her. She felt that there was so much more to see in the people of New York City. Without focusing on their small, minute details, they'd look like blurs quickly moving by her. But details were what she slipped into when honing in on specific features or attributes of people. *Big nose. Ugly hat. Bright eyes.* She'd whisper the things that caught her attention or say them in her head.

One particular gentleman, tall and slender, wearing a black wool coat down to his shins, caught her stare. *Creepy,* she thought to herself. As the crowd moved by, so did this man. But he was as fixated on little

Luella as she was on him. He was looking down at her, their eyes meeting as he walked by. The rest of the world drowned out when he caught her attention. It was the way he looked at her that rattled her and sparked the subtlest fear. He intently watched her as she noticed him and as he moved past her, she smelled his scent: musk and cigarettes. She got caught in the cloud of smoke he'd been exhaling as they passed each other, and as Luella turned around she saw him also turning back. Luella felt her heart begin to race and her palms begin to clam up. She felt scared. In the instant of realizing the feeling of her palms, she quickly looked down at her hands, realizing that her hands were without Vinny's. She had broken from the chain with her brother and her father. In the few seconds that ten-year-old Luella was alone on the streets of New York City, the faces had never looked more frightening. She spun around five, six times, panicking, looking in every direction for her brother and her father. She spun her head over her shoulders so quickly that the brown locks in her ponytail whipped her face, poking her in the eye, catapulting her into hysterics. Right before she could scream for her father, she felt arms around her.

"Luella!" Vincenzo grabbed Luella so quickly from the crowd and into the safety of his arms.

"Vinny!" Vincenzo yanked Vinny closer to him, moving them to the far side of the sidewalk, leaning against a building to get out of the way. "You never, ever let go of your sister's hand!"

Vinny's eyes began to fill with tears, feeling regretful and sad to learn that if only for a few seconds, he lost sight of his younger sister.

"I'm sorry, *Papa*! I'm sorry!" Vinny's voice was shaking, his tears now falling.

Vincenzo squeezed Luella in his arms, lifting her slightly off the ground. He pulled Vinny closer to his side before kneeling down in front of them.

"You two never leave each other's side. Not for one minute! You hear me?" Vincenzo's own eyes now began to water. Eye-level with his children, witnessing the fear and sadness on both of their faces, he let the panic dissipate in his own chest. Both of his children were safely in front of him.

"*Papa*! Never leave me!" Luella wailed as she threw herself into his arms. "Never leave me, *Papa*!

Vincenzo grabbed both Luella and Vinny, pulling them in close. Hugging them both so tightly that he felt their bodies press into his.

"I will never leave you. Either one of you. I am always with you." Vincenzo went back and forth, kissing both children on their cheeks two times. "We are always together. *Ti voglio bene.*"

Vincenzo wiped the tears from their eyes first, and then his own before standing up. He grabbed each one of their hands in his, kissed them both, and the three of them began to walk.

Chapter 39

1987

Luella made her way through the hallway from the backdoor of the market as she had done so many times before. She flicked on the switch, lighting the front of the original *Il Mercato de Greco*, the place where she had grown up. She slowly walked to the kitchen, allowing her fingertips to graze along the stucco walls, that for so long her father cooked within. The walls that heard him in every capacity that one could be heard. It was within these walls that Vincenzo had his highest highs and lowest lows. *This* is where she felt her father. Vincenzo's bare hands built the market into the operation it is today. It was he who had the vision when he first came to America. To serve the people of his community the food of their homeland. To offer those who were not of Italian descent, a slice of the European way. Vincenzo raised his entire family within these walls and now, his ghost would haunt them.

It was a Thursday, and the family had buried Vincenzo earlier that day. At eighty-seven years old, Vincenzo died of heart failure four days earlier. Luella wasn't sure how to live life without her father, nor did she want to figure it out. Vincenzo was Luella's constant, as so many parents are for their children. He was both her father and her mother. He played the role of two parents in such a way that Luella only on occasion found herself yearning for a mother's love. Vincenzo had given both of his children so much warmth, adoration, and attention, that they felt completely full and wholesome with the love of only him.

Walking over to the oven, she stopped herself. She allowed herself to listen to the silence, and in that, she could hear Vincenzo's laughter. She closed her eyes and imagined him singing operatically in Italian, flouring his countertop generously to knead his dough for the bread he'd make. The bread that people came to know. It was the scent of his bread that drew customers into the market. They'd want something savory when they initially intended on getting something sweet upon coming in. It was the bread that she first learned how to make when she was just a girl. Vincenzo would prop her up on the countertop and have her watch his meticulous process. She'd question each step as he explained it to her, partially in his native tongue and partially in English, leading her to only be able to articulate the how-to in a mix of Sicilian and English. As she basked in the energy left all around her after Vincenzo's departure from the physical world, she heard the back door open.

"Hello?" She questioned from the kitchen. At this time of night, the only person likely to show up was her brother.

"Hey, Lu," Vinny said, turning the corner.

"Hi, Vin. How are you doing?" Luella hugged her brother and they both cried. There was no need for a response. They knew how the other was doing.

"I just can't believe it," Vinny started. "I know everyone has to die. I'm a sixty-one-year-old man, I figured that out a long time ago." Luella chuckled at Vinny's insertion of humor, even in times of immense pain. "I just never thought *Papa* would die. Isn't that silly?"

"It's not silly," Luella tried to compose herself. "It's not silly at all, Vin. He's all we've ever known. He was our whole world before we started creating worlds of our own. And even still, he was the universe that we were able to live within." Luella looked for a tissue for herself and her brother to help fight off their uncontrollable stream of tears.

"I knew we'd both end up here tonight. I wasn't sure if it would be the same time, but I knew we both would." Vinny assured as he reached over the counter for a roll of paper towels. He handed one to his sister before taking one for himself.

"So, now what?" Vinny asked.

"Now? I'm not sure. But what I do know, is as much as it hurts, we'll be okay." Luella grabbed her brother's shoulders, then placed her hand gently under his chin. "We'll be okay, Vin. He's with us. He's all around us. The pain is overwhelming and we'll never be able to fill the void that he left, but I promise we'll be okay."

"You're so strong, Lu. I'm so proud of you and *Papa* always was too." Vinny smiled at his sister. "Luella. *Warrior.*"

The two of them sat in the kitchen, talking until the early hours of the morning. They talked about life, death, and all of the in-between. They laughed and cried and held onto their father in the time between when the sun set and when a new dawn began to rise. They knew that they had each other. They knew that as they had so many times before, they'd recreate themselves. They'd reshape their lives ever so slightly to fit into their new normal as one so often does. The Grecos had their hearts broken and put back together, time and again. Each time, slightly taking a new shape, but with each new shape, they learned about acceptance. They morphed with the years and transformed into the people they were. Now, with Vincenzo gone, they'd morph again.

Chapter 40

1987

The months following Vincenzo's death were uncanny and uncomfortable times for the entire family. Vinny, Luella, and their spouses jumped right back into the market as they were used to, ensuring both the Jersey and the New York City locations were running smoothly and up to par with Vincenzo's expectations. The pressure, now more than ever, not to miss a beat was carried by each one of them. They wanted to honor Vincenzo and to instill in their children and now grandchildren, that this was who they were - this market, the walls within which they'd created memories, friends, and family, was their life, too. It was in the very makeup of them. Whether they grew to want to be involved in the daily operation, or step in occasionally, it was theirs. It would shape them.

As the months turned to a year, they adapted to the new normal. Time was waiting for no one and the world kept going. With that, *Il Mercato de Greco* did, too. The customer base was expanding, and changing. The regulars from the past forty-plus years had begun to look a bit different. Like Vincenzo, some passed. The regulars that had supported Vincenzo when it was just him and his young children had also lived full lives and were no longer. The customers that graced the market with the opportunity to serve them, laced themselves into the very DNA of Greco's. Now, it was their children, and their children's children who would frequent. The customers were what kept the business alive, thriving, and growing. It was their loyalty, their belief in Vincenzo Greco and what he created and shared with them, that kept them more than afloat.

"Grandma!" Luanna's voice raised as she walked through the front door, making eye contact. Her arms stretched far out in front of her miniature body, reaching for Luella. Once kindergarten started, Maria made a ritual of stopping in the market on the walk home from school with Luanna. Luella cherished this. She'd wait patiently until 12:15 p.m. for the immense joy of seeing the bright-eyed, curly-haired child burst through the door. The excitement was reciprocal.

"*Ciao,* my baby!" Luella nearly ran around the counter, scooping up Luanna in her arms. This is what she did every day, if she wasn't actively engaged with a customer. "Come to Grandma!" Luella planted kisses repeatedly on Luanna's full cheek as she giggled and squirmed in her arms. The loud smack of kisses was emphasized by design as Luella embraced her grandchild, knowingly causing her to laugh.

"Hi, Ma. How's everything going today?" Maria followed behind Luanna, waiting to greet her mother with a kiss on the cheek, not to disturb the reunion between her and her daughter.

"Hi honey, it's been slow. *Zio* Vinny is in the kitchen and *Zia* Elena is in the office. Your father is in the city with Joey."

Things had begun to feel normal, to a degree. The customers' familiar faces unblurred themselves as time passed from the day Vincenzo had died. The market began to feel like the old days, when Vinny and Elena were just married. When Joe and Luella had just gotten together. The energy of the four of them being back at the helm of the store, but now, with their own families, was dynamic. It was a bittersweet transition-allowing Vincenzo's memory to live on through his creation of the market while also making it a bit of their own.

"And Anna? I left her a message yesterday and she never called me back. I haven't seen her or the babies in a week!" Maria tried very hard to keep a close relationship with her siblings. They were still closer than most, but Maria wouldn't rest easy if she didn't see her sister or brother and their families over a period of a few days.

"I'm not sure, honey. She called me this morning. Maybe she just got busy. The twins are always a lot to manage. Why don't you try her again later. I'm sure she just got caught up. Plus, we'll all be together Sunday."

Anna ended up marrying the young man that Maria and John set her up with- Paul. They married in 1982 and had twins a year and a half later, named Carla, in honor of her deceased sister, and Paul, honoring her very much alive husband. The family still gathered at Luella and Joe's house every Sunday for dinner. Now more than ever, Luella felt the importance of keeping the tradition of spending the day together. She felt fortunate to have had the experience growing up as closely as she did with her brother and father, that she wanted the same for her children and grandchildren.

Maria rolled her eyes and waved her mother's response off. "I'm not waiting until Sunday, Ma. I'll call her now."

Luella looked at Luanna in her arms and pressed her forehead against the little one she was holding. "*Madonna mia*! Your mother is a silly one, isn't she?" Luanna giggled and covered her mouth.

"And Joey? My brother couldn't call me before work today? My God. Is it too much to ask that I get five minutes to catch up with my brother and sister?" Maria, standing behind the counter, calling Anna from the phone on the wall, was clearly offended. It didn't take much. Maria hadn't worked since she had Luanna. She was used to being busy with her daughter all day long and then tending to John when he returned home from work, but now that Luanna was in kindergarten, she found herself aching to feel a closeness with her siblings. She wanted to spend the short time that Luanna was in school catching up with them.

"Honey," Luella started as she and Luanna came back behind the counter, Luanna now walking, holding her hand. "It's okay. What are you getting so worked up for? They're busy. You're busy." Maria cocked her head to her mother with her gaze fixated on her. "Alright, so you're not busy when Luanna's in school. I know, you're adjusting. But your brother and sister have their own lives, sweetheart. They've got a lot to juggle, just like you. You can't expect them to be able to drop what they're doing to talk to you in the middle of their mornings."

"I know." Maria hung up the phone by the third ring. "I know, you're right. I just feel like before we know it, all of these kids are going to be in school and off doing their own thing, and I want to embrace it and enjoy this time in our lives while we're going through it together."

Luella put her hand on Maria's shoulder and began to rub her arm. "I know you do, sweetie."

"Hey! I knew that was my beautiful niece." Vinny came out from the kitchen with the freshly baked bread ready to be neatly stacked into place in the baskets on the walls. "Where's Luanna?" Vinny knew where Luanna was. This was a part of their regular routine. He'd ask where she was as he'd see her peeking around the counter, anticipating his question.

"I don't know where she is, actually," Maria said, looking in the direction of her daughter.

Vinny shrugged his shoulders, "Hm." And he continued to place the bread in their appropriate baskets.

Luanna did her best to tiptoe and slowly creep behind her great-uncle, attempting to startle him. When she got close enough, she'd widen her stance and puff her chest out before tugging on the back of his apron. "Boo! Here I am!" She shouted.

"*Ahh*!" Vinny's voice reflected acting. "Oh my goodness, you! You scared me!" He said as he grabbed a hold of his chest, pretending to calm his nerves.

Yes, this was the new normal. It was chaotic at times, but it was full. The family was spending their time there whenever they could and they were finding the light in their days. They would allow themselves to face the sun and feel the warmth of it, embracing the joy that being together brought them. This was exactly what Vincenzo would've wanted for *Il Mercato de Greco,* and for his family.

Chapter 41

1953

When Luella went back to painting, she'd completely lose herself in her art. In the beginning, when she first uncovered her natural, raw talent, she'd play around with different color palettes. She'd try new brushes, and push herself to get comfortable with various strokes. She'd sit at her easel with a blank canvas and just stare blissfully into the untold story that she was about to tell. The smallest thing could be her inspiration. When she felt it, she'd begin. She'd start painting and move quickly and effortlessly across the canvas. She'd go back and forth rather ferociously, between dunking her brush in water and dipping it into a new color. She'd allow herself the freedom to feel rough yet gentle. She'd stand or sit, she'd turn her body whichever way she felt necessary to allow herself the best position to paint what was coming to her and through her. She often could not explain what her vision was before she began to create it. It was less of a conscious thought and more of a feeling.

Luella had realized long ago, when Mickey introduced her to painting, and she picked the brushes up for the first time, that this was it for her. When she felt them in her hand and ran her fingers across the top of the bristles, feeling the difference in texture and length, she knew she'd never be the same. She'd known, back then, that Mickey had given her something she'd never be able to thank him for. Mickey introduced Luella to who she was. He had given her the key to the door that had been locked within her, unbeknownst to her. When she found the key, it was unlocked forever. She was a creator. She was a painter. *She* was an artist.

When Luella painted, she came alive. Her art was her outlet and it allowed her to focus on everything and nothing all at once. It was to her what strumming a guitar is to a musician. It was calmness and tranquility, yet the only thing that made her feel alive inside. She'd known other things, explored other hobbies, but this... this was not a hobby. This was who she was. It was the very makeup of her being. It was her soul's work and what she felt to be her sole purpose at times.

When Luella started to share some of her work, her family would tell her she should sell it. Vincenzo, her biggest supporter of them all, had pushed Luella to enter art competitions and have features in local art shows. Everyone wanted her to be recognized for the beauty she created and how she could make people feel just by looking at her work. It was eclectic and seemingly had a place for everyone. But Luella didn't want to sell it. She didn't want the one thing she truly loved to become work or a source of income. She did not want the pressure or vulnerability of finding out whether or not the world felt the same way about the pieces she had created as she had. She figured her family was biased, just rooting for her and applauding her for doing something different. She knew the work she created was beautiful, but she didn't think any of it would be worth anything. At least, that is, to anyone but her loved ones. So instead of trying to publicly display her art, or feel as though she was handing over her most prized possessions, she painted only for herself. She'd paint depending on her mood. She'd allow her emotions to dictate what was going to pour out of her and onto the canvas. In the good times, her work typically tended to be bold, bright, enigmatic even, but hopeful. One would look at a piece she painted when she was having a good day and they'd, too, feel like they were having a good day. It was unexplainable. Conversely, when she was in a dark place, her work was raw and unhinged. It was as if she'd cut herself open and instead of paint, used her own blood from her wounds. It was heavy and dark, but it was still beautiful. It still drew someone to it.

Luella had a talent that was unlike anything anyone in her family had seen. It was unlike anything she knew she was capable of and yet, she kept it mostly locked away. It was her outlet for so much, yet she'd allow it to be just that and that was it. As the mood passed and the paint dried, she'd decide whether or not it made the cut to swap out one of the few pieces she'd hung around the house. If she had created something that really moved her, she'd give it a spot in the house. Otherwise, they'd go up to the attic and remain stacked. The varying sizes of what were once white canvases now covered in paint would overlap one another, neatly lined up like dominos from the wall out to the middle of the floor. Each of them there, unintentionally collecting dust, never sure if they'd see light, or remain hidden away forever.

Part Four

Chapter 42

2003

As the years passed and the children grew, Luella and Luanna's bond deepened. While she had a slightly different relationship with each of her children and grandchildren, Luella had a unique connection with Luanna. Perhaps it was because she was her first grandchild, or maybe it was because of her name. It was her personality that stood out to Luella. Unlike the rest of her grandchildren, Luanna thought deeply about how her grandmother grew up. She was inquisitive and wanted to know all that she could about her. She'd grown up spending an immense amount of time under Luella's care, but it was more than that. It was more than the fact that they were close in proximity. Luanna was drawn to her grandmother, fascinated by the stories she'd shared and the way that she'd lived her life thus far.

"Gram," Luanna was looking through Luella's closet, inspecting what seemed like every piece of clothing Luella had hanging.

"Hm?" Luella questioned, watching her granddaughter from the bed on the far side of the room.

"What the hell did you used to wear to a wedding when you were my age?"

Luanna was twenty-two years old and in school for fashion design. She was fascinated by the decades and how styles changed. Yet like anything else, she knew it was only a matter of time before history repeated itself, and fashion was no exception to that rule. So, when she had a big occasion coming up, before going to the mall, she'd search her grandmother's closet in the hopes she'd find something she'd be able to repurpose or reconfigure into something just as elegant or more modern than it was when it was last worn.

Luella laughed at her granddaughter's question. "Well, I guess I'd wear a nice dress and pair of heels."

Luanna looked back, breaking from sifting through the tightly condensed hangers. "I know you'd wear a dress. It was the fifties! You had no choice," she said facetiously. "What style? What color? How would you wear it? Come on, you know what I mean." Luanna pleaded.

Luella laughed and stood. She walked out of the room they were in, the guest room, where they kept old articles of clothing, baby stuff, and things that Luella and Joe had collected over the years.

"Where are you going?" Luanna asked, not yet ready to break away from the closet.

Luella walked down the hall and into the other guest room, where she kept her art supplies neatly on display. In her art studio room, there was a closet big enough to keep storage bins on one side and clothes hanging on the other. Luella called for Luanna. Luanna came in holding a lilac drop-waist chiffon dress up over her head.

"Yeah, gram?"

"Come," Luella said from inside the closet. "Come help me pull this bin out."

Luanna hung the dress over the top of the door as she dutifully listened to her grandmother.

"Grandma, what the hell? What's in these? I don't think I ever knew this closet had this much room." Luanna began to take the first of three bins stacked atop one another down.

"Which one do you want?" She asked after she removed one of them from the pile.

Luella popped the green lid off of the first bin and rummaged through it quickly. Luanna peered over her shoulder, looking back to try and get a glimpse of what it was her grandmother was looking at. There were boxes inside the storage bin. What seemed to be paperwork, old receipts, and perhaps Christmas cards. Nothing that Luanna had any interest in delving into at the moment.

"No, it's not in here," Luella said as she popped the lid back on. "Let's see the next one." Luella gestured to Luanna to get the second box in front of Luella.

Luella yet again took the top off and unveiled neatly stacked articles of clothing.

"*Oh, la la,*" Luanna said, stepping over the boxes to get closer to her grandmother. "What do we have here?"

Luella started unraveling some of the folded garments and picked through the stacks of clothes until she got to the bottom.

"I think this is it." Luella pulled from the bottom of the pile, carefully using one hand to keep the stack of clothes from falling out of place.

When she pulled it from the bottom of the bin, it revealed itself to be a burgundy satin a-line dress with the tiniest, delicate stitching on it, displaying a subtle flower pattern.

"Oh, Grandma! It's beautiful!" Luanna gently took the dress from her grandmother, holding it up against herself and walking quickly to the mirror.

"Oh, it's gorgeous. I'll get it dry-cleaned and perhaps take the shoulders out to pull them down a bit. Give it a little off-the-shoulder, modern-day edge. What do you think?"

Luanna looked back at her grandmother.

"I think that'll look lovely. And if that's what you want to do, it'll be great."

"It's perfect, Gram. Thank you." Luanna helped her grandmother to the daybed up against the wall and kissed her on the cheek. "What would I do without you?"

Luella laughed and patted Luanna's leg. "Oh, you'd be just fine."

"Hey, don't say that," Luanna said, teasing. "I would not. And listen, I know I can't stay too long today after we have lunch, but next week maybe we can go through the rest of those bins. I can't believe you've been holding out on me!" Luanna nudged her grandma's arm. "You've got gold in there! I can repurpose so much of that. Oh, and whatever those papers are, I'll look at those too. You know me, always looking to get into something of yours."

Luella grabbed her granddaughter's hand, rubbing it gently. "Whatever you want, my dear. It's yours." She coughed slightly before continuing. "I'm sure those bins would take more than just a few hours to get through. There's a lot of history in there."

"Well," Luanna acclaimed, "All the more reason for me to see you more then, isn't it?"

"I'd love that, sweetheart."

Chapter 43

2003

For as long as Luella could remember, she'd loved Joe. Joe Andriotta had given her a beautiful life. Together they had navigated the highest of highs and the absolute lowest of lows. They'd witnessed the ugly, tragic part of life that most people would want to hide from, and yet, they'd managed to last. Their love conquered some of the most difficult challenges that life could throw one's way. They not only overcame, but they prevailed. They fought against all odds. They found each other again after separating, they worked through the unthinkable and unbearable loss of a child. They dealt with the aftermath and infidelity. They created a beautiful home and a lovely family. They raised strong, respectful, loving children who became spouses and parents. They knew that their love was deep and powerful. It was soft and comforting. After fifty years of marriage, they had become one.

As Luella and Joe lay in bed, Luella allowed herself to embark on the trip her memory was bringing her on. She felt herself slipping into an unconscious awareness as she was falling asleep. Her mind's eye was like a movie. Scene after scene flashed on a screen in her head, showing parts of her life. The memories were like a reel, not knowing what she was going to see next. She saw faces vividly. She pictured her father, Vincenzo, and her brother Vinny. She retraced the steps she took with her sister-in-law on her wedding day. She saw her and Joe on their first date, then in the walls of Saint Anthony's, a dream in white. She pictured her children, all of them. Carla, Maria, Anna and Joey. She envisioned what Carla would be like now and she saw the adult version of her so clearly. She pictured her doting grandchildren, each of them just as if they were standing in front of her. She saw Luanna, her special girl. Luella saw herself for a moment with Mickey. She saw the tall, slender build and the reddish brown hair wisp in the park. She felt his laugh and his touch. She felt the presence of them all, near her, as if they were in the very room she was in.

As Luella drifted off to sleep, she felt a sense of peace and serenity wash over her. She felt her eyes roll further and the weight of her body sink deeper into the bed. She felt the sensation of the cold sheets on the tips of her fingers and through the ends of her toes. She fell asleep, comfortably and tranquilly in her bed, lying next to her husband as she had countless nights before.

When Joe woke the next morning, he rolled slightly, closing the gap between him and Luella. He reached for her arm, tenderly, as he so often did. But when he grabbed hold of Luella's hand, he noticed something felt different. He lifted himself slowly from his pillow and put his arm around his wife, trying not to disturb her. As he did, he realized she felt cold. The air had left her lungs and her soul had left her body. He knew, in that instant, that his wife was gone. The love of his life, the love of their family's life, had departed. Joe did not wail, he did not waver. He simply laid down next to her, held her close in his arms, and breathed all of her in for the last time. It was as if he already knew she would be gone.

"I love you, Luella. I love you, I always have and I always will." He continually kissed her cheek, moving to her neck, her ear, her head, and back to her cheek. "Luella Andriotta, my beautiful wife. Thank you for all that you've given me. I will never walk this earth the same without you." And as Joe had done so many years before, he rolled off of the bed and onto the floor, next to his lifeless wife, rocked himself into a ball, and began to cry.

Chapter 44

2003

In the weeks following Luella's death, the family helped Joe clean out the house and make it more liveable, tossing what needed to be purged, and divvying up keepsakes for the children and grandchildren. Luanna spent time alone in the guest room that had doubled as Luella's art studio. She ran her fingers across the easel that her grandfather had bought Luella. She grazed the bristles on the brushes and let her fingertips trace the painting that was on the canvas. She walked to the closet, filled with the storage bins she had, only a few weeks ago, gone through with her grandmother. She knew she wanted her garments. She wanted to wear what her grandmother had worn. She wanted to give life to the clothes that once draped her grandmother's body. She wanted to feel the closeness of having something that hugged her grandmother's skin, hug her own. Luanna opened the closet and pulled out the first bin. As she popped the lid open, she remembered the first one was stacked with what seemed like paperwork. She figured it'd be things her grandfather would want to keep. Perhaps it was old bills, or medical records, that as you become older, seem to become more useful. She couldn't help but to start to pick through. She thought that perhaps there was something in there worth finding. Worth keeping, for herself as a little piece of her grandmother that no one else knew about.

The first small cardboard box inside of the storage bin was filled with hospital records, birth certificates of her mother, aunts, and uncle, and the death record of Vincenzo, her great-grandfather. She quickly moved through, seeing bits and pieces that caught her eye, but nothing worth reading closely. She moved down to the second cardboard box before noticing underneath them all, was a manilla envelope, worn and tattered. It had a blue ribbon around it that seemed weathered. She carefully pulled it out from the bottom of the pile and laid it on her lap. As Luanna cautiously untied the ribbon, unsure of what she'd find, a small, wallet-sized photo fell from it. It was of her grandmother, much, much younger with an unrecognizable man. From the photograph, it seemed as though her grandmother was close to this man. They were facing the camera, but their bodies were turned in towards one another, hugging each other lovingly. The man was not her grandfather. He was tall, and slender and wore a baseball cap. She couldn't make out the details of his face, but she knew it was no one that she'd been introduced to. It didn't seem like a friend of Joe's, or anyone's for that matter. This felt like an intimate photo. Although nothing of scandal was showing, it was the way her grandmother was clinging onto this man, laughing at the camera. Her eyes beaming and her smile wide. The man returned the hug in such a way that it seemed he was protective of Luella. His long, lanky arms wrapped tightly around her, keeping her in the crux of him. Luanna, intrigued, continued to explore what was in the folder. She placed the photo on the floor and opened the flap. Inside, were stacks of folded pieces of paper, handwritten and scarred with wet marks. Some were in her grandmother's handwriting, and some were wrapped still in envelopes addressed to her grandmother. She moved to the bottom of the letters and grabbed the first one from underneath the rest.

October 10th, 1952
My Sweet Luella,
    I know that what we had was special. I know that while it was only a short time, you left a mark on me that I'm not sure I'll ever be able to come across again. The days I spent with you, though limited, were some of the happiest days of my life. You proved to me that I could fight through my bad days and find the good. That there is more to life

than just wallowing in my sorrow and guilt for what I'd done when I was a child. You taught me that giving the gift of happiness to other people is how I will feel fulfilled.

You, Luella, are the most beautiful woman I've ever met. Your eyes are thoughtful, your smile, intentional. You've got the most beautiful face a woman could have, and yet, there's more to you. Your heart is pure. Your kindness and drive inspires me. When I first saw you light up at the gallery, and fall in love with the art, I knew that you were talented, too. When you began painting I fell more in love with you. I fell in love with your creativity, your passion, and your persistence. I knew that through your determination to find what it was that you loved to do, I'd only become a better musician.

I hope you know that I only want the best for you. I imagine you've moved on with your life, or back to the way things were before you and I met, and that's okay. I hope you did. Because Luella, of all things you've taught me, you've taught me that I can never truly fulfill someone else. Not entirely, at least. You've taught me that I am somebody to love from afar, because I will never be whole on the inside.

I wish you a happy life, Luella. I wish you all of the love and adoration one can receive. I want you to know how special you are and how impactful your presence is. I want you to know, Luella, that I loved you. Every minute of every day we spent together. For those few months, I loved you every step of the way and I will love you every step I've still got left to take. I hope that at the very least, when you find yourself thinking of me, the memories are of happy times. I hope that you know while our time was limited, it was pure.

I love you, Luella, and I always will.
Love always,

Mickey

"Mickey?" Luanna whispered to herself as she put the letter down. Eager to discover this love her grandmother had that she knew nothing of, she picked up the next letter.

May 19th, 1953
Dearest Luella,
I thought of you today. While I know this is going to sound absurd, I met someone. I met a lovely woman who I will probably spend the rest of my life with. Her name is Bridgette and she's a really swell gal. She's beautiful and tall, and she's got the bluest of eyes. But she's not you. And I'm okay with that. I've accepted that I will never find you, Luella. I don't go searching for you in women I meet, you merely come to me in various forms. You take shape in women I look at. It's as if I look through them to you. Like you're standing right in between me and anyone else. I know you've moved on and started a family of your own. I hear you married Joe Andriotta and had a daughter. I'm sure she's beautiful, just like you. I hope that one day, even from afar, I can catch a glimpse of you as a mother. You probably make a wonderful mother.

I know it's silly, me writing letters to you that I'm unsure if I ever have the intention of sending. But somehow, it helps me feel connected to you. It allows me to still feel connected to the only thing I've ever knowingly truly loved. Whether they ever reach the postman, I'm not sure. But this is me keeping that love I felt somewhat alive. Continuing to breathe air into its lungs, I suppose. Sounds quite silly when I write it on paper and repeat it back to myself.

I suppose, Luella, knowing I'm going to propose marriage to Bridgette is me saying goodbye to you. Goodbye to you in my mind's eye, and I will see you in my memories. I will only hope that I can be the kind of man to Bridgette that she deserves.

Love always,
Mickey.

July 21st, 1963
Dear Luella,

 It's been years since I thought of writing you one of these letters. A letter that I know will probably never make its way to you. However, I couldn't imagine not writing to you now.

 I saw you, the other week, at the racetrack. You were there, beautiful and confident as ever. You were mothering your children, what seemed to be three. I saw you from a distance, and perhaps, that's how I've always admired you. From a distance. Perhaps our love has always been something of a distant memory, a distant thought.

 I saw you and I thought of the news I heard of your firstborn daughter. How she had passed at such a young and tender age. How heartbroken I was to hear the news. How compelled I felt to reach out to you once I got wind, but I didn't. I just prayed for you, from where I was. Hoping that you felt the warmth of my thoughts with you. Your family looks lovely, and you look happy. God, I hope you're happy, Luella. I think I am. I married Bridgette, and we have a son, Noah. He's a year old and he brings me so much joy I feel it pour out of me every day. I just hope that I can be the father he needs. I hope, every day, that I can teach him to be strong and resilient, yet empathetic and thoughtful. I'm not sure what kind of a husband I am. I treat my wife well and I love her deeply, but the love that I have for my son is unmatched. I know you understand this.

 It made my day to see you, Luella. Maybe, one day, I'll grow the courage to say hello. I don't want to cause any type of disturbance in your life, or problems with your husband. He seems like a nice fella and a good man. Maybe one day, Luella.

Love always,
Mickey

Luanna could barely contain herself as she ripped through, letter after letter. She found herself lost in the love she had just discovered this man had for her grandmother. How confused she felt reading these notes. This man loved her grandmother, year after year, and seemed to have never forgotten her, no matter how life separated them. She continued to the last letter addressed to her grandmother from Mickey.

March 22nd, 1981
Dearest Luella,

This will be my final letter to you, along with the rest of those I've loved. I am saying goodbye. I've made peace with the fact that although life has been grand to me, I will never know the pure happiness and joy that I know a normal person should experience. I know that no matter how much I run, or hide, my past will haunt me. It haunts me more deeply now than ever. My son is now a man, and I can't imagine my burden beginning to weigh on him. I can't tell my son what I did so many years earlier. I can't tell him that I accidentally took another man's life. I don't want him to know that his father is capable of such a thing. But I must tell him. I must instill the lessons I learned from my mistakes into him so he does not make the same ones. I want to avoid him feeling life's remorse at any expense.

I've decided to tell him, though, in a letter. My guilt hangs on me every minute of every day. I don't want my son to be burdened with the truth and have to figure out how to love his father after he finds out what a monster I am. Plus, I just found out that I'm on borrowed time. My doctor told me that I am living the last of what could only be a few months. Cancer. Pancreatic cancer that's spread like wildfire with no sign of water. So, I decided to tell my son the man I really am. I decided that I will let him know, and then I will end my life so that he doesn't need to worry about how to forgive me.

I wanted to also write to you, Luella. I wanted to thank you for giving me such happy times. When I was with you, I felt peace. I felt openness and honesty. You did not waver in your feelings for me when I told you what I did and you forgave me, unequivocally. Thank you for giving me that gift. So many years ago, you gave me the slightest window to feel joy. My son brings me joy, but much different than the joy you brought me. My wife brings me joy, but she and I never connected the way you and I had. So, thank you.

This is my goodbye, Luella. Maybe in another life, or in another universe, I'll get to love you longer. Maybe, our souls will find each other in another world. And maybe, just maybe, you'll be mine forever, one day.
Love eternally,
Mickey

April 13th, 1981
Mickey,
I don't know where to begin. I don't know how to comprehend what I've just learned. Your son, Noah, came to find me and give me your letters. He delivered your letters along with utter heartbreak in the news of your death. Mickey, I'm so sorry.

I wish I could've been a friend to you throughout your lifetime. I wish we would've stayed in touch, if only to check in. Then maybe, just maybe, you'd still be here.

Your son looks just like you. It's rather striking, really. I didn't see it, until that was all I could see. He seems like a sweet boy with a good head on his shoulders. You and your wife should be very proud.

I read your letters and found myself angry. I was angry with you. I am angry with you. I'm angry that you didn't try to remain in contact with me. I'm angry that when you'd see me, or hear about me, you did not try to reach out. We were so close yet so far. I'm angry that you didn't seek help.

    Joe never knew about you and I. Sure, he probably had assumed that perhaps I saw other people in between him and I breaking up, but he never knew to what extent. He didn't know that you were the one who had the patience and yearned to help me find out who I was, who I am, the way you did. He didn't know that although our time was short, it was sweet. The love that you and I shared was something many people only dream of. I don't know if it was the type of love made to have lasted forever, but it was true, honest, and pure. You cared about me the way women dream to be cared for. It was a burning love that you and I shared. It was that of a rocket ship, or a shooting star. It's fast, and the heat can be suffocating if you're too close, but it's typical to burn out quickly.

    I thought of you a lot when my daughter Carla passed. I thought of the way you would've cared for me and tended to my needs. How perhaps you would've been more patient than my own husband was when she died. How I needed someone with the empathy and charisma that you had. How I needed someone like you.

    I thought of you, that day at the racetrack. I heard your name and smelled your scent. It was as if I knew you, too, were there. Somewhere in the stands where crowds of people were coming and going. How funny it is that life tried to reconnect us. In various random gestures, the fates tried, for some reason, to have our paths cross again. I don't know, Mick. I don't know what would've or could've been. All I know is that I'm happy to have known you.

    I will look for you on the other side. I can only pray to reconnect with you in whatever way that may be possible,

someday. Who knows, maybe we could be together...
Forever, one day.
   A piece of me will always love you.
Love endlessly,
Luella

Luanna sat back against the wall, the pages scattered across the floor, wet from her tears reading the exchange that never saw the other intended person. She held the last page of her grandmother's letter to her chest and quietly let out an exhale. She knew her grandmother had a life before she was the matriarch of their family, but she didn't know the extent of it. She had a love in between her grandfather, and this love seemed to have shaped the person she became. *What if they had run into each other over the years?* She thought to herself. Her imagination created scenarios playing out in her head, of her grandmother in a parallel life with another man. Her fingers lightly brushed through the pages on the floor before picking back up the first letter. *The paintings.* Her grandmother's art, which this man helped her discover, had still not been looked at since she passed. All of her pieces collecting dust in the attic.

Luanna sorted the letters neatly in sequential order and placed them, along with the photograph of her grandmother and the now-known Mickey, back in the manilla envelope. She tried her best to tie it back up with the ribbon, and she placed it in her overnight bag across the room. She poked her head out of the hallway to hear some of her family downstairs talking about memories over coffee, and her mother and aunt in the other guest room. She knew there was no quiet way for her to get into the attic using the ladder that had to be pulled down, so she made her endeavor public.

"Ma, I'm going to look at Gram's paintings. Does anybody mind if I have a few minutes up there?" She announced, already pulling the string hanging in the hallway.

"No, honey, of course not. Just be careful. And perhaps, don't pull what you want quite yet. I don't think Grandpa has been up there in years and I'm sure the rest of us will want to look." Maria responded from down the hall.

Luanna climbed up into the dark, full space before reaching for the light. She knew what was up there; baby cribs, baby clothes, and paintings. All of the paintings her grandmother never deemed worthy enough to share. Luanna began to pull the sheets off of the canvases lined up against the walls. She uncovered what seemed to be a beautiful depiction of each era of Luella's life. She found paintings dated to the fifties, when her grandmother first started painting. Happy, bright, hopeful, and carefree. She uncovered paintings that showcased dark agony and muddy hues that were very clear when her Aunt Carla must've passed. She watched as she placed herself in her grandmother's shoes at each stage in her life. She found herself turning and spinning, moving and shuffling canvases out of their position to see them more clearly in the light.

"Oh my God," Luanna whispered to herself. "These are fucking beautiful." Luanna could not contain her tears or her astonishment. Her grandmother was an artist. An undiscovered talent that had a gift that should be shared with the world. She wanted everyone to see, to know what was hiding in the attic. The gift her grandmother had her entire life that was never at the forefront. She could've sold her work, and had it featured in galleries and exotic art shows. Her pieces were unique, abstract, and elegant. They were magnificent portrayals of what people could connect to.

"Ma!" Luanna shouted, holding one of the paintings in her hand. "Ma! You gotta come up here. Tell Aunt Anna and Uncle Joey, too." Luanna stared at the paintings in awe. "Your mother was unbelievable!"

Epilogue

2022
New York City

"I don't know what it is I'm looking for exactly," a woman said to the gentleman at the desk. "I just know that I need a piece to fill a very empty space in my home. I want it to be the focal point, though. It has to be moving, and impactful. I need people to walk in and it screams back at them BAM!" She used her hands to emphasize the power behind her description.

"Okay, well what style do you like?" he asked.

"Style? I don't know. Perhaps I'll know it when I see it. I just know that this home has had some negative energy and I need something to rid all of that. I need something that takes all of the pain away that was once stored at the large, oversized, family portrait that was hanging there."

The young man figured as much. A divorcé was not hard to spot in an art gallery in Soho. He figured it was infidelity. They probably lived in a penthouse, she probably didn't work and he probably worked too much. She probably nagged him and he probably got bored. He probably cheated, and she probably got a shit load of money. Typical.

"Why don't I show you a few pieces back here?" The man led the way as he continued to guide her through the paintings he was about to showcase. "This is an artist you've probably never heard of, but she was a *real* talent. Someone very much ahead of her time and she has *mood pieces* as we like to call them. She's certainly what we'd describe today as abstract Impasto." He stopped walking and gestured his arm to the woman as if she were to go ahead of him and look.

The woman stepped into a corner of the gallery and was instantly transported. The canvases hanging from the wall varied in emotion. They were compelling and spoke to her. She found herself pulled to a piece that wasn't just powerful; it *was* power. The image wasn't recognizable, but it was bold. The dark grays and blues meshed together and brought her eyes back and forth. There was black tying it all together with the glimmering bit of hope, cast in the shade of a shining gold paint that danced its way across the entirety of the canvas.

"*This*," The woman started, "this is what I need. This is everything all in one. This is magnificent." She traced the painting with the very tips of her fingers, barely grazing as her hand and her eyes made their way to the bottom right-hand corner.

In the corner, ever so faintly, was a signature and timestamp in black.

Luella Andriotta, 1953

Made in United States
North Haven, CT
08 March 2025